Legendary Lover

SUSAN JOHNSON

Bantam Books
NEW YORK TORONTO LONDON SYDNEY AUCKLAND

LEGENDARY LOVER
A Bantam Book / May 2000

ISBN 0-553-57867-7

Published simultaneously in the United States and Canada

Bantam Books are published by Bantam Books, a division of Random
House, Inc. Its trademark, consisting of the words "Bantam Books"
and the portrayal of a rooster, is Registered in U.S. Patent and Trademark Office and in other countries. Marca Registrada. Bantam Books,
1540 Broadway, New York, New York 10036.

PRINTED IN THE UNITED STATES OF AMERICA
OPM   10 9 8 7 6 5 4 3 2 1

Dear Reader,

The evolution of the Duras family began by chance. Andre Duras came to life in *Taboo* as the alter ego of Andre Massena from *Wicked*, because I became infatuated with Massena, a real historical figure, and wished to add some fantasy elements of my own to his life. Often as I'm finishing one book the next generation appears in my consciousness—although the creative impulse doesn't always follow a sensible chronology. But in the course of time Pasha Duras had his own story in *A Touch of Sin*, and *Legendary Lover* now showcases Pasha's daughter, Venus.

I like Venus. She's sure of what she doesn't want but unreservedly open to the other possibilities in life. Jack Fitz-James, on the other hand, *always* knows what he wants. They make a darling couple. I hope you like them too.

Best wishes,

Susan Johnson

Legendary Lover

Chapter 1

—❦❦❦—

THE MARQUIS OF REDVERS CAUGHT SIGHT OF the Honorable Sarah Palmer and her aunt Lady Tallien before they saw him, and quickly slipped away down the nearest aisle. The crowds at the Great Exhibition offered him refuge, the daily attendance of forty thousand a veritable crush beneath the glass barrel vaults of Paxton's brilliant design.[1] Taking no notice of the exhibits, he moved swiftly through the throng, concerned only with putting distance between himself and the two ladies. Sarah, newly out, had set her cap for him—always reason for evasion—while her aunt Bella, one of his many lovers, had begun making demands of him of late. Definitely time to move on, now *and* in the future.

Quickly glancing over his shoulder, he detected no telltale bobbing pink bonnet feathers in the mass of humanity behind him and, gratified, he determined to make his unavailability crystal clear next time he met the Palmer ladies. But not today, not after two nights of women and carouse; he was damned tired. And if Sarah Palmer didn't understand he wasn't in the market for a wife, her aunt certainly should, as did anyone in the ton with half a brain.

Swiveling around a second too late, he crashed into a lady reading a brochure. She began to pitch backward, her astonished cry swallowed up in the din of the crowd. Reacting instinctively, he caught her arms, pulling her hard against him to keep them both from falling. Her eyes flared wide at the impress of his muscled chest against her breasts, his powerful thighs braced against hers. Stunned, she looked up into dark eyes suddenly regarding her with interest.

She was exquisite—golden-haired, dazzling, graphically voluptuous—and even after two sleepless nights of debauch, the marquis's senses instantly came alert. "Pardon me," he murmured in a deep, low, fascinated tone.

"You're pardoned." A modicum of reserve underlay her words.

But he didn't let her go. Her lavish breasts, shapely thighs, and wide-eyed beauty were too intriguing. "You're French," he said.

"Unhand me, please." Her voice was cool now, her arms held out wide.

A gentleman despite all his profligate ways, he released her and stepped away. But he took note of the brochure in her hand, the machine on the cover a vast conglomeration of gaslights and mirrors. The exact one, he reflected, gazing over her shoulder, on display in the booth behind her—the apparatus set at the head and foot of an operating table. "I've been thinking of buying a dozen of those," he remarked, pointing at her brochure, his smile gracious.

Her surprise showed.

"For my tenants' hospital," he mendaciously added.

"You must have a very large establishment." She was wary. He'd never seen that look before in a woman; his reputation for pleasing women was well known.

"Just a small one at each estate," he improvised.

The caution left her eyes, replaced by a spark of interest. "Do you employ doctors, or just nurses? I've found that nurses often . . ."

Her conversation became quite animated at that point and, guiding her to one side of the stream of traffic, he replied to her questions with answers that further encouraged her passionate interest in the very odd field of patient care. He was infinitely charming, but then he'd had enormous practice.

Was she equally animated in bed? he wondered, debating how best to discover that fact for himself. And if the purchase of a dozen of those light contraptions might entice this dazzling woman into his bed, he decided it would be money well spent.

He invited her to dinner—just a small party of relatives, he spontaneously devised—and her hesitation was rather that of propriety than disinterest.

"You may know my aunt, Lady Markham," he offered. Her dress and manner were of his world; he understood the requirements of protocol.

"My father does," she replied. "Her husband brokered the treaty between Greece and Turkey."

"Your father?"

"Pasha Duras."

"Ah . . . the freedom fighter." Pasha Duras had served in the Greek government for a time; his name was well known in Europe. "I could send a carriage for you at nine."

"Will your aunt be there?"

If he had to drag her from her bed. "Yes," he said.

"Well, then . . . I'd like that." She finished with a smile that outshone the operating room lights. "My name is Venus."

Perfect casting, he reflected, wondering if she'd inherited her namesake's amorous persona as well. "I'm Jack Fitz-James."

"The Marquis of Redvers," she said with distaste. "I'm afraid I'm busy tonight. If you'll excuse me." And turning abruptly, she walked away.

But the marquis never withdrew from a challenge. Apparently she was planning on staying in London for another fortnight at least. Plenty of time, he mused, watching her disappear into the crowd, for a leisurely seduction.

FOUND A NEW WOMAN?" NED DARLINGTON quirked his brow in sardonic query as the marquis approached the Turkish exhibit. Pushing away from the glass display case filled with the weapons they'd come to see, he added, "Is she blond or blond?"

Jack's gaze narrowed in mild scrutiny. "How the hell can you tell?"

Baron Darlington's tone was indulgent. "How long have I known you?"

"Long enough, apparently." The marquis slowly smiled. "But this one's utterly gorgeous."

"Aren't they all?"

Jack's smile only broadened. "So cynical, Ned, when I'm enchanted."

"No doubt that single-minded fascination accounts in no small measure for your success with the ladies."

"I do like 'em. That's no secret." The marquis's dark brows flickered with pithy import. "The lady calls herself Venus."

"How appropriate, considering your reputation for fucking."

"I rather thought it auspicious."

"So when are you joining her in bed?"

"Since she cut me cold, it might be a few days."

The baron chuckled. "Losing your edge, my fine stud?"

"She's French."

"And obviously doesn't know of your special talents for pleasing the ladies."

Jack's perfect white teeth flashed in a grin. "Apparently she does, and that's the rub."

"So you'll have to change her mind."

"My thought exactly."

"French ladies know what they want. Maybe you're not her style. Have you thought of that?"

"We were having a very pleasant conversation until she discovered my name."

"Along with your propensity for vice." Ned shrugged. "If she's prudish, don't waste your time."

"But I want to."

"You want to assail the impregnable citadel? Since when?"

"Nothing's impregnable," the marquis softly murmured.

The baron cast his friend a speculative look. "That comment almost calls for a wager . . . and if I didn't know your unerring seductive skills, I'd hazard my money."

"She just has to come to know me better," Jack Fitz-James said with a disarming grin.

"I expect she will. Have you ever been refused?"

"Not until today."

*B*UT REGARDLESS OF NED'S WISDOM IN NOT betting on the outcome of the marquis's seduction, he related the story of the lady's refusal with droll merriment to some friends, and many of them were less prudent or perhaps less discerning. Or maybe simply ripe for any scandalous wager. By the time the marquis entered Brookes that evening, gossip apropos Venus Duras had preceded him, and the betting book was filled with an array of wildly extravagant wagers. Understanding the speed with which gossip swept through the ton, he received all the ribald and licentious comment with equanimity. But he took notice, as well, that there were those who had put money on the lady—on her ability to deter his advances.

He spent most of the evening gambling and won as usual, drank with his renowned and notable capacity, and adroitly deflected most of the conversational gambits having to do with his interest in Miss Duras. Until later that night, when everyone was well into their cups and discretion vanished along with tact.

"She's at the Duchess of Groveland's ball tonight," one of his gambling companions remarked with a waggish arch of his brow. "Why aren't you there?"

"You already missed the dinner," another noted with a grin, for the marquis's disinterest in society dinners was well known.

"Are we gambling or discussing my sex life?" Jack drawled, looking up from his cards, surveying his companions with an open gaze.

"Both," the young Viscount Talmont cheerfully retorted, signaling the dealer for another card. "Did you know the untouchable Miss Duras has turned down two dukes and a passel of earls in the last fortnight?" Undeterred despite Jack's blank look, the viscount remarked, "Think you can do better?"

"I'm not offering her my title, Alastair. I hope that's clear to everyone."

"Don't have to be clear to us, Redvers. Although I don't suggest you mention the transience of your interest to the lady straight away." Lord Halverstam cast a sportive look around the table.

"I'm also not in the market for advice," the marquis murmured, "although I'll take some of your money if that's the best you can do." He nodded at the man's cards spread out on the green baize.

"Damn, Redvers," Charles Givens muttered. "How the hell do you do it hand after hand?"

"Just lucky," Jack pleasantly replied, scooping in the markers from the center of the table. "Or maybe you're paying too much attention to my love life and not enough to your cards."

And for the next several hands, with varying degrees of inebriation, everyone concentrated on the cards— without any better results. The marquis won another twenty thousand by the end of the hour, and after glancing at the clock on the wall, he waved a footman over and ordered a bottle of brandy. Gathering his winnings, he handed them to another servant, bid his adieus, and rose from the table without explanation. Taking the ordered brandy from the footman just short of the door, bottle in hand, he raced down the stairs.

He'd promised the Duchess of Groveland he'd come and dance with her before midnight, and he had only ten minutes to make good on his promise.

Chapter 2

⸺❦⸺

THE MARQUETRY CASE CLOCK IN THE CAV-
ernous entrance hall of Groveland House was striking
midnight when the Marquis of Redvers strolled through
the opened doors. He handed his brandy bottle to
Peggy's majordomo, whom he greeted with genial familiarity. "Don't bother announcing me, Oliver," he added.
"I'll cut in on the duchess."

"As you wish, my lord," the august butler replied, his
mouth twitching into a restrained smile. "She didn't
think you'd arrive on time."

"Don't I always?"

"My words exactly, my lord. Lord Redvers is to be
depended on, I told her."

"How much did she lose?"

"Ten guineas, my lord," the majordomo replied with
obvious pleasure.

"Only women are always late, eh, Oliver?"

"It rather seems the case, sir. Would you like some of
your usual vintage?"

"In a few minutes, perhaps. And I forgot my damned
gloves again."

"I could procure some for you, sir."

Jack shook his head. "Hate those damned things.
Peggy won't mind."

"I'm sure she won't, my lord. Since the duchess considers you the finest dancer in the ton, she'll be pleased to dance with you, gloves or not."

"Well, then," the marquis said with a grin, "I'm off to do my duty by my godmother."

"Very good, sir." Offering the young marquis an impeccable bow, he watched the object of his employer's affection stroll to the staircase and ascend to the floor above. Then, snapping his fingers for an underling, he saw that the marquis's favorite champagne was sent up to him.

The Marquis of Redvers stood in the doorway to the ballroom, surveying the numerous guests twirling to the strains of a waltz, the crystal chandeliers illuminating the gilded room, the glittering light contending with the sparkle of jewels, the shimmer of silken ball gowns and gleaming coiffeurs ornamented with flowers and feathers, the satiny glow of bared shoulders and décolletages—all the grandeur and brilliance of the fashionable beau monde assembled under the duchess's splendid Tiepolo ceiling.

And one by one, those guests took notice of the gloriously handsome young marquis standing in the doorway. His splendid height was attributed to the Fitz-James connection with Charles II, as were his excesses, although his dark good looks, everyone agreed, came from his mother's family. The DeLanceys had contributed beauty to England's bloodlines since the time of the Norman invasion. The faultless hand of his tailor was evident in the fit of his evening rig, the fine wool smoothly flowing over his lean, muscled form, his damask waistcoat subtle in tone, eggshell rather than white, calling attention even in its understatement to his taut, honed torso. Eschewing the hirsute fashions of the time, he was clean-shaven, his bronzed skin evidence of his devotion to the sporting life. But what most attracted attention and gave him his special cachet beyond his notoriety were his eyes. He had gypsy eyes, black as ebony, sensual, magnetic; some said it seemed as though he could see right through you. But those who knew him best saw the laughter and mischievous sparkle more often than not.

"Darling! You've come!" The duchess's jubilant voice rose above the diminishing hum of conversation as everyone regarded the infamous young lord who was here tonight, they hoped, to make good on their wagers. Arms outstretched, Peggy Hexton crossed the large ballroom with a beaming smile on her heavily rouged face. The duchess had been a great beauty in her day, and retained the less subtle cosmetics of her generation. Her hair was brightly hennaed and she wasn't svelte anymore, but she was cheerfully enamored of life and embraced each day with enthusiasm.

"Would I stay away from you?" Jack replied, taking her hands in his a moment later and offering her a warm smile. "When my favorite waltz is playing?"

"Every waltz is your favorite, you sweet boy," she lightly retorted, pulling him onto the dance floor. "And now that you're here, I'll have someone decent to dance with."

The duchess had been on the stage before she captured the duke's heart, and while he was long dead and she could have had any man with her fortune, she'd never remarried. She preferred her freedom, she always said, but Jack knew hers had been a love match, and while he didn't precisely understand the concept, he envied her the obvious bliss she'd enjoyed.

"I intend to keep you by my side for a good long while," she warned as they moved into the first turn.

"I'm here as your cicisbeo, darling." The marquis winked wickedly. "You may order me about at your will."

"What if I order you to make amends to Miss Duras?" she archly said.

"I would, of course. But for what do I need to make amends?"

"She seems angry with you."

"She's here?" He'd not seen her, but then the crowded ballroom limited visibility.

"I had her beside me at dinner. She's a very remarkable woman."

"I'm not sure I like that particular tone of voice."

"What tone?"

"That matchmaking tone. I'd recognize it in the roar of a hurricane." Or on the last day of the apocalypse, he reflected, any inference of matrimony having the same effect on him as a vision of hell.

"Good God, Jack, she's more than a match for you. She doesn't want to be married, either. You should have heard her at dinner. Although she was completely charming, there was no doubt of her disinterest in marriage."

"Are you humbugging me?" he said, swinging them in a double twirl with flawless precision. "There isn't a woman born who doesn't want to be married."

"She wouldn't agree with you."

More than intrigued, for he'd not stopped thinking of Miss Duras since their meeting, he debated the possibility she might be available for a liaison outside the normal courting rituals. Not that he hadn't perfected evasion of those rituals to a fine art, but were her disinterest in marriage true, how much more pleasant their relationship could be.

He didn't question his ability to persuade her to become closer friends. Only the timetable was in debate.

"You'll have to introduce me, then." His smile lit up his face, for he knew his godmother's propensity for gambling. "I suppose you have some money riding on this."

"Perhaps a little." Gazing up at him, she lifted one hennaed brow with a dramatic flare reminiscent of her days on the stage.

"I hope it's not more than a pony," he challenged. "I can't guarantee swift results."

"Or any results, some are saying," she murmured, playfully tapping his shoulder with her fan.

He scrutinized her for a moment. "Did you bet on the lady?"

"What if I did?"

"Traitor." But he was grinning.

She made a small moue. "I didn't, of course. Knowing you so well." She refrained from saying the beautiful, intelligent Miss Duras would give him a merry chase, though. He'd find that out soon enough. It was about time someone resisted the young boy's surfeit of charm. And on the obverse side, the young lady might find Jack's unconventional attitudes refreshing.

At base, of course, she really couldn't resist a bit of matchmaking.

———

While all the guests at the duchess's ball waited with bated breath for the marquis and the Frenchwoman to meet, the lady in question, unaware of the speculation rife in the air, was enjoying the evening. She loved dancing, and the duchess, so warmhearted and cordial, had become a comrade of sorts at dinner. She seemed to understand what so many nobles didn't—that the poor deserved respect, compassion, and, rather than moralizing, a decent chance to earn a living. The duchess had also donated a generous sum to Venus's latest charity hospital, being built in Paris. Additionally, she'd offered her men to relay the new hospital equipment Venus had ordered at the Great Exhibition from the warehouse to the docks, saving on dray fees.

During dinner, too, when a female guest had rudely asked Venus about her lack of a husband, the duchess had come to her defense. "Don't mind Clara," the duchess had said, sotto voce. "She's green with envy over your looks." And for some time they'd spoken quietly about the advantages and liabilities of marriage, agreeing that if a woman had her own fortune, there was little reason to marry simply to be married.

"Wait until you're swept off your feet," the duchess had counseled, and when Venus had remarked that that was highly unlikely considering the men she'd met and known, her hostess had winked and said, "Sometimes it happens when you least expect it."

When the dancing began, Venus was besieged with partners, and while all the men she danced with were solicitous and affable, some gallant to the extreme, none touched her emotions. But then no man ever had. On occasion over the years, she'd questioned her lack of interest, concerned she was some aberration of womanhood. Not tonight, however. She was having a marvelous time dancing and if her suitors didn't spark her fancy, they certainly were offering her immense pleasure.

Shortly after one, her escort conducted her into the supper room where buffet tables had been set up for the guests' refreshment. After seating her at a small table, he left to bring them each a glass of chilled champagne. Leaning back against a gilded chair, Venus gently fanned her heated cheeks, her gaze surveying the extravagant display of colorful ices on the nearest buffet table.

"Darling, bring us all some of that pineapple ice."

Hearing the duchess's voice, Venus turned around with a smile that froze on her face when she saw the man beside her hostess.

"Go now, Jack, and do my bidding as you so gallantly promised you would." Peggy Hexton shooed him away with her ivory-and-silk fan. "You look as warm as I feel," she went on, dropping gracefully into a chair beside Venus. "Are you enjoying yourself?"

She wanted to say, *Until now*, but in the interests of courtesy, answered instead, "Yes, very much. Your musicians are wonderful."

"You dance well."

"I like to dance."

"Then you should dance with Jack. He's the very best."

"I'd rather not."

"He's really quite harmless, my dear. And you'll enjoy his skill immensely. I always insist he come to squire me at my balls."

"I'm afraid I generally avoid men of Redvers's ilk."

"I doubt you've ever known a man like Jack. Come, darling, it's only a dance."

How rude would she be if she continued to resist her hostess's coaxing? Would she be thought unduly rigid? Could the marquis really be as notorious as gossip attested? "We'll see," Venus evasively replied, taking note of the duchess's piloting away of her returning escort with a stern look and a wave of her hand. She realized it wouldn't be easy to withstand her willful hostess.

Satisfied with her maneuvering, the duchess was in good spirits, regaling Venus with humorous descriptions of some of her guests. When Jack returned with their ices, she said, "I was telling Miss Duras about Lady Clara's prim daughter, who, thank God, couldn't come tonight."

"Amen to that," Jack lightly replied.

"Lady Clara has set her sights on Jack for her daughter, you see." The duchess shot a facetious glance at her godson.

"Peggy finds humor in my misery," the marquis observed, pulling up a chair beside his godmother.

"Surely you have to marry someday," the duchess playfully said.

He cast her an oblique glance. "I see you're bent on torturing me. I'm sure Miss Duras would prefer some other amusements."

"Not necessarily."

He found her sardonic smile captivating, but then everything about her was extremely fine, like a magnificent work of art. "Then consider me at your disposal, ladies," he offered.

"I'm donating some money to Miss Duras's hospital," the duchess abruptly said, as though having seen the incipient rapport between the two young people she wished to further put the lady at ease. "You've plenty, Jack. Give her some for her charity."

He smiled. "That sounds very like an order, Peggy."

"Damned right it is. You're as rich as Croesus. Tell him how much you need," she directed, nodding at Venus.

"That's not necessary, really, but thank you, Lady Groveland."

"Stuff and nonsense," she snorted. "You needn't be polite with Jack. He likes plainspoken people—like me," she added with a grin that creased the rouge on her cheeks. "And you need cash for that hospital."

"Why don't I send you a bank draft in the morning," the marquis suggested, rescuing Venus from his god-mother's commanding enterprise.

"Make sure it's sizable." The duchess struck his hand with her sorbet spoon.

"Yes, Peggy. Now are you through ordering us about?"

"Take Miss Duras for a dance and I'll be silent the rest of the night."

"There's an offer we can't refuse," the marquis said, turning a beguiling smile on Venus. "Once around the floor, Miss Duras, and we're free of Peggy's interference."

"Not forever, mind you," the duchess quickly inter-posed.

"For tonight at least," he countered with a piercing look meant to arrest her persistence. He didn't need help enticing a woman.

"For tonight," she reluctantly agreed, clearly in her element when ordering others' lives.

"Would you mind, Miss Duras?" Rising from his chair, he offered his hand to Venus. "In the interests of calm and tranquility for the remainder of the night, I remind you." An impudent light sparkled in his eyes.

Understanding her hostess wouldn't be gainsaid, Venus capitulated. The beauty of the man was truly breathtaking at close range, dancing with him would be far from an ordeal. "A laudable reason, Lord Redvers," she said. "I'm a proponent of calm and tranquility."

But when her hand touched his, any probability of maintaining calm and tranquility vanished.

They both felt the same inexplicable thrill, and his fingers closed over hers with more force than he intended. "Excuse me," he instantly said, but he didn't release his grip. Instead, he placed his other hand under her arm and drew her from her chair as though she were more fragile than moonbeams.

They stood very close for the briefest of moments before his better judgment roused itself, before he remembered where they were, before he moved back a half-step and said in a normal voice that took enormous effort to produce, "Come dance with me."

The duchess was smiling as they walked away.

Venus wasn't aware of walking into the ballroom.

Lord Redvers was particularly aware of the hush that descended on the room when they moved out onto the floor.

But a second later, all the gawkers and voyeurs and gamblers who were counting their winnings disappeared from his perception. She was smiling up at him, a temptress in flowered yellow mousseline and he felt it in more than the obvious places. He felt it like a jolt, a primal hammer of arousal and excitement, and if Peggy wouldn't be so smug, he'd tell her tomorrow she was right.

"You like me," Venus murmured with a smile, the fragrance of her hair swirling around them.

"I'd say no if I could."

"If your interest wasn't so obvious, you mean."

She was smug, too, but oddly he didn't care. "One of the great merits of the waltz."

"You're a very good dancer," she calmly remarked as if his erection wasn't hard against her stomach as they glided into a tight turn. "Is that why we're alone on the floor?"

His brief hesitation was answer of a kind.

"Tell me. I'm quite unflappable."

"You know how shallow the interests of the beau monde."

"And?"

"I don't want you to become angry again."

"Again?"

Her tone of voice didn't bode well. "How much do you want to know?"

"The truth would be fine."

He swore softly under his breath, debating the various levels of truth. "There's a wager concerning . . ."

"This dance?" She glanced at their rapt audience. "I feel as though we're on stage."

"Do you mind?"

Her mouth quirked faintly at his politic courtesy. "Being on stage or being with you?"

"Both, I suppose."

"That depends on the degree of scandal in this wager."

Wagers, he silently corrected, recalling the lengthy list in the betting book at Brookes. "How unflappable are you?"

She chuckled at his discomfort. "Good God, Redvers, just tell me. Or do you stand to lose a large sum of money?"

"Hell, no, the wagers aren't mine."

"Wagers?"

"Could we talk about this in a degree more privacy than this dance floor allows?"

"You don't wish to be embarrassed before the entire ton."

With his rash, impetuous conduct, he'd long ago learned to ignore public speculation. The lady, however, might not be so blasé. "Yes," he lied. "If you don't mind, we could find a measure of quiet in Peggy's library."

"Because these people don't read."

He nodded. "We're assured privacy."

"Do I dare be private with you?" The smallest hint of flirtation scented her words.

"I'm not sure," he said honestly, when he'd always viewed honesty as de trop in dalliances.

"Then I shall have to be on my guard." The tip of her tongue wetly traced her lush bottom lip, and he wondered for a split second who was seducing whom.

Having been given further impetus to leave the ballroom, he guided them in wide, sweeping circles to the least populated section of the dance floor and, taking her hand, forced a passage through the bystanders. She followed him without demur, scarcely looking at the avid spectators. Once they were in the outside corridor, she laughingly said, "If ever I'm in a burning building, I'd like you for a guide."

"People always move out of my way." He turned to the left, drawing her alongside him.

"I noticed. Do you have a reputation for violence?"

He paused for the briefest second; at first he thought she'd said vice and he was trying to decide how to answer. "Violence?" he said, understanding now. His smile was benign. "Not unless I'm provoked."

"You sound like my brother. He claims he's the innocent in all his duels."

"It's against the law to duel in England."[2]

"Please. I'm not a schoolgirl." She knew Viscount Coleridge had just settled a dispute with Lord Ferrers on the beach at Brighton.

"Since I don't care to live on the Continent," he said, smiling, "I don't admit to dueling. Here we are." He stopped before a door, glancing up and down the hall before turning the door latch and ushering her in.

A splendid, Italianate gas chandelier illuminated the room, and a small fire glowed in the grate. The light, however adequate for a normal space, was subdued in the large, high-ceilinged chamber. All the corners were in shadow, the heavy, leather-covered furniture like great hulking shapes in the dimness.

He stood for a moment just inside the door, not entirely sure how to deal with Miss Duras when his feelings were so curiously out of character. With anyone else, with all the women in his past, he would have quickly found the darkest corner and the softest sofa and had the lady under him and panting in short order. Instead, he politely inquired, "Where would you like to sit?" offering her a choice with a wave of his hand.

His closeness sent an irrepressible shiver up her spine, and she turned to him as though trying to gauge the reason for such a sensation. There was no explanation for her fevered susceptibility, nothing in her past to serve as yardstick or measure.

"*If* you'd like to sit," he added in an exquisitely soft murmur that meant something else entirely.

A touch of flame from the fire was reflected in the depths of his eyes. He was so near she gave in to a tantalizing urge, reaching up to run her fingertip over the silken blackness of one brow.

He raised his hand slowly, understanding she might be easily frightened, and lightly clasping her upraised hand, he brought it to his mouth and placed a warm kiss in her palm.

She made the softest of sounds, muted and low, and he felt it deep in the pit of his stomach and in his pulsing erection. Sliding his free hand around her waist, he gently drew her against his body.

Neither spoke, the utter silence of the room broken only by their breathing, his deep and rhythmic, hers lightly labored as if she were caught in a turbulence.

He didn't know her, knew nothing about her, only that she'd rebuffed him when last they met, so he proceeded with caution, not rushing the lady, lowering his head to hers slowly, deliberately, so she could change her mind if she wished.

When their lips touched, when the velvety, brushing contact first registered in their brains, they both sighed as if the world had briefly vibrated on its axis and they were the recipients of that delicious oscillation. Her arms drifted around his neck a second later and she molded herself against his hard, muscled body, like a flagrant invitation to pleasure—when she never, never allowed herself such license, when she should have known better with a man of his repute.

"I think it's your cologne," she said against his lips.

"Good," he whispered. "Then I'll bathe in it."

She laughed, the sound smothered by his kiss, and when next he lifted his mouth from hers, she was panting. He knew the sound, understood the nuances of female arousal to perfection. Slipping his hand under her legs, he lifted her into his arms and carried her to the darkest corner and softest sofa and placed her on the satiny leather. He followed her down because she didn't release her hold around his neck, and when she said, "I need more kisses," he obliged.

The sofa was broad and long and more than sufficient to hold them both, despite her voluminous petticoats and flounces and froth of a gown. For a brief moment between kisses, she wondered if she'd gone mad to be doing what she was doing in a stranger's house with a man she scarcely knew. If she'd not been so unmoved by the hundreds of suitors in her life, all vying for her attention, she might have considered being prudent. But she knew better than most how rare these sensations were, how miraculous these heated feelings, and she was liberated enough to want what she wanted.

A woman of independence for many years now, reason her only guide, she was familiar with making her own decisions. But even unconventional as she was, it took a dramatic, fevered passion for her to so cavalierly disregard her scruples. She even said, "Maybe we shouldn't," as he began unhooking her bodice, and he stopped, well-mannered even half-breathless, even under duress. But the throbbing between her legs was so profound, she couldn't resist her carnal longing for more than a second, and when she said, "Never mind," and arched up to kiss him, he drew in a deep, steadying breath and resumed what he did so well.

He'd undressed her to her chemise and stockings when she frantically whispered, "The door!"

He responded swiftly to her fearful cry, springing up in a fluent flow of muscle and long-limbed grace. Captivated, basking in a sensual glow, she watched him cover the distance to the door and back in record time, thinking him wholly too beautiful for words, from his gleaming black hair and starkly handsome face down his lean, athletic body to his silk-stockinged feet.

He smiled at her as he reclaimed his place at her side, unaware of her scrutiny, or too familiar with it to take notice. Brushing her lips in a gentle kiss, he murmured, "Now you're safe."

"Or in great jeopardy, depending on your point of view," she whispered, smiling up at him.

"Never that," he breathed, "with this kind of pleasure." He slid the strap of her chemise down her shoulder, kissed the mounded plumpness of her breast and, pushing the fabric aside, covered her taut nipple and aureole and gently sucked.

She couldn't breathe for several moments, but when she could, she whispered, "More . . ." as she shakily unfastened the bow at the neckline of her chemise, wanting that exact sensation again—the touch of his mouth on her breast miraculously traveling downward to the heated, throbbing core of her body.

He stripped her chemise away so gracefully she felt as though it were removed by gossamer wings, and she lay before him unclothed except for her white gartered stockings.[3]

He didn't know how much longer he could wait, whether he could continue with his amorous play now that she was nude and waiting, a siren with creamy thighs and a welcoming smile. Only an iron will had restrained his lustful urges thus far; he'd been ready to take her on the dance floor.

"Take *all* your clothes off," she softly urged, her hips restlessly rolling from side to side, her large breasts quivering with the movement, her eyes hot and fevered, glowing with emerald fire. "If you don't mind," she added in a sultry murmur.

He was partially undressed, his shirt studs loosened, his coat and cravat discarded, his shoes kicked off under the sofa. "A rhetorical question, no doubt," he said with a smile, slipping his forget-me-not-embroidered suspenders down his arms.

"I certainly hope so." Rolling on her side, she propped her head on her hand and surveyed his disrobing with interest.

"Do you like to watch?" For the first time since he'd seen her in the supper room, the thought of other men struck him. Obviously he wasn't the first, not with her explosive, swiftly roused passions and the bewitching sorcery in her eyes. For a dissolute man, he was curiously offended. "Do you?" His shirt arrested halfway down his arms, he frowned at her.

She looked wildly desirable lounging on the leather sofa, her thick, magnificent hair undone and falling on her shoulders in a fragrant tawny mane, her sumptuous cleavage ostentatious and showy in her odalisque pose, as though her large breasts had been confined in her gown bodice with only the most repressive constraint.

"I do right now." She shifted slightly so the curve of her bottom was more highly defined in pale profile against the dark leather. "Hurry . . ." she whispered.

"And if I don't?"

"Don't be temperamental. Were you expecting a virgin?"

A flash of annoyance heated his brain even though she was right, even though he avoided virgins like the plague. "You're no shrinking violet, are you?"

"Hardly your type, I expect. Are we having our first fight?" Her brow arched in amusement.

She was a veritable vision, voluptuous, enticing, the kind of woman seen only in paintings. Definitely his type. "Forgive me." He slid his shirt off and dropped it on the carpet. "I seem to have lost my mind for a moment."

"Then we're not fighting."

"Perhaps tussling, as soon as I get these clothes off."

"Ummm . . . a lovely promise."

"I can promise you something else as well," he said with a salacious grin, unbuttoning his trousers.

"Is this where I should blush and assuage your sense of propriety?"

He shook his head, not sure why he'd reacted so oddly a moment ago. "You're perfect, really. I mean it sincerely."

"I didn't know rogues were sincere."

"I didn't know women were sincere."

"Then we both have something to learn tonight."

"Is this a teaching lesson then?" he teased, stepping out of his trousers.

"I doubt I can teach you anything. And you'd be angry if I did," she playfully added.

He tipped his head, his look sportive. "In my more benign mood, that's damned tempting."

"*You're* very tempting, standing there in your silk underwear with your beautiful, rampant penis rearing its head." His drawers were short, the China silk covering only his upper thighs, the evidence of his erection barely concealed beneath the light fabric. "Do come closer."

"I don't suppose there's a man alive who would decline that invitation."

"Nor many women who can resist your intensely virile charms."

None as of this moment, but well-bred and gallant, he said instead, "As long as you can't, I'm content."

"Contentment wasn't exactly the sensation I was looking for." Crooking her index finger, she motioned him closer.

"Something more feverish?"

"How clever you are."

She was utterly natural, frank and unself-conscious. Asking for what she wanted without ceremony. After the surfeit of coy and artful society belles sharing his bed, pretense and artificiality their forte, she was delightfully refreshing.

As he moved toward the sofa, he slipped his fingers in the waistband of his underwear, about to slide them off.

"Let me do that." Her voice was a husky low contralto that touched him like velvet across the small distance, adding dimension to his erection.

He came to a stop inches from the leather couch and waited, feeling overwrought with a rare, reckless delirium, as if this were his first time. It unnerved him briefly, the effect she had on him, he never felt more than an impatient lust. When she sat up, gazed up at him from under a fall of gold-streaked curls, and reached out to stroke the enticing outline of his erection, he sucked in his breath and began counting backward from a thousand.

He tried to shake away the sense of losing control, reminding himself she was just one of hundreds; this wasn't his first time, not by the farthest stretch. But then she began sliding his silk drawers down his hips and he felt a wild desperation to bury himself deep inside her without further wooing or preliminaries. "I'd better do that," he said in a strained voice, forcing himself to master the rash urgency impelling him, brushing her hands away with as much courtesy as he could muster.

"You're impatient—good." Her whisper was understanding, approving, as if the sight of white China silk sliding to the floor were a personal present. "Then I don't have to wait."

For the merest pulse beat he questioned his frenzied need for her, but relentless lust immediately voided introspection and a second later, he eased her down on the sofa and climbed between her outspread legs. He was beginning to move forward, when she pressed hard against his chest and breathlessly murmured, "I almost forgot. You need a condom."[4]

Already in full rut, he ignored her, forcing her hand aside, adjusting himself for penetration.

"No!" she cried, shoving at him harder, and the enormity of what was required of him finally registered in the tumult of his mind. It took a moment more to compel his body to understanding, then another second for him to bring some order to his thoughts. Marginally rational, he found enough breath to whisper, "I won't come in you."

"That's not good enough." Her gaze was challenging.

His body still at ramming speed, he drew much needed air into his lungs. "I'm absolutely dependable." He was going to die, he thought, or explode, or do something unforgivable.

"I'm sorry, that's not good enough either."

His brows came together in a scowl and looking daggers at her, he swore and rolled away. Sprawled against the sofa arm, his chest rising and falling in agitation, he hotly said, "Is this some fucking game?"

"Haven't you ever heard of a condom?" she snapped, as frustrated as he with the interrupted pleasure. "A man like you who fucks everything in sight?"

"A hot little cunt like you—I'm surprised you didn't bring your own."

"Go to hell." At twenty-five, she'd seen enough of the world to take on anyone as an equal. Not to mention being a member of a family who faced challenges undaunted. She scrambled up into a seated position and reached for her chemise. "I should have known a man like you only thinks of his own pleasure. Selfish bastard."

"Not as selfish as you. We could have both climaxed without any problem. I mastered the art of withdrawal a decade ago."

She snorted. "I doubt it." Pulling the chemise over her head, she thrust her arms into the armholes and let the embroidered silk fall into place. "How many children have you left in your wake?"

"None. If you'd done your homework better, you'd know that."

"I was pursuing you? Is that what you think?" Incredulous, she swept up his shoe and threw it at him.

He deftly caught it, replaced it on the carpet. "You

certainly weren't running away, Miss Duras," he rudely said. "How long was it between the supper room and this sofa? Ten minutes?"

"Ohhhh!" she bristled, clenching her fists. "I could hit you if it would do any good, you smug bastard. If you must know, it's been a year since I've made love. So, acquit me of being lured by your irresistible charms. I was in heat, that's all."

"Then I have a suggestion." His voice altered, his eyes turned seductive, his fury was abruptly curtailed.

"I'm not interested in your suggestions," she tartly replied, grabbing one of her petticoats from the back of a chair.

"If you haven't climaxed in a year and if you'd like to, I could help you out—short of intercourse."

His voice was like the most bewitching sorcery, his words an overt promise of pleasure. The thought of assuaging the tremulous pulsing that still heated her body shamelessly tempted her. She swung the lacy petticoat in a lazy arc and looked at him straight on. "And what will you get out of this charity?"

"Nothing if you don't wish, but—"

"There's always a but," she mocked.

"I *could* find a condom among the men at Peggy's ball." He glanced down at his conspicuous erection. "And we could both enjoy this . . ."

Her body instantly responded. If the thought of being brought to orgasm manually was tempting, his second choice was wildly provocative. It had been so long, she thought, or she wouldn't even consider his brazen invitation, however seductive his tone, however tantalizing his enormous penis. She *should* say no, though, she reflected. He was too self-assured . . . and too damned beautiful, and much too familiar with women always saying yes. She should refuse him out of hand. "Under one condition," she said instead.

He smiled. "Look at me. I'll agree to anything."

She couldn't help but smile at his candor. "So we'll each be charitable."

"Something like that, although this is the first time I've ever bargained for a fuck."

"How interesting," she sardonically replied. "When this is my thousandth time."

"You *are* a little bitch."

"Not little," she sweetly said.

His gaze traveled slowly down her tall form and then back again, coming to rest on her splendidly large breasts. "No," he softly drawled, "definitely not little."

There was a conspicuous silence, while both struggled with their principles and lust, neither sure they were actually talking about rutting as though they were negotiating for a leasehold. But the marquis was less familiar with delaying satisfaction—the lady's year-long celibacy a case in point—so he cast aside principle first and said, "So, then . . . do we agree?"

"On a condom?"

"On that."

She nodded. He tipped his head and swiftly rose from the sofa.

"Wait here," he said, reaching for his trousers.

"You'll need these." She picked up his silk drawers from the floor.

"I won't be gone that long."

She took a deep breath. "Maybe I won't want to go through with this by the time you come back."

He glanced at her sideways, swiftly buttoning his trousers. "I'll change your mind."

"I don't know . . ."

He was beside her before her words died away, and lifting her arms before she could protest, he slid her chemise off, swept her up into his arms and, walking to the couch in front of the fire, placed her on the cushions.

"Now think of me fucking you here," he murmured, slipping his fingers inside her heated dampness, "a dozen times. And then after that," he whispered, bending his head to lick her nipple, "I'll fuck you a dozen times more . . ." He stroked her sleek tissue delicately, deftly, with infinite skill and patience, and before long, Venus had forgotten her uncertainties, all her doubts dissolving in the heat of her arousal. He left her just short of orgasm, easing away from her heated embrace with whispered promises of satisfaction once he returned. "Lock the door behind me," he whispered. "I'll knock twice." And he dressed with such speed, she didn't know if she should be charmed or offended by his expertise in leaving.

But ultimately she wanted what he could give her, and disregarding his reputation and past, she sensibly decided there was time enough to take offense after her climax. Her smile elicited a brief query from the marquis, but she only said, "Hurry back and I'll tell you." Locking the door behind him, she poured herself a glass of sherry from a tray of liquors, returned to the warmth of the fire and, lying on the sofa, sipped on her drink while she waited for her sexual salvation.

She wasn't a novice to amorous pleasure. She'd had lovers, but none who brought her to this frenzied heat.

And if she was in a speculative mood—which she wasn't at the moment, physical pleasure of more import—she might have questioned the reasons for the marquis's significant appeal. Other than the obvious. She smiled faintly. While women always politely said size didn't matter when talking of their lover's prowess, size did matter, of course. And in that regard, Jack Fitz-James couldn't be faulted.

Chapter 3

———◦◦◦◦———

AT A HALL MIRROR, THE MARQUIS CHECKED the degree of disarray in his appearance before entering the ballroom, decided he was presentable if not too closely inspected, and entered through one of the lesser-used doorways. Moving around the perimeter of the dance floor, he avoided conversation with cool politeness, his focus the card room in the adjoining chamber. Once he'd passed through the gauntlet of female attention, he allowed himself a small sigh and, standing on the threshold of the card room, surveyed the paneled interior looking for the likeliest prospects.

Most of the men of his class were relatively unconcerned with other than their personal pleasure in making love. Their position and wealth allowed them that prerogative and most took full advantage of it. But he knew one or two peers who were concerned with protection for reasons of health, and he searched them out in the busy room.

There was no manner in which this could handled discreetly. He knew his peers too well; gossip was the lifeblood of the ton. His only hope, he decided, was that Miss Duras was unconventional enough to ignore whatever rumors surfaced. When his scanning gaze stopped on Lord Alvers, he swore under his breath at the sight of so many of his friends at the table. But highly motivated, he moved forward, determined to secure what he'd come for.

Standing behind Lord Alvers a moment later, he leaned close to his ear and quietly explained his needs.

The young earl swung around in his chair, a smile already forming on his mouth. "In a hurry, are you?"

Jack wasn't smiling. "Do you or don't you?"

"I might," Alvers replied, smirking.

"If you'll excuse George for a minute," Jack politely said, ungently lifting the young man out of his chair and leading him away with a viselike grip on his arm. Finding a quiet corner, the marquis said, "I *am* in a hurry, so kindly hand them over and remain silent about this if you value your sister's reputation."

Alvers bristled. "Just a minute, damnit. What *about* my sister?"

"I'm not discussing it, and if you don't, no one need know. Hand them over."

"You'd better not have fucked my sister," the young man muttered, but he was already pulling two condoms out of his coat pocket.

Jack hadn't, but then George didn't know that, and he didn't have the nerve to ask his sister. The fear of scandal should keep him silent. "Thank you very much. My lips are sealed," Jack said with a smile. "Give my regards to Sally." And with his prize in hand, he flew from the card room, brushed off a dozen overtures to converse as he strode through the ballroom, and with his heart pumping at double speed, passed down the hallway to the library.

His two brisk raps weren't immediately answered and

he shifted restlessly, concerned she might have changed her mind and gone.

"Who is it?" Venus called out a lengthy while later.

His frown disappeared. "The delivery boy," he cheerfully said.

She was smiling when she opened the door. "You're very speedy."

"I had good reason," he softly replied, taking in the lush beauty of her nude form as he eased through the half-opened door. Turning to lock it, he held out the two small packets on the palm of his hand. "That's all there is, I'm afraid. I didn't want to make a scene."

"Are we missed?"

"No one seemed to notice."

"How very nice."

"With three hundred or more here tonight, it's easy enough to become lost in the crowd."

She thought of saying, "I don't normally do things like this," but decided it would sound disingenuous, considering she was standing nude in Peggy Hexton's library in the midst of her ball.

And he thought of saying they would surely be missed soon, but decided it would be counterproductive, considering his plans.

"Your cravat is awry." Moving a step nearer, she reached up and set it to rights. "There. I should have noticed before you left."

He laughed and swung her up in his arms. "When I need a dutiful wife, I'll let you know."

"If I ever need a husband, I'll be sure not to call you." Her voice was playful, her green eyes filled with laughter. "I can see any help from a woman is misconstrued."

"Years of running makes one wary." His grin was very close, then luscious and heated as he kissed her.

And when his mouth lifted several moments later, she breathed, "Do let's try one of those packets . . ."

He carried her to the sofa near the fire and set her down on the warm leather. Placing the two paper packets on the sofa arm, he said, "I'm glad you didn't leave."

"Temptation overcame scruple." She lifted her brows. "Although I expect you hear that often."

He'd already stripped to his shirt and pants. "No more than you, I warrant." She was temptation incarnate lying waiting for him, gilded by the firelight, voluptuously female, a sense of anticipation in her gaze.

"No one will bother us, will they?"

The provocative question, the expectation in her tone flared through his senses. "No one will dare." He stripped the pearl studs on his shirt free with a jerk of his wrist.

"Because of you?" She'd seen how everyone stepped out of his way in their passage from the ballroom.

"Because my being with you is no one's business but ours." Pulling out his shirttails, he slid the fine linen down his shoulders and arms.

She smiled at his polite cavil. "And what a pleasant business."

"Soon it will be. I'm sorry for all the delay." His answering smile was intimate, as though it were specially bestowed on her. His trousers joined his clothes on the carpet.

The sight of him nude momentarily took her breath away. "I appreciate your understanding," she replied in what she hoped was a normal tone of voice.

His smile broadened. "It's not as though I had a choice."

"Or I, as it turns out." He was utterly splendid, like some Dionysian god: tall, bronzed, his musculature perfectly modeled, his erection monumental. "Would you think me terribly forward if I said I need that"—she lifted her hand pointedly—"right now?"

"If you wouldn't think me boorish if I agreed."

She shook her head. "I'd say benevolent."

He was already reaching for a condom; as he tore the packet open, his penis surged higher.

She squirmed, her body opening in readiness, a frisson of anticipation rippling through her vagina. "I find this unnerving," she breathed, her gaze on the prodigious size of his erection. "I'm not usually—"

"I know," he said on a suffocated breath, sliding the rubber sheath over the swollen crest of his penis, an incredible lust beating at his brain. "I haven't done this for anyone."

Her eyes flared.

"You can't feel much with these," he muttered, moving closer. "You see how much I want you."

"A mutual obsession, Lord Redvers."

A flicker of understanding registered in his eyes at the use of his title; she was distinguishing the act from the irregular circumstances. "Perhaps it's the pineapple ice making us reckless."

"I wish it were so simple."

"But then I don't want it simple." With the extraordinary state of his arousal, he wasn't in the mood for brevity tonight, nor for any form of simplicity.

"Now are you sure you don't want to slow this down?" He moved between her legs with a casualness she found intriguing, as though he'd done this often enough to feel no awkwardness in a conceivably awkward situation.

She lightly touched his rampant penis. "Do you?"

"It was my last politesse."

"Before?"

"Before I give in to this insanity."

"No need to be polite on my account."

He grinned. "Where have you been all my life?"

"Perhaps waiting for this."

"I'll be coming in then," he whispered, his voice husky with desire, and gently spreading her thighs wider with a brush of his hand, he slowly entered her. Conscious of his size, he invaded her with caution, gauging her receptivity. But even with the vulcanized rubber condom exerting more friction, his progress was one of ease.

As his enormous length filled her, as he plunged deeper into her throbbing tissue, every pulsing nerve quivered in expectation. Could one die of lust? she wondered. All sensation centered in the shimmering heated core of her body, and she lifted up to draw him in more deeply.

As if he needed encouragement with the rapacious urgency burning through his blood, spiking through his brain. His hands on her hips tightened and once he was completely submerged and she was flushed and trembling, saturated, he withdrew marginally against her whimpering protest, only to sink back in, deeper still.

She cried out, the sound echoing in the shadowed room.

His muted groan gave indication of an equally feverish response and, sliding his hands under her bottom, he drew her closer, impatient to possess her completely.

Sweeping her hands down his back, she traced the taut curve of his flexed buttocks, exerted pressure with her palms, lifted her pelvis against his weight . . . and exhaled in a low exultant sigh.

The enticing sound added inches to his erection. Her eagerness was enchanting, his own vaulting need so fierce the rhythm of their desire soon turned to an unbridled flux and flow that brought them quickly to a tempestuous, shuddering climax.

Too quickly, Jack disgruntledly thought.

"I want more," Venus breathed, as if in answer to his discontent.

He crushed his mouth against hers and she returned his fevered kisses, both famished, insatiable, overcome by prodigal desire.

She swiftly felt him hard again inside her, and turning her mouth away, whispered, "Get the other condom. Hurry!"

For a man who'd never taken orders, he hesitated only briefly. Quickly withdrawing, he sprang up from the couch, discarded the used condom, and wiped himself quickly with his shirt. A new condom was in place in seconds, his arousal impressive for a man who'd only recently climaxed.

That must be why he was so much in demand, Venus thought—with only a fleeting resentment, because she needed his renowned prowess and stamina, her impatience matched only by her astonishing lust.

She'd never understood untrammeled passion before, dismissing it as poetic license or the result of an overheated imagination. But she was utterly ravenous for his touch, wanting to have sex again when he was so notorious for his profligacy she should be ashamed of herself.

Perhaps she'd consider principle later—after another climax, after she no longer burned with such longing. Understanding how rare her feelings were and how finite time, she selfishly wished to indulge herself. "Do I have to come and get you?" she murmured, restless, impatient.

He chuckled. "Give me a minute to catch my breath."

Instantly contrite, she apologized, although her words dissolved at the last in a trembling sigh as he returned to her embrace and kissed her. Gently lowering himself between her legs, he whispered, "Round two," and slid inside her welcoming warmth.

"Just in time," she breathed, her eyes already half closed, her legs wrapping around his back, the sleek heat enclosing him a degree of nirvana not previously attained.

She was a ravenous temptress, her desire in avaricious sync with his, a woman after his own heart, he thought, matching his rhythm to hers. She was hot, hot, flame hot, demanding, without the coy affectations he was used to. And unlike all the other women he'd known, he found her exhilarating—and disturbing as well. She suddenly bit him, her teeth sinking into his throat, and his unease was instantly swamped by a lust so acute he forgot everything but sensation.

Her panting indicated a level of arousal that required concentration and he leaned into his downstroke, ignoring her nails sunk into his back, deftly meeting her thrust for thrust. And they settled into a glorious driving rhythm, as if they were mating on some instinctive primal level beyond the bounds of reason.

She moved to please him and he her—their sensibilities so violently inflamed the world disappeared, awareness disappeared, only raw feeling prevailed. Until, gasping for air, they convulsed in a soul-shattering, divine, unearthly orgasm.

"Incredible." Breathless, his chest heaving, Jack lay braced above her, eyes shut. "Don't . . . go . . . away," he said, a smile on his mouth.

"I couldn't . . . if I wanted to." The remnants of her climax deliciously strumming through her body, she brushed her fingertips against his broad chest.

His eyes came open and he smiled down at her. "I won't let you, anyway."

Her lashes faintly flickered. "You might have to. The condoms are gone."

"So?"

"Don't be difficult." Her voice changed, cooled.

"Don't worry so much," he soothed.

"But *I'm* the one who *has* to worry."

"Not with me, you don't."

He was too calm or unconcerned—indifferent probably, given his past. "Somehow I'm not assured," she murmured, her palms braced against his chest, problematical issues in the fore. "Get off."

His brows rose sharply. "Do your lovers actually respond to that tone?"

"*Get off.*"

Although he considered her concerns grossly exaggerated, he chose not to argue. With a shrug, he complied, easing away, dropping to the floor, and leaning against the couch. "You're too nervous," he casually noted, discarding the condom and reaching for a decanter of liquor on a nearby table. "I have no intention of coming in you for selfish reasons of my own. Would you like some?" Swiveling around, he held up the decanter. "It's sherry, I'm afraid."

"You're too cavalier about this, Redvers. And I don't know if I want a drink."

"Jack, and if you want to come again, let me know."

"I don't think so."

But he noticed she didn't move from her languorous pose, and when he handed her a glass of sherry, she took it.

He lifted his glass to her in salute a moment later. "Tempted?"

"I can't afford to be tempted." She spoke like a teacher might to a recalcitrant pupil.

A mischievous gleam appeared in Jack's eyes. "Such little faith."

"In a man with your reputation? I think I have good reason to be skeptical."

"I don't have children."

"That you know of."

"I'd know. They'd ask for money."

She made a moue. "So cynical."

He shrugged, not about to disagree about his cynicism.

"Well, you don't have to worry about me asking for your money."

"I'm not. It's your anxieties I'm trying to assuage." Reaching over, he lightly trailed his fingertip up her calf.

"That's high enough."

He politely stopped. "Is your pussy still throbbing?"

"No."

But she'd answered too quickly, her gaze evasive. "Let me see," he murmured, sliding his hand over her knee, his warm palm coming to rest on her lower thigh.

"I'd rather you didn't." Her smile held a restive constraint. "For safety's sake."

"This can't be dangerous. Relax." He slipped his hand between her thighs. "How does this feel?"

"I don't feel anything," she lied, knowing she shouldn't allow him to touch her, knowing a simple brush of his hand was disastrous to her resolve.

"How about this?" He slid his middle finger over her swollen labia with infinite delicacy and he could feel the muscles of her thighs clench. "Let me take that glass," he murmured, lifting it from her hand, continuing the bewitching massage, promise in the enchanting drift of his finger. "You're really wet," he said a few moments later, kneeling beside the couch, the liquid evidence of her arousal drenching his fingers. "Why don't I let you come?"

Mute against her mortifying desires, shamed by her wanton response, she raised her hips, incapable of defense against her longing, against his consummate skill. He seemed to know exactly where to touch her, how lightly, how slowly, how deeply. She moaned as his fingers sank knuckle deep inside her.

She arched upward against his hand, wanting more, seeking surcease. Spreading her legs wider, he bent his head, ran his tongue over her throbbing labia, found the swollen tip of her clitoris.

She cried out.

His lips closed over the taut, erectile nub and he gently suckled, his fingers still buried deep inside her.

The passage of time seemed momentarily arrested as riveting sensation bombarded her brain. Her vagina pulsed, throbbed, roused to fever pitch, his mouth so artful and pleasing on her clitoris, she was panting, seconds from climax. And then he bit, lightly, delicately, as if he knew how to push her over the edge and she died away in a sweet flood of pleasure.

After a lengthy interval, her lashes slowly lifted and, searching for Jack, she saw him lounging in a chair near the fire.

"That was safe enough, I trust?" he amiably said.

"You needn't look so smug."

"*Au contraire.* Far from feeling smug, I'm horny as hell and not sure how far my courtesy extends."

"I'm sorry. I wish I could help, but—" His splendid penis lured her gaze, the erect length extending past his navel.

"Maybe we could negotiate something," Jack murmured, aware of her gaze, not sure he was capable of gentlemanly behavior for long.

"I can't take the risk."

"How can I assure you of my trustworthiness?"

"You can't." But she could almost feel him inside her as she gazed at him, the swollen veins of his erection prominent in the firelight, her strange new psyche inattentive to everything but carnal gratification.

"I don't suppose testimony from witnesses would serve."

She smiled. "You'd call them in from the ballroom?"

He grimaced, moody under his afflicted desires. "Damn you. I should be able to curb these impulses."

"It's my fault?"

"Yes." He had a reputation for superb self-control—

too much control, those ladies unable to attract his attention would attest. But that restraint seemed to be lacking in Venus Duras's company, and for the first time in his life he considered the possibility that female sorcery might actually exist. "Hell and damnation," he growled, coming out of the chair in a fluid surge of muscle and power. "I'm done talking."

She came up on her elbows. "What are you doing?"

"I'm going to put this stiff prick into that hot little cunt of yours."

"How *charming*," she sarcastically said.

"If you don't like it, I'll stop."

She had to look up a very long way; he towered over her, his rigid erection particularly difficult to ignore. "Jack, don't even consider force majeure. I won't allow it, I—"

He stopped her protest with a heated kiss, settling between her legs with such ease, he rightly questioned who was seducing whom.

"Trust me," he whispered against her mouth and plunged into her dewy wetness, burying himself hilt-deep with a contented sigh.

Instantly, shamefully, like the most scandalous wanton, she climaxed with a whimpering cry. Disgraced, ingloriously humbled, she felt all the certainties in her past swept away. "Oh, God," she whispered, distrait, bewildered.

"Hush," he murmured, gently kissing her. "It's allowed." Sliding his hands under her bottom, he forced himself deeper. And desire quickened within her again even while saner counsel chastised her irresponsible hunger.

But fretful anxiety soon faded in the heat of passion.

His penetration increasing until he'd buried himself to the most profound depth, he moved delicately, deliberately, skillfully, on his best behavior since he'd never resorted to brute force before. He soothed her apprehensions, mollified his own scruples, and brought her to climax twice more before he finally allowed himself to come on her stomach.

Into the hushed aftermath, Venus whispered, "I shouldn't have let you." But her tone was benevolent, her sensibilities replete.

"I shouldn't have either. Forgive me."

"If I weren't so blissfully content, I'd muster up the energy to chide you."

"Chide me next time." Sprawled against the opposite end of the sofa, he smiled at her.

Her languid sensibilities snapped to attention. "No," she firmly declared, coming up to a seated position. "There are percentages of risk, my darling man, that I don't care to contemplate."

"And degrees of pleasure, my darling lady, that you should experience."

"Absolutely not. You're not going to win this time."

"It's not about winning. It's about hot sex."

"Don't." But she felt an immediate titillating response.

"You always *seem* to like it." Confident in his ability to persuade, he gave her a tolerant smile.

"That I like," she said with a charming frankness, indicating the undiminished vigor of his penis.

"We're at your service, mademoiselle."

"A pleasant thought. However—" She glanced around. "What time is it? I should be going."

"I think I'll keep you for a while yet."

"You'll what?" Shock resonated in her words.

"I'm not finished yet."

"No, absolutely not." She scrambled to her feet and held up her hand as though the gesture would forestall his rash inclinations. "I'm not taking any more chances tonight. Enjoyable as the sex is, the consequences are too serious."

"You're hard to convince. I didn't come in you. I won't come in you."

"Sorry, I'm just more practical—for obvious reasons."

"Then I'm sorry, too," he murmured, slowly coming to his feet.

"Jack, no—Jack!" She slipped under his outstretched arm and darted away. Finding protection behind the sofa, she guardedly watched him.

"I'm completely dependable," he said, moving forward.

"Jack, no, I mean it!" Gripping the couch, she struggled to check her sexual urges. Limned by firelight, he was breathtakingly male—broad-shouldered, tall, honed to a level of fitness rarely seen. And beautifully aroused.

Suddenly leaping, he cleared the sofa in a graceful vault, landing lightly beside her. "Now about that no."

"You can't just take what you want." Her eyes were hot with affront. "Have you no manners?"

"Don't need 'em. And I always get what I want."

"Not this time," she snapped, annoyed by his insolence.

"Why don't we see how your hot little pussy feels." His smile was cheeky. "I have the distinct impression she likes me."

"You arrogant bastard!" Her palm met his cheek in a stinging blow.

"Your temper's as hot as your cunt," he murmured with a faint smile, quickly capturing her hands in his. "Now, let's see if you're still interested in fucking." Twirling her around, he pressed her into the sofa back, holding her firmly in place with his hand on the small of her back. Slipping his other hand between her legs, he eased two fingers inside her drenched passage. "Mmmm, wet cunt . . ."

She squirmed against his hold, but the resulting sensations were so intoxicating she instantly quieted.

He'd heard her suppressed moan and, slipping his fingers out, he leaned into the warmth of her back and traced his damp fingers over her plump breasts. "You're always ready, aren't you?" His mouth was close to her ear, the length of his body pressed hard into hers, his erection like an iron rod between them. "It must be your French blood."

"What's your excuse?" she snapped.

"My long-ago DeLancey ancestors, I presume. And don't pretend you don't want this, because I know better." He slid his erection between her thighs. "Feel how much I want you."

He was rock hard, magnificently long. The ache between her legs indelible evidence of his allure, she felt hot-blooded desire overwhelm her senses.

"Bend over."

He moved his hand up her spine and helped her. Her rosy bottom suddenly raised to him, her pouty labia lush and welcoming, was like the gates of paradise open for his pleasure.

Guiding his erection to her sleek cleft, he penetrated minimally, only the swollen crest of his penis partially submerged. Her silken labia closed around him, anticipation taut between them—cross-grained temper adding to the heat.

"Tell me you want this," he softly ordered, adverse to being alone in his mad, unquenchable frenzy.

"Damn you," she panted, quivering with need, resentful, her feelings in tumult. But she swayed back, wanting more, impatient to feel the full extent of his arousal even while she cursed his brazen conceit.

"Tell me what a hot little piece like you wants," he growled, resisting her enticement, unnerved by his irrepressible cravings, needing her capitulation.

Silence enveloped them, lengthened . . .

"You," she finally whispered, hating herself for wanting him so desperately.

"Good," he muttered, the single word sanction, satisfaction, exoneration for all the ambiguities. And he drove into her, lifting her with the ferocity of his thrusting stroke, plunging in over and over again with a mindless, impassioned fever that overlooked limitations and good judgment and years of casual sex. Braced against the sofa back, she melted around him, insatiable, eager for the dizzying impact of each driving invasion, caught in a torrent of rapacious need so shocking in its intensity that shame, will, reason were all silenced by sensational lust.

She came once, twice, three times until, near swooning, he took his own pleasure at last, coming on her back. Sated—at least momentarily—he lowered his head to kiss the silken nape of her neck, his mouth like a hot brand. "I'm going to fuck you all night," he breathed.

She didn't protest or take issue.

She only purred deep in her throat.

※

*M*UCH LATER, THEY LAY ON THE SOFA, THE coals of the fire a soft red glow on the hearth, contentment glowing through their senses as well. Half reclining against the sofa arm, he held her lounging form between his legs, her back against his chest, the silk of her hair brushing his chin, the gentle rise and fall of her breathing a delicate friction on his forearms.

He'd glanced at the clock on the mantel some time ago, but felt no inclination to move even though the hour was getting late. Most of the guests would be gone by now—perhaps an asset rather than a liability. Although those who remained would be badly in their cups, and unpredictable.

"I'll send you flowers in the morning," Venus murmured, swiveling enough to gaze up at him. "You definitely deserve them."

"I was thinking you might like something with emeralds to match your luscious eyes."

"No wonder you're so much in demand, my dear, sweet, darling Jack."

"Don't be flirtatious." His voice was gruff.

"Whyever not?" She twisted around in his arms so she lay against his chest, her back gracefully arched beneath his palms.

"I know flirtatious women by the score."

"So?"

"So—" he took a small breath, not quite certain why he felt nettled "—don't play the coquette."

"I may want to." She looked at him with a mild query. "Are we going to fight?"

"We're not fighting," he tautly said.

"Will you make love to me tomorrow, then?"

He didn't answer immediately, too long conditioned to avoid commitment.

"Am I not supposed to ask? Is that a male prerogative?"

"No," he gently said. "No, of course ask, and yes, I will. With the greatest of pleasure."

"Your place or mine?"

"Where are you staying?"

"My family has a house in Belgrave Square. I'm quite alone."

"No chaperon?"

Her trill of laughter annoyed him.

"Not for a very long time, darling. Why would I possibly want or need one?"

"For propriety's sake, of course."

"How starchy and prudish you sound, when you make love to all the ladies in the ton under their husbands' noses."

"It's different for a man."

"Perhaps in your world. I live very much as I please."

"And you make love as you please."

"Hardly a question for you to ask. Did you win your wager, by the way?"

"It's not my wager."

"Whose is it?"

He hesitated. "I'd rather not say."

"Does it concern me?"

His hesitation was longer this time. "In a manner of speaking."

"Then I'd appreciate knowing what I'm involved in."

"Jesus," he muttered. "Don't ask."

Pushing away from him, she eased into a seated position. "Tell me so I'll know what everyone is tittering about tomorrow."

"I thought you did as you pleased."

"I do. I simply wish to be forearmed."

"Let's just say you're going to be barraged with admirers."

"I already am. That's not a problem."

"With leering admirers."

"Because of this wager?"

"I had nothing to do with it."

"Good God, Jack, stop this unnecessary evasion. Just tell me."

"There was some question whether you were unassailable."

"And you disagreed."

"Yes."

"Well, you won your wager. Why is that so appalling."

"It wasn't my wager."

"Then whose was it? Whom do I have to cut with a scathing look?" she facetiously queried.

He debated telling her the truth, but she'd be forewarned at least if he told her. "A couple score men at Brookes," he said with a sigh. "It's in the betting book."

"Along with their friends and acquaintances." Her gaze suddenly turned cool. "And you couldn't resist."

"I hadn't planned this."

"Tonight, you mean."

He had the grace to look discomfited.

"I know men like you. You'll share the story of your conquest over drinks and cards. How fucking juvenile," she tartly said, swinging her legs over the side of the sofa.

He reached out to stop her, grasping her arm. "It's not that way."

"Yes, it is. And I should have known better. But thank you for the excellent fuck. I'll recommend you if anyone asks." Shaking his hand away, she rose to her feet.

"I wish you'd let me explain." But he didn't move, because he had no intention of doing anything more than apologize. He'd escaped too many marriage traps in the last decade. Caution gave him pause; affronted womanhood could be very expensive in terms of personal freedom. He knew men who were married for less than what he'd done tonight.

"No explanation is necessary," Venus replied, beginning to dress.

"Would you like me to escort you—"

"No, I would not." Crisp, unequivocal words.

Silenced, moody, ill-humored, he watched her dress. He didn't feel as though he were entirely to blame—neither for the wagers he had no part in, nor for the lady's open-minded, very receptive sexuality. And as she stood at the mirror, fully clothed and pinning her hair back in place, he said, "Is this exclusively my fault?"

"I don't want to talk to you."

"I have no intention of speaking about this to anyone, if you're concerned."

"You'll lose your wager."

"It's not my wager, damnit. It never was."

"Fine. I'm sure you're right," she added, readjusting a curl over one ear. "I'm just sorry I ever met you."

"You didn't seem sorry an hour ago."

She rounded on him with fire in her eyes. "Yes, you're very good, Redvers. Is that what you want to hear?

You're fucking unbelievable. But then my life doesn't revolve around sex the way yours does, so I'll manage just fine without you. I wish all the ladies good fortune with you."

She slammed the door when she left. Loudly. The crash thundered down the hall.

If he wasn't so surly, he would have smiled at her disregard for appearances. Venus Duras, apparently, had no intention of quietly sneaking out of Groveland House.

Chapter 4

⊶⊷

THE DUCHESS OF GROVELAND WAS HOLDING court on the verge of the ballroom. The dance floor was still awash with dancers despite the late hour, but dancing until dawn was common enough, and while the great bulk of the guests had departed, a goodly number still remained.

Venus walked up to the group and, bowing, thanked her hostess and bid her good night.

"I'll see you to the door," the duchess quickly replied, rising from her chair with astonishing vitality considering her age and the late hour.

She waited until they were alone in the corridor outside before saying, "I'll apologize for Jack if need be." She'd seen the strain in Venus's eyes when she'd said her good-byes, although her demeanor and voice had been composed—and Venus and Jack had been absent for a very long time. "He's rash at times, but goodhearted for all his scapegrace ways."

"No apologies are required."

"He didn't offend you, then?"

"No, not at all," Venus calmly lied as they approached the staircase.

"Good. I wouldn't want Jack to interfere with our friendship. I'm deeply interested in your hospital. I commend you for thinking of more than your newest dress or parasol, like so many of these empty-headed ladies."

"Life would be very boring if one relied only on the fashionable world for entertainment." Venus descended the marble stairs slowly so the elderly duchess could keep pace with her.

"My thought exactly." Lady Groveland added with a smile, "Although I do like a dance now and then. As to my offer of help, if you agree, my men will be over in the afternoon to help transfer your hospital supplies. Say two o'clock?"

"Thank you very much. Two o'clock will be fine."

"Don't be angry with him." The duchess had the feeling her godson and this unusual Frenchwoman were oddly alike.

"Forgive me, Duchess, but I'll be angry with him if I wish." Reaching the base of the stairs, Venus turned to her hostess with a gracious smile. "Thank you again for a lovely evening. I'll expect your men at two."

"AND SHE WALKED AWAY AS COOL AS CAN BE," the duchess said. Having tracked Jack down in the library, she sat in a chair near the fire with a glass of port in her hand and cast him a penetrating look. "You misbehaved, didn't you?"

"I'm not going to pour out my heart to you, Peggy, so don't even try." He was sprawled on the sofa, still half dressed in trousers and a partially unbuttoned shirt, his black mood undiminished. A half bottle of port since Venus left hadn't help lighten his mood.

"I can smell sex in this room. I'm not asking you for details. Only what you did to offend her."

"That's the damned rub. I didn't do anything. It's people like you, my dear gambling maniac, who had to bet on this. I don't need incentive to bed a woman."

"You told her about the wagers?" A hint of incredulity colored her voice.

"I couldn't avoid it. She'd hear soon enough tomorrow. I thought at least she should be warned."

"And now you're drinking away your sorrows."

"No, I'm not." Each word dripped with affront.

"It look to me as though you are."

"Well, you're wrong."

"She walked away from you and you can't stand it."

"I'm not that vain, and you know it."

"So why are you sullen, like a little boy who's lost his favorite toy?"

He mockingly tipped his head. "Just put the knife in and twist it, Peggy. Be my guest."

"Why do you like her?"

"I don't like her," he gruffly muttered.

"Let me reword that. What tantalizes you?"

He grimaced. "I'd like to tell you to fuck off."

"But I'm right."

"She's unlike all the rest. There. Happy?"

"And you're intrigued."

"You might say that. A day too late, a ha'penny short . . ."

"I'm going to see her tomorrow."

"And you'll make everything right. You *are* a damned romantic, Peggy."

"I always have been, I don't deny."

"But then I'm not interested in romance."

"Men never are, until it's too late."

"Jesus, Peggy, don't play matchmaker. I'm intrigued

maybe, but not demented. The day I willingly take a wife will be the day I sail to the moon. Promise me you won't interfere."

"Very well," she reluctantly murmured. "I promise."

Although the sun was breaking over the horizon, the library was still clad in shadow. Otherwise Jack might have seen the duchess's crossed fingers.

*T*HE SPRING DAWN WAS MUCH TOO BEAUTIFUL for her sour mood, Venus thought, descending from her carriage at the gate to her home in Belgrave Square. It should be overcast, with a pelting cold rain and the hint of snow in the air.

But nature overlooked the resentments of puny man and the warm sun rose in a brilliant golden haze, illuminating the world in shimmering splendor. The fresh new leaves on the trees gleamed, the fragrance of early roses filled the air, and even in her chafing resentment, she couldn't help but stop to admire the glorious blooms on the wisteria climbing up the wall trellis.

The door opened as if her staff were on alert for her return, and her butler stood framed in the opened portal. "Good morning, Miss Duras," he murmured with a punctilious bow. "Did you enjoy your evening at Groveland House?"

"Yes, Charles," she said, turning away from the splendid flowers. "Thank you."

"Chocolate is waiting in your bedchamber, mademoiselle."

"I'll need bathwater."

"Very good, my lady."

"And something hearty for breakfast. I'm famished."

"Perhaps the chef's special scrambled eggs with caviar. He received the fresh mushrooms from France yesterday."

"Some Provençal sausage, too."

"And strawberries with cream?" Charles suggested, familiar with his mistress's tastes.

"Perfect," she said with a smile. "I adore you, Charles. You know my every mood."

When her breakfast was delivered, shortly after her maid had finished drying her after her bath, Charles had seen that the chef included her favorite yeasted sugar cake with crème fraîche, as well.

She ate the sugar cake first, seated at a small table near the open windows, and then the scrambled eggs, savoring the pearly caviar as it slid over her tongue. She drank two cups of Mexican chocolate with raw piloncillo sugar, a great favorite of hers, and picked daintily at the strawberries swimming in heavy cream.

The delicious food helped to soothe her resentments, as did her refreshing bath and the lush spring morning. She was able to review the evening with less bitterness—with none, after her third cup of chocolate.

After all, she reflected in her more benign humor, she'd been well sated, luxuriantly, lavishly by a man who knew exactly what a woman wanted. She smiled faintly at the heated memory. And if one wished to be utterly practical, she was now fully replete after a year of celibacy. Definitely a charming benefit.

She sighed. A shame one had to always deal with male egos.

Leaving instructions with her maid to be wakened at one, she lay down and went to sleep instantly.

But her sleep was restless, her dreams of a dark-haired

man with smiling eyes and a ravishing sexual expertise. Fevered, tantalized, she dreamed of that ravishment, softly moaned as she felt his hands and his body giving her pleasure, tossed and turned in the grip of his enchanting sorcery, until she came awake at her maid's call with a start of surprise.

Glancing down, she saw she was in her own bed.

And softly cursed Jack Fitz-James's much-used talents.

*J*ACK DIDN'T SLEEP, OR IT SEEMED AS THOUGH he hadn't slept when Ned came calling and woke him.

"Go away," Jack muttered as Ned pulled back the drapes and let the sun into his bedchamber.

"Rise and shine! We've an appointment to see some prime horseflesh at Tattersall's." He jerked another drape open and moved to the next window.

"Go without me." The marquis's voice was muffled by the pillow he'd pulled over his head.

"Lord Simon is selling his racers. And you want that big black of his. Or last I heard, you did. I suppose we can let Blandford buy it instead."

Ned's gibe elicited a string of oaths from under the pillow.

"Is that a yes or a no?" Lord Darlington cheerfully queried, when he knew very well Jack would crawl a hundred miles rather than let Edward Dunlow buy a horse he wanted. "Maurice is sending up very black coffee, but don't hurry, we still have twenty minutes."

"Someday I'm going to strangle you." The words were utterly clear now, for Jack had flung the pillow at Ned.

"Watch my hair, damn you!" Ned yelped, smoothing

his sleek blond hair behind his ears. Vain of his overlong curls, he fancied himself an amateur poet in the mold of Lord Byron, although his poetry was intended more to impress the ladies than to express a sincere interest.

Fully awake now, the marquis rose from his bed with a sigh, feeling more fatigued than when he'd gone to sleep. But knowing Tattersall's wouldn't wait, he moved toward his dressing room. "Thanks for reminding me of that black." He yawned and stretched. "I just wish like hell it wasn't so early."

"It's past one, Jack," Ned said, following him. "Since when did you need more than a couple hours of sleep?"

"Since last night apparently. I'm exhausted."

"Is that my opening to say, 'And why is that?' I hear you and Miss Duras disappeared for several hours last night."

The marquis pushed the dressing room door open. "Lord God, this town is restricted in its interests."

"But you entertain us all so well, my boy. What would the gossip mills do if you decided to take up fishing instead?"

"Maybe I will," Jack muttered, walking over to the special shower-bath he'd installed in his home and turning on the tap. "I'll move to the country."

His friend chuckled. "That would elicit huge odds at Brookes. Mostly on how long you'd last in the country."

Shooting his companion a black look, the marquis stepped inside the tower-shaped framework composed of numerous pipes spouting water from hundreds of perforations. Standing under the hot water, he wondered how much he really wanted Lord Simon's black. He was tired or weary or both, and still surly about the events of the previous night.

He'd probably drunk too much. He didn't allow himself to admit a craving for the lovely Miss Duras. Such an admission would set his comfortable life at risk.

"Have you fallen asleep in there?"

Ned's brusque query disrupted his discontent. "I *do* need to sleep one of these nights," he grumbled, lifting his face to the overhead spray.

"After Tattersall's," Ned briskly replied. "Once we're finished with the auction, we'll go and see if Mme. Robuchon has any new girls, and you can nap there. Ah, here's Maurice with our coffee."

THE MEN REACHED THE AUCTION HOUSE JUST as the first lot came on the block, and then waited for nearly an hour before the black Jack wanted was brought forward.

The bidding was furious. The horse had taken a dozen firsts last year. But those with lesser fortunes fell away before too long, and Jack and Lord Blandford brought the sum up to staggering levels in short order.

The marquis didn't care how much he paid for the racer. His nabob wealth had come from the East India Company in the last century, although the Fitz-Jameses had been equally well endowed by Charles II's generosity to his mistress. And as one of the largest landowners in Gloucestershire, the family had never worried about money. Additionally, Jack had invested in railroads very early. He could buy a dozen Lord Blandfords without bringing a sweat to his bankers' brows.

Deciding to finish the bidding, Jack offered ten thousand over Blandford's last bid, and Edward Dunlow's face turned black with fury.

"Damn you, Redvers. I need that horse in my stable," he raged.

"Then you should have stayed the course," Jack calmly remarked.

"As you did with the French lady last night. How long did you ride her?"

"I went home early last night, Blandford, and if you wish to question my word on the matter, name your seconds."

The Earl of Blandford wasn't known for his courage. A small, rawboned man, he preferred his footmen fight his battles. "Fuck you, Redvers."

"You're not my type. Perhaps if I'm drunk enough, we could talk," Jack drawled.

"Maybe the French lady would welcome other suitors," Blandford spitefully suggested.

"Be my guest, Blandford. She's quite capable of making her own decisions on suitors." But despite his casual reply, he had to restrain an urge to knock down the bloody sod. As if he'd let the damned bastard touch Venus, he thought, thin-skinned and moody.

Fortunately, the auction clerk approached him then, or he would have had to question his novel feelings of possession.

Chapter 5

———✷———

ENUS HADN'T EXPECTED THE DUCHESS TO accompany her serving men, but there she was riding beside the driver of the dray wagon when the vehicle arrived in Belgrave Square. Dressed in a plain natural linen gown and a utilitarian straw bonnet, bereft of her usual heavy layers of rouge, the duchess looked as though she were planning on working along with her men.

Venus greeted her with a smile, charmed by the old lady who viewed work as a feasible activity. A rare instance for those in the fashionable world.

"Come ride with me," Peggy offered, making room for Venus on the broad, wide seat. "And give Will directions to the warehouse."

Leaving her majordomo standing dumbfounded on the pavement, Venus climbed up onto the high seat of the wagon with help from one of Peggy's men and, seating herself beside the duchess, found herself in extreme good humor. "How nice to see you again," she said. "I didn't realize you wished to help."

"I look forward to doing something productive for a change. Teas and visiting and parties become wearisome after a time."

"Don't they, now," Venus agreed. And after giving

directions to the driver, the ladies discussed the two hospitals Venus was financing in Paris. The duchess queried her on a number of details, not content to simply give her money to a charity and feel that she'd done her duty. She was even more impressed with Venus after she'd disclosed the number of patients who were treated each day at the charity hospitals.

"My heavens, with that many patients, your expenses must be considerable. Did Jack send his bank draft yet?" the duchess inquired.

"No, but it's not necessary. I'm sure he was only being polite. My family has resources enough."

"Additional funds are always useful, my dear. I'll see that some others of my friends help out as well. And if you'd be so kind and give my steward some advice on how to begin such a project, I think I'd very much like to do the same here."

"One feels an enormous sense of accomplishment at seeing a small child cured, or a young mother given adequate care during birthing, or an injured workman who would otherwise be invalided nursed back to health. I derive great pleasure from my work, although my parents sometimes think I should lighten my schedule."

"You're young and energetic. Why not do what you like when you have vigor. I still recall my days on the stage with great delight, although we worked long hours in sometimes difficult conditions. But I wouldn't have given up the experience for all of Cyril's money."

"Jack said last night that yours was a love match. How wonderful."

"Cyril was the most perfect of men. I consider myself

very fortunate to have found him in this rough-and-tumble world."

"Have you been alone long?" Venus didn't wish to pry into the details of the duke's death should the memory be painful.

"Ten years now, and I still miss him every day. He ignored his family's outrage to marry me. He was very brave."

"He was very fortunate, I think."

"We both were much in love for forty years. Tell me of *your* family. Everyone knows of your father and grandfather. Do you have brothers and sisters? I'm told your mother's from Kent."

For the remainder of the journey to the warehouse, the women spoke of their families. The duchess had two children born late in her marriage. Her son was currently in Egypt on a desert trek, while her daughter, married to a diplomat, was posted in Vienna.

"They'll both be back in England this fall. Do you intend a lengthy visit?" the duchess asked.

Venus shook her head. "Another fortnight, perhaps a month, but no more. I came to buy some of the new equipment displayed at the Great Exhibit, and once I've accomplished my task, I'll return to Paris."

"You and Julia would have suited wonderfully, although she's somewhat older than you. She believes in independence for women, you see, although I can't imagine where she acquired such radical notions." The duchess's smile was teasing. "And should my son show the faintest inkling of taking a wife someday, I'd try to induce you to stay and meet him. Although his father was nearing forty when we married," she reflected. "I suppose Geoffrey feels he still has ten years before he needs to take a wife. Julia's given me my wonderful grandchildren, for which I'm grateful. If I were to wait for my son to produce an heir," she said with a small sigh, "I'd be long dead."

Wishing to keep the conversation on a happier note, Venus asked the duchess about her grandchildren and was regaled for the remainder of the journey with their glowing achievements.

The ladies spent the afternoon overseeing the removal of the supplies from the warehouse to the Duras's ship, and once their task was completed, the duchess cajoled Venus into returning to her home for tea. "No need to dress, my dear. We'll be quite alone. And you haven't seen my garden yet, so I won't take no for an answer."

After the duchess's generous donation and help, it would have been difficult to refuse, but Venus found her likable as well. "If you promise I shan't have to meet anyone of fashion in this dirty gown," she replied, trying to brush a smudge from her skirt.

"Only my own fashionable self, my dear." The duchess spread her arms wide, displaying her own dusty gown, smiling as she might have years ago on Drury Lane's stage.

"Then I accept with pleasure, although I warn you, I'm extremely hungry. I'll make a shambles of your sweets and sandwiches."

"How shocking," the duchess said in mock horror. "A woman who eats. My female acquaintances all nibble like so many tame squirrels. Do you like lemon-curd tarts?"

"I adore anything with lemon curd."

"I do think we must be related." The duchess patted

Venus's hand. "Come now, we'll have Will drive us back."

*A*T GROVELAND HOUSE, THE DUCHESS OFFERED Venus a sunny lady's chamber adorned in aquamarine damask and pale Empire furniture in which to refresh herself, suggesting they meet in the garden in ten minutes.

Which gave her only a few moments to send a note to Jack.

As Lady Groveland dashed off her message requesting his presence for tea, she ignored high-minded principles in the interests of matters of the heart. Call it kismet or sorcery, she'd recognized an affinity between her profligate godson and the extraordinary Miss Duras and she intended to meddle. So she lied without a qualm, asking Jack to stop by briefly to help her decide on a bequest for her grandchildren. The marquis served as her surrogate advisor in business matters when her son was absent.

"Find him, wherever he is," she ordered her footman, standing beside her at the ready. "Check Mme. Robuchon's first if he's not at home. Lucy's is his favorite afternoon retreat."

The duchess well understood the ways of a fashionable buck. Her husband had lived a bachelor life for two decades before they'd met; her son had followed his father's pattern. She knew how wealthy young men spent their leisure time. She also kept abreast of all the gossip through her lady's maid, Molly, who could tell you by noon each day who had had breakfast with whom.

The duchess gave instructions to her maid, her confidant in all things. "The minute Jack arrives, have him brought to the garden."

"He's going to be right furious with you, my lady," Molly warned, her eyes wide with alarm.

"Not in front of Miss Duras, he won't be."

"Sure enough, he might," the maid disagreed. "You know his temper."

"I also know he was melancholy last night when Miss Duras left, whether he cared to admit it or not. Why shouldn't I give him a nudge in the right direction?"

"You're ever so brave, my lady," Molly declared. "Melancholy or not, the marquis is frightfully hot-tempered."

"I've known him since he was a suckling babe," the duchess observed, tucking a hennaed curl into place. "I can handle him. You just see that he comes into the garden. And then after a decent interval, call me in with a message. Now, not a word from anyone that Miss Duras is visiting when he arrives."

"My lips are sealed, my lady."

"See that the rest of the staff's are as well."

And so saying, the duchess twitched her skirt into place and sailed from the room with the stage presence of an accomplished actress.

THE GARDEN WAS PEACEFUL AND SERENE, tucked away behind serpentine brick walls covered with cascading roses. A spreading magnolia planted by some long-ago Groveland shaded one corner where a tea table had been arranged.

Venus was lounging on a silk-cushioned chaise, the cream tussah a perfect foil for her golden beauty and fern-green muslin gown. She waved at the sight of the duchess descending the terrace steps, and Peggy cheerfully waved back.

"I told Oliver we deserved our best champagne after all our hard work this afternoon," the duchess said as she approached.

"I've already been served." Venus held her half-empty glass up for her hostess to see. "Your butler insisted I try the lemon-curd tarts too. You see," she went on, indicating the depleted plate, "I took him up on the offer."

"Tell me what I can do to help tomorrow," Peggy declared, pouring herself a glass of champagne. "I haven't had so much fun in ages. Perhaps you could instruct me concerning some purchases for my own charity hospital."

"I'd be delighted. I plan to return to the Exhibition tomorrow for my next round of purchases."

"Capital! Let me replenish your wineglass." The duchess had deliberately chosen to have their tea without servants in attendance. She had every confidence the marquis would be found, and she wished no spectators when he appeared.

The ladies had finished one bottle of champagne, the lemon-curd tarts, and half of the salmon sandwiches, and their discussion of the recently appointed poor-law board was in full swing, when Jack arrived on the terrace. Having positioned her chair so the terrace door was in sight, the duchess rose from her chair immediately and waved in welcome.

Venus turned to see who was arriving, and a warm flush immediately colored her face.

Jack's descent was arrested midway down the terrace

stairs when he saw Peggy's guest and, for the briefest moment, he debated turning around and leaving. Grandchildren's bequests indeed. Now he knew why Peggy's footman had been so insistent, why he wasn't willing to have Jack come to see the duchess that evening.

Damn Peggy's guile, he irritably thought. He couldn't cut and run, of course, and she knew it. Bloody hell, this was going to be awkward.

But he was urbane and gracious as he made his bows to the ladies, and after a small hesitation, he sat at Peggy's invitation. He had no intention of refusing the duchess's offer of champagne. He might need several glasses to survive this clumsy, misguided scheme.

Peggy cheerfully maintained the flow of the conversation, chattering on about their afternoon at the docks, going off in raptures over the sleek, racy Duras vessel being used for transport, extolling the virtue and reward in undertaking a charity hospital, repeatedly refilling Jack's glass as he emptied it.

Outside the duchess's relentless stream of garrulousness, the marquis and Miss Duras found themselves oppressively aware of each other, acutely conscious of all that had passed between them last evening. Assailed by inopportune feelings, traitorous memory, ill-defined longings, they responded vaguely to Peggy's attempts at conversation.

Venus had the wholesome look of a country maid in her light muslin gown and undone hair, Jack testily thought—fresh and ripe, infinitely tempting—and he cursed his godmother's conniving intent. Who the hell could resist such toothsome allure? He held his glass out for a refill, as if he could drink himself into some obliv-

ion where he'd no longer be susceptible to such tantalizing sensuality.

Jack smelled of a woman's perfume, Venus crossly
thought, as though she had a right to be angry, as
though her anger could protect her from her desires. His
dark beauty and lean, muscled body, his unquenchable
virility irrepressibly lured her while he lounged in his
chair, seemingly unaware of his powerful allure. She
vowed to resist her unconscionable longing, refusing to
yield to his seductive appeal like every woman he'd ever
known.

Molly's shout shattered the increasingly taut unease.
"A message for you, my lady!" she cried, waving a sheet
of paper from the distant terrace.

"I can't imagine what's come over Molly," the duchess said in mock indignation. "I thought I'd trained her
better than to scream like that. If you'll excuse me for a
moment." She came to her feet, waving back at her
maid. "Jack, pour Miss Duras more champagne. Her
glass is empty. I'll be back in a minute."

As the duchess crossed the green lawn, the marquis
rose to refill Venus's glass. "I take it you weren't aware of
Peggy's machinations." Her discomfort had been obvious.

"Hardly," she curtly replied. "I don't know what she
expects to accomplish. Please—" she held up her hand
"—I really don't want any more champagne."

"In that case, I'll drink it all." Bottle in hand, he
dropped back into his chair.

"Uncomfortable, are you?" Venus sardonically murmured, grateful he was as disconcerted as she.

"God, yes. Peggy brought me here on pretext of business. I should give her a tongue-lashing."

"Do you think it would do any good?"

He found himself laughing. "Hell, no."

"Please don't stay on my account. I'll tell Peggy not to waste her time and ours in future." She spoke briskly, his laughter reminding her too much of last night. She wanted him to leave and save her from temptation.

He should have been relieved at her words, but oddly he wasn't. "Maybe I'm not wasting my time."

"You are, I assure you. I don't care to be the subject of any new wagers."

"No one collected on their bets. I denied everything. And if anyone wishes to dispute my account, they're free to challenge me."

"No one will."

He shook his head.

"How chivalrous, Redvers. I should thank you, I suppose, but then you smell of perfume in the middle of the afternoon."

He looked at her over the rim of his glass. "Does it offend you?"

"Don't look at me like that. And yes, it does."

"I was just accompanying a friend of mine. I didn't participate."

"Don't explain. What you do with your time is of no importance to me."

"But you don't like the scent of perfume on me."

"Because of what it implies of your indolent life. Have you no other interests?"

"Would it matter if I did?"

"Of course not. I don't know why we're even having this conversation."

"Probably because I'd like to make love to you again, despite every warning bell going off in my brain—and if you don't think me too immodest, I suspect you do as well."

"I certainly *do not.*" But her cheeks turned pink and she wouldn't meet his gaze.

"I'm not saying we would, only that we'd like to. I'm as unwilling as you to give in to these unprecedented feelings."

She heard the word *unprecedented* and took a deep breath, as though she could still the flutter in her stomach by such simple means. The word echoed her own disobedient emotions, filled her brain with expectation, flared hotly where she didn't wish to feel any heat. "Yes, unwilling. I agree."

His gaze sharpened. He knew that sound. And it suddenly became a question of whether he cared to act on his feelings.

For the lady was willing, whether she acknowledged it or not.

He softly swore, not familiar with curbing his desires. "I dislike these sensations."

"I think you should leave."

"Or we should leave together." The words seemed quite independent of his wishes.

"It's impossible . . ."

But there was ambiguity in her tone. "I've a river house, not too far away," he slowly said, choosing his words with care, as if he needed justification for what he was saying. "It's wholly unfashionable and rustic. No one would see us there."

"I hate this. I hate you for making me feel this way."

"You could chastise me to your heart's content upriver," he replied with a faint smile.

"How can it even signify who you take there? How can you distinguish anymore?"

He seemed not to have heard her. "I should have left when I first saw you. I don't know why I didn't."

"How smoothly charming you are."

He shrugged. "I'm sorry for my candor. I generally prefer dissimulation in these arrangements. It's so much easier."

"You find it difficult to consider making love to me?"

"I find it unnerving in the extreme."

She gazed at him for a tremulous moment. "I understand completely," she whispered.

"We're damned tyros at this . . . shocking susceptibility."

Her heart beat wildly. "Absolute novices."

"Peggy is peeking through the drawing-room curtains, along with Molly," he noted, dipping his head in their direction. "Shall we make love here and delight their little hearts?"

"Acquit me, Redvers, of your exhibitionist tendencies."

"Jack," he murmured.

It took her several seconds to reply. "Jack," she finally said, very low, sumptuous possibility in the word.

And rising, he held out his hand.

Chapter 6

NO ONE APPROACHED THEM AS THEY LEFT save Oliver, who handed the marquis his hat and cane.

"Tell your mistress, who's hiding in the drawing room, that she will suffer my wrath at some more convenient time."

"Very good, sir. I'll relay your message." The majordomo's face was impassive.

"And thank the duchess for her tasty tea," Venus offered.

"She'll be pleased you enjoyed yourself, my lady." Oliver played proxy for his mistress with suave civility.

"Give her a further warning," Jack added, hoping to curtail any additional interference. "If she meddles again, I won't come to her next ball."

"Your message will be conveyed, my lord."

Jack took Venus's hand and drew her toward the door. "She won't listen, of course, but perhaps she might hesitate a moment or so and give us time to escape her watchful eye."

"You mean she'd have us followed?"

"God only knows with Peggy. She lives her life with more drama than most. And I'd just as soon reach my river home without observation."

But the duchess had no intention of following the

pair of lovers, understanding the lady's reputation was best preserved with complete privacy. But she and Molly had a well-disposed little coz once the marquis's carriage had departed, both ladies pleased with their part in the reconciliation.

𝒟O YOU THINK WE SHOULD DO THIS?" VENUS had been having second thoughts as the carriage bowled along the streets of London. "I'm not altogether sure anymore."

They sat on opposite seats in the luxurious interior, the marquis having chosen to sit across from her when he'd entered the vehicle. Indicating his own level of reserve.

Instead of answering her question, he ambiguously said, "I need a drink." Reaching under the seat, he opened a compartment filled with bottles set in a sturdy padded rack.

Venus took in the array of liquors, as well as his non-answer. "You wouldn't want to run out."

"I travel to my country home on the spur of the minute occasionally."

"And it's a long drive?"

"Would you rather I not drink?"

"Did you hear what I said?"

"About changing your mind?" He nodded.

"Well?" She leaned back against the black leather upholstery, her eyes holding a sharply interrogatory look.

"That's why I need a drink," he murmured, inserting a small corkscrew into a brandy bottle. "I'm also racked with indecision."

"Drinking helps?"

"It postpones a decision. Helpful in a way." He offered her the opened bottle. "Would you like some brandy?"

"Do you have anything else?"

His gaze came up as though she'd cracked a whip in the air and then he broke into a grin. "You see how unnerved I am. I'm susceptible to the most benign double entendre. But to answer your question, I have a variety of wines— a damned good claret for one, and some Rhenish wines that taste as though the sun is glowing in your mouth."

"You've convinced me—"

That hard-eyed gaze again pinning her to the carriage seat.

"The Rhenish wine, if you please," she went on, finding it suddenly titillating that she could stir such trepidation in a man of his finesse.

"Keep it up, darling," he murmured, a husky resonance in his voice, "and we might not reach the bed at my rustic folly."

"Feeling better, now that you're back on familiar ground?"

"Are you?" Taking out a bottle of wine and a small silver cup, he began uncorking the bottle.

"Yes. Don't ask me why."

"Gladly."

"You'd rather not talk about our—"

"No." Anything prefaced by *our* terrified him immensely. Handing her the filled silver cup, he said, in lieu of facing his feelings, "Do you fish?"

"Not often, but I have with my brother."

"I fish a lot."

He could have said "I decorate ladies' boudoirs," and she wouldn't have been more surprised. Although, on second thought, he did perform that office in his own special way. "I wouldn't have suspected," she pleasantly remarked, taking a sip of her wine.

"My father's gamekeeper taught me. I spent more time with him than I did with my father. A decided advantage, if you knew my father."

"He was difficult?"

"Luckily he died young."

Apparently she wasn't going to hear any further details, so she said, polite and conversational, "What kind of fish do you prefer catching?"

"Brown trout."

"With wet lures or dry lures?"

His gaze came alive in a distinctly enchanting way— a young boy's open, warm gaze. "Wet ones. Which do you like?"

She never would have thought talk of fishing lures could be so agreeable, so gratifying and sweetly sensual. He was a completely different man as he described his particular favorites, the special flies he tied himself; his practiced charm was replaced by an artless candor that touched her.

"We'll go fishing afterward," he murmured, leaning over to replenish the wine in her cup, the heat of his smile warming her entire body.

"Or we could go before," she teased.

"Not likely." He wasn't sure suddenly whether he could wait until the river.

"Don't I have anything to say about it?"

"No."

The single word strummed and rippled through her

with such delectable intensity, she wondered how she could have ever debated her carnal interest in him. "Am I supposed to just submit?"

His dark gaze slowly traveled down her body. "As I recall, you weren't particularly meek."

"The way I'm feeling right now, I'm wondering if you can keep up."

His low chuckle warmed his eyes. "It would be damned pleasant to try." He quickly glanced out the window.

"How much farther?" she asked, understanding his intent as though their minds were one.

"How long can you wait?"

"I'm not entirely sure. When will we reach your folly?"

"Nor for another half hour at least."

She groaned.

"There's no need to wait."

She exhaled softly, shocked at her sudden avid lust. "I don't suppose you have—"

"No, but I don't need them. Did I ever come in you last night?"

He hadn't. He'd been scrupulously trustworthy after the two condoms had been used. But habitual caution impelled her. "I don't know . . ."

"I could find some in the next village."

"Thank you, I'd be more comfortable."

"Certainly," he politely replied.

But she couldn't wait, and by the time they reached the next village, she was seated on his lap facing him, his erection buried deep inside her, and with her climax peaking, she took no notice of the storefronts flashing by.

"I don't know what's come over me," she whispered moments later, lounging on the seat beside him, the remnants of her orgasm a pink sunset on the fringes of her consciousness. "I'm completely without judgment, utterly rash, senseless in my ravenous desires. Tell me everything will be all right."

He gently stroked the silk-stockinged legs resting on his lap. "Everything will be perfect." He bent to kiss her rosy cheek, not so sure that they both hadn't been lost to reason. His orgasmic passions had been so fierce and shattering, he'd been nearly incapable of withdrawing in time. But he had—just barely.

"I'm not sure I like to feel this way. Or else I want to feel this way for the rest of my visit," she murmured, reaching out to touch his cheek.

"Just so long as you know what you want," he teased.

"If only I did. But I feel terribly adolescent, indecisive . . . thinking I do, I don't, now, not now, later, forever . . ."

At the word *forever*, he looked up.

She smiled. "How easily I can alarm you."

His mouth quirked in a grin. "I forget how different you are."

"Not out to shackle you in marriage, you mean?"

He nodded. "Among other things." He began buttoning his trousers.

"I thought you said we had a half hour."

He began unbuttoning what he'd buttoned.

"So accommodating, Redvers."

"It's not purely unselfish, darling."

They both took note of his endearment.

She with pleasure—being his darling had distinct advantages.

He with a modicum of shock—not at the word so much, but at the way he'd said it.

"Then I think I'll take my shoes off this time," she lightly proclaimed, civilized and cultivated, knowing better than to question an extemporaneous caprice. She began untying the ribbons at her ankles. He assisted, discarding her green kid slippers, sliding her garters and silk stockings off.

Helping her to move over him, he brushed aside her petticoats and skirt. "Once we reach the river, we'll get rid of these cumbersome clothes. I'll take you swimming."

"Will we go fishing, too?" She could feel his arousal gliding into her, filling her.

"Eventually." He moved a delectably blissful distance.

"How do you know that's the absolute perfect place?" She softly sighed, moving her hips in the faintest of undulations.

"Just lucky," he whispered, though luck had nothing to do with it. He flexed his hips upward again exactly the same way so her small moan warmed his cheek.

"Maybe I won't let you go back to London for a long time," she said in a heated whisper.

"Maybe I won't want to go back to London." He adjusted her minutely, holding her hips and pressing down slightly.

"Oh, my God . . ." Her voice trailed away in a delicate whimper.

HE HELPED HER DOWN FROM THE CARRIAGE when they reached his thatched cottage, and after escorting her into the parlor, he left to dismiss his driver. Sam usually stayed above the stables when he came to the river, but Venus had indicated she was more comfortable alone, so he obliged. Returning shortly, he found her gazing out the leaded windows.

"I can see why you like it here. The river is beautiful, peaceful. You're quite alone."

"I like it even better now." He came up behind her, slipping his arms around her waist. "You're the perfect addition to my paradise."

She leaned back against his tall, strong body. "I'm very glad I decided to go to the Exhibition that day."

"The fates were kind to lead me to you. Even though you refused me."

"The notorious Lord Redvers wasn't my type. You turned out to be very different."

He shrugged faintly. "There are certain presumptions in the fashionable world that aren't necessarily correct."

She twisted around in his arms. "You don't deserve your reputation?"

"Not particularly. A bachelor simply elicits a certain degree of gossip."

Although a wealthy, handsome bachelor, adored by women of passion, no doubt merited the gossip. She gazed at him with a more exacting regard, as if she could separate truth from celebrity. The dissolving, golden light from the windows softened the contours of his face, an unobstructed purity of modeling suddenly revealed. "How old are you?" she abruptly inquired.

"Old enough," he pleasantly said.

"A precise answer, please." His lashes were extravagantly long, thick, and lacy, like those of a Botticelli youth.

"Twenty-four."

She exhaled with relief. "You looked very young for a moment. I was hoping I'd not miscalculated."

"Miscalculated?"

"Your maturity."

"Are you questioning my maturity?"

"Only in an amorphous, within-the-bounds-of-convention way," she said with a smile.

"Would I be mature enough to invite you into my bedroom?" he roguishly queried. "The view is equally good from there."

"Don't tease. I'd just be uncomfortable if you were very young."

"A little late for that, isn't it?" His eyes were amused. "Would you have gone back to London?"

"Are you really twenty-four?" she quickly asked, his drollery disconcerting.

"Peggy will vouch for me. But you'll not know for certain, will you, 'til we return. Will it be different fucking me, do you think?" he whispered, leaning down to lick her upper lip. "Come, see my bedroom, and we'll find out." He gently pushed her in its direction.

"I should say no . . ."

"If you could." He compelled her forward with a hand on her bottom.

"Are you calling me wanton?" She cast a playful glance over her shoulder.

"I certainly hope so." His grin was enchanting. "If mademoiselle would instruct and edify an innocent young man, I promise to be a diligent pupil."

Spinning around, she tried to punch him.

Laughing, he grabbed her fists and, lifting them to his

mouth, kissed her knuckles. "I've never played the innocent before."

"That I believe." She jerked her hands away. "Now
behave or I'll go home."

"And miss fucking me for days on end . . ."

The insinuating heat, the delicious promise in his
words stirred her senses, whetted her impetuous passions, riveted all her quickening attention.

"That's what I thought," he whispered, trailing his
finger up her throat, over her jaw, along her cheek, following the rising flush pinking her delicate skin.

"You're much too smug." The throbbing between her
legs had settled into an undeniable, hard, steady
rhythm.

"But ready to fuck you again."

"That's your specialty, isn't it?"

"Yes," he softly said, holding out his hand. "Let me
show you my bed."

She hesitated, piqued by his shameless assurance.

"You can chastise me later," he gently noted. "Right
now, I'll make you come."

"Or I'll make you come," she insolently offered.

"Better yet."

Turning, she walked into the bedroom as if she were
Queen of the Nile and he followed, charmed by her
feisty challenge, intoxicated by her sexual need, looking
forward to the tempestuous and mutual heat of their
passion.

"I want to know something—and don't lie to me,
because it doesn't matter that much." She was standing
against the heavy footboard of the oak bed, grasping the
carved center roundel.

"You're the first woman I've brought here."

"That's much too glib. I haven't asked you yet."

"I could tell by the fire in your eyes. And it's not glib, it's the truth. Ned's been here fishing with me, but no one else. Now don't be angry with me. I adore the thought of having you in my bed."

She softly sighed, her grip on the footboard relaxing. "I dislike this inexplicable need."

"As do I, but—" he shrugged "—what's the point?"

"You make me feel insatiable. It's disturbing to my peace of mind."

"We'll be insatiable together. I share the feeling—for the first time as well. Better?" he softly said, moving toward her. "Knowing you're not alone in this insanity?"

"Much better," she whispered, feeling the heat of his body against hers, circling her arms around his waist. "I've always been able to walk away."

"You're speaking to a master on that subject, but don't worry, we'll explore this fantastical *outre-mer* together."

"And we've never actually made love on a bed," she playfully noted, consoled that he was as equivocal as she.

"Reason enough to test this one out."

He undressed her while she stood docile under his hands, returning his playful kisses, smiling at his teasing, delighted to be sharing her afternoon with him. She lounged on the bed while he discarded his clothing; a young lady of wealth and fashion, she didn't think to help him.

He took note of her indolence and thought how suited she was to the sumptuous leisure of carnal play. In a way, her self-indulgence matched his, her earthy acceptance of passion as generous and open, her desires as greedy. They fit in temper and disposition, he thought, unclasping his belt, and rather than being unnerved by the prospect, he found it agreeable.

The lady's disinterest in marriage, no doubt, assuaged his habitual caution. He didn't allow himself to consider the more startling assumption that perhaps they indeed suited.

"This bed is deliciously soft," Venus said, stretching languidly. "I may just stay here until we leave."

"Sounds good to me."

How dark his skin was, she thought, as he stood before her, half nude. How pleasing he was to the eye. "You'll have to wait on me, then."

He looked up from unbuttoning his trousers. "I might be persuaded."

"Although you did promise me fishing."

"And swimming." He stripped off his trousers. "I'll carry you to the river. It's quiet in the evening. You won't have to dress until we return to London."

"Mmmm . . . To be waited on and serviced by a man of your . . . charming proportions. I feel like a sultan's favorite."

"You're definitely mine. I should thank Peggy . . . for her insight."

"As should I. I was sure I despised you."

"I almost walked away when I saw you in the garden."

"And now we're here."

"In hot rut, if you'll forgive my plain speaking."

"I prefer plain speaking. The way I prefer your cock to everything at the moment. I'm completely in thrall to licentious feeling. I want you now and in five minutes and then again in a few moments more. How tiresome it must be to always hear that from women."

He walked to the bed. "But never tiresome from you." His gaze traveled from her undone hair spread on the pillow, slowly downward, and then up again to her smiling face, thinking himself the most fortunate of men.

"Do I pass muster?"

"You pass on every conceivable level. Although perhaps that's obvious from the state of my arousal." His glance flickered down.

"It pleases me to please you," she murmured with dulcet coyness that brought a grin to his face.

"God Almighty, you're going to wear me out. Not that I'm complaining." Dropping into a sprawl beside her, he twined his fingers through hers and stared at the whitewashed ceiling. "Who would have thought when I ran into you yesterday—"

"That we'd be lying here, shamelessly filled with lust."

He chuckled. "I was going to say that we'd enjoy the same things."

"So polite, darling. Personally, I've never lusted for a man like this—never."

"Hmmm," he breathed, gauging the exactitude of his feelings. Lust, of course, was a constant in his life.

"I expect something polite in response." She came up on one elbow and regarded him with a smile.

He shook his head. "It's not that. I was distinguishing this lust from—"

"All the other women?"

He shook his head again, his dark curls in stark contrast to the white pillow cover. "No, to the myriad other emotions you provoke." He traced a finger down her arm, his brows drawn together. "My emotions are *never* involved."

"Don't be alarmed. I don't *want* anything from you." Her lashes fluttered. "Besides that." Cupping his heavy testicles in her hand, she bent and touched her warm mouth to the gleaming crest of his arousal.

Quickly pushing her back on the bed, he rolled over her and eased between her legs. "That's enough foreplay," he whispered, a half-smile quirking his mouth.

"I also adore your sense of timing."

"We're without finesse. I almost feel as though I should apologize."

"No apologies required—provided I come to climax in the next thirty seconds."

"A sweet bitch in heat," he affectionately murmured.

"I hope you can oblige me."

"Or?" His expression sharpened minutely.

"Or I'll wait until you can. My lecherous tastes seem to be centered on you."

Gratification softened the set of his mouth, his rare possessive impulse mollified. He glanced at the clock quietly ticking on the mantel. "Do I have some leeway on the thirty seconds?"

"You can have anything you want." Indulgence was delicious in her voice.

"Then I want you under me for the indefinite future."

"Indefinite—how tantalizing." She arched up to kiss the fine curve of his mouth.

"I may never let you go," he breathed.

"The way I feel right now, I may be willing." She gently moved her hips. "Are we done talking?"

His gaze was amused. "Thirty seconds and counting."

Her arms twined around his neck, her thighs fell open and, lifting her hips, she met the first silken penetration with a low contented sigh.

She had what she wanted. He gave her swift, bewitching surcease in the prescribed time, and then again ten seconds later, the particular specificity of his blissful penetration so exquisite she wondered how long it had taken him to become so skilled. But a few seconds later, renewed passion obliterated thought and she was swimming through a gossamer cloudbank of ecstasy. And when she came out the other side and opened her eyes, he was gazing down at her.

"More?" he softly asked, his dark gypsy eyes heated.

"No . . ." Dazed, half numbed by excess, she barely moved her head.

"Sure?" His lower back flexed.

And she uttered a low, feverish moan.

"Just a little more," he whispered, gliding deeper. "How does that feel?"

As if she were falling off her gossamer cloud, she thought, the heat beginning to curl upward again, her body melting around his long, rigid length as though she had no control over her senses. "You should stop," she whispered, not sure she was capable of withstanding another orgasm.

"After this . . ." His driving descent stretched her wider, the tension in his arms caught in the rhythm of his body. "After we both come . . ." His head moved down close to hers and he gently bit her ear, marking her, tasting her, making her skin tingle.

She moved against him, desire building within her again, coursing through her blood, hot and glowing, insatiable. Whatever he was making her feel was so impossibly fine, so pure, she wanted to tell him how good he was.

But he already knew.

Making love was his specialty.

And for an instant she hated all the women before her with a mindless, useless jealousy that didn't make any sense with a man like Jack.

He wasn't looking for praise or flattery or resentment in bed. He was here only for this.

His hands suddenly closed over her hips, holding her captive, his next plunging downstroke disintegrating conscious thought. Ravenous desire took center stage in her mind, exhilarating pleasure racing faster and faster, her heart beating wildly.

Their entwined bodies moved in a frenzied, intemperate taking and giving until the first trembling shudders grew by exquisite degrees into a hotspur, ferocious orgasm, and this time they both climaxed.

Almost immediately, Venus fell asleep in his arms, exhausted. Covering her with a quilt, Jack offered up silent thanks to Lady Luck, who'd brought him the delectable Venus Duras. They had at least two uninterrupted days of solitude before Sam would be back, and after that he'd see what their schedules would allow. Although he had no intention of letting her slip away.

Not just yet.

Easing away after a time, he left the bed and poured himself a brandy. Lounging in a chair near the windows, he surveyed the tranquil river view, the gardens running down to the river ablaze with poppies. The peace and beauty of the scene always offered solace to his restless spirit.

Today though, the interior scene was one of equal peace and beauty. He turned to his sleeping guest and smiled. Her legs were uncovered, their slender length perfection, pure in line and form and only recently wrapped around him in the heat of passion. Instant lust stoked his sexual desires, and he wondered how soon he could wake her or how impolite it would be to make love to her while she slept.

She was unbelievably tempting, her beauty dazzling, but he knew beautiful women by the score and none appealed so intemperately. Perhaps her candor and frankness intrigued him, a novel concept in the ranks of women who'd passed through his life.

He raked his fingers through his hair and looked away to the river as though a change in scene might curtail his unease. He disliked feeling this intense craving, this irresistible need. And while his shift of focus may not have assuaged his disquieting thoughts, three brandies better served to soothe his disconcerted emotions. When Venus woke, Jack was pleasantly relaxed, once again in his normal dégagé mood. "Ready for a swim?" he pleasantly inquired.

She said, "In a minute," her voice still soft with sleep.

Her tawny hair tumbled down her shoulders, her flamboyant breasts rose above the crumpled quilt, her heavy-lidded gaze held a delicious, sultry warmth.

Drawn to her like a magnet to the poles, he set his glass aside and rose from his chair. Walking to the bed, he sat down beside her and touched her rosy cheek, tracing a finger down her silken flesh to her pouty mouth. Sliding the tip of his finger over her lips, he gazed at her with affection. "I can't get enough of you."

Her knowing smile moved beneath his touch, and raising her hand, she grasped his finger and gently nibbled on it. "Then we'll have to see that you get what you want."

"Everything?" His eyes measured her response.

"Anything at all," she softly breathed. "You're not the only one who feels intemperate."

"Anywhere?"

"Anywhere."

He slowly smiled and ran his hands down her arms as if vetting the corporeal feel of her. "Are you sure this isn't a dream?"

"I don't care if it is, so long as it doesn't end." She glanced down at his arousal. "Maybe we could begin the next installment of this dream right now."

"What do you have in mind?" His eyes held a hint of teasing.

She pulled away the red-embroidered quilt and slid her middle finger down her silky cleft. "Putting something I like here . . ."

"Let me." He lifted her hand aside, replacing her finger with his, stroking up and down in a lazy, slow rhythm.

The air suddenly seemed palpable on her skin, her tactile senses charged, and she braced her hands on the bed and gave in to sensation.

But he'd waited too long for her to wake and in short moments he lifted her up, swung her over his lap, and guided her down his erection. Wrapping her legs around his waist, he rose from the bed and began walking from the room.

"Ummmm," she remonstrated when she realized what he was doing. "I like the bed." But her protest died away in a suffocated moan because he'd stopped at the door and, leaning against her, pressed her back against the solid oak and thrust into her hard, hard until she ached with longing—until she came.

When he carried her outside, she clung to him, her arms wrapped tightly around his neck, her face buried in his shoulder, the dissolute heat of passion a fever in her body. "The neighbors . . ." she murmured, not sure she cared to be a performer onstage.

"There aren't any neighbors. I own five miles of river. You can open your eyes." Turning his head, he bent to lick the lobe of her ear. "Look."

She didn't at first, not so much from shyness as from lack of concentration. With each step, his erection thrust upward with such force she was immune to everything but the driving invasion, every sense dominated, enthralled, focused on the delirious sensation. And on the long walk down to the water, she climaxed twice.

When he came to a stop, she was given momentary respite and, feeling the cool breeze from the river, she turned her head on his shoulder and opened her eyes. Willows bordered a secluded inlet, the riverbank brilliant with pink astilbe, the grass so green if there was ever a facsimile of paradise, this watery bower would be in the first rank.

"The grass might be cool," he warned, dropping to his knees, leaning forward, following her down.

"I'm hot." Impaled, in the grip of ungovernable cravings, her mind was consumed with desire, her body in thrall to this man who serviced her with such skill. The arctic itself wouldn't have felt chill at the moment.

"Then we're good," he whispered, moving inside her with such delicacy she felt tears come to her eyes.

There should be a word to describe the indescribable, she thought. Good wasn't enough, but her mind wasn't thinking very precisely, absorbed as it was in experiencing passion and lust and hot-blooded wanting.

Jack entertained her that afternoon and evening with blissful regard for the rarest of sensation. They made love on the grass and in the water, under the sun and later in the light of the rising moon, with languor and ferocity, with the most tender kisses. She'd never been kissed with such warmhearted joy, nor had he ever kissed a woman with such benevolence.

Later that night when they returned to the cottage across the dew-wet grass, they stood in the doorway, wrapped in an embrace, gazing at the moon, reluctant to put an end to their enchanting idyll.

Chapter 7

⬥⬥⬥⬥

*H*E MADE BREAKFAST FOR HER IN THE MORNing. The compact larder was well stocked, and fresh eggs, milk, two crusty loaves of bread, and fresh churned butter had been left in the small root cellar near the back door. When she asked how anyone knew he was there, he told her he had caretakers who checked each morning.

"You come here that often?"

"Sometimes several times a week."

"For the fishing."

"Mostly."

She'd already noticed two well-filled bookcases in the parlor, watercolor paints and paper scattered on a table, a small spinet near the fireplace. He was a man of surprises.

He cooked on a nickel-plated wood stove, while she drank hot chocolate he'd made for her with the cream from the top of the milk. She wore his robe, the quilted red linen trailing on the floor when she walked, the sleeves rolled up several times, the belt wrapped twice around her waist.

He'd slipped on a pair of twill trousers, well worn and faded to a fawn color, and after a night of sustained and impassioned sex, she wondered that he could arouse her still with no more than a glance at his lean, bronzed body.

"I wish you'd put more clothes on."

"I'm too hot." He glanced over at her, his dark tousled hair falling over one eye. He brushed it aside with the back of his hand, his fingertips wet from the eggs he was cracking into a bowl. "And I mean it in every possible way. It's your fault completely I'm still in full rut after fucking you all night."

"What if I get pregnant?"

The egg he was cracking smashed against the bowl with unforeseen violence, oozing down the side and onto the tabletop.

"Sorry," she murmured.

"My fault," he said, wiping his hands on a damp towel and cleaning up the mess, his expression startlingly blank when he turned around. "If that should happen, let me know."

"My apologies for even bringing it up, but I'm normally overly cautious on that account." She smiled. "I'm reasonably logical again in the light of day, although watching you in half-undress is highly stimulating."

"Eat first." He turned back to the stove. "I'll walk into the nearby town later and get some condoms."

"I'll come with you."

"If you don't mind the distance. We probably should have kept the carriage."

"When is your driver returning?"

"I told him to check in two days."

She grinned. "So confident, my lord. Am I your prisoner, then?"

"I think I'm yours."

"How sweet."

"I'm not so sure about being sweet, but I'm damned infatuated. Now make yourself useful and cut us some slices of bread."

In short order, they carried their breakfast to a small flagstone terrace facing the river, where a weathered teak table and chairs were positioned for a view of the water. They ate under the spring sun, talking idly of the few acquaintances they had in common, of their plans for the day, their walk into town, fishing, swimming. It seemed as though they'd known each other for a very long time, a sense of ease and tranquility both comforting and in stark contrast to their heated night.

Later, while they enjoyed their coffee and chocolate, Jack said, "I've been thinking that I really should buy some hospital supplies for my tenants. You could advise me on how to set up an infirmary at Castlereagh, and I could duplicate it at my other properties."

"Don't feel obligated."

"Not at all. I just never considered setting up a hospital on my estates."

"I'd be happy to help, of course."

"Good." He could keep her for a time, he thought, personal motive auxiliary to his duties as a landlord. "When we go back to the city then, I'll take advantage of your expertise."

"*What* expertise?"

The male voice heard at close range was all too familiar, and Jack braced himself for their visitor. A second later, Ned Darlington strolled around the corner of the cottage still attired in evening dress, his sartorial disarray bespeaking a night of carouse.

"I hope you're alone," Jack brusquely said.

"Of course. Would I trespass on your secret hermitage with a stranger? Although it looks as though you've relaxed your stringent rule concerning women." Ned glanced at Venus with a broad smile, his bow mildly unsteady. "And yes, thank you very much, I'd love something to eat," he drawled, pulling up a bench and joining them. "You must be Venus."

"Darling, this is my oldest and rudest friend," Jack declared, his reluctance obvious. "Ned, may I present Miss Duras—whom I trust you'll not remember having met when next we see you."

"My lips are sealed." He mimicked locking his mouth and tossing away the key.

"See that you recall your promise once you're sober again," the marquis warned.

"Won't be sober 'til tomorrow at least. It's Lily's coming-out party tonight, and I'll need a bottle or two to get through that boring affair. Need you there, too. Reason I came all the way out here to find you. You promised Lily." He reached for Jack's coffee.

"Is that tonight?"

"Damn right." Lifting the cup to his mouth, Ned drained it.

Jack exhaled in frustration. "You're sure?"

"Sure as judgment day. Maman sent a footman to remind me yesterday. Wrote the date large on her note-paper and gave my valet orders to see that I'm there dressed and ready. It's tonight. Word of God."

"Merde."

"My feelings exactly, but Lily is all atwitter, so have to do our duty, my friend. Like a fool, you agreed to lead her out in her first dance."

"What time?" The marquis was already gauging the hours remaining for them at the river.

"Dinner at eight, I suppose. Mostly family, but Maman will be expecting you."

Jack offered Venus a quizzical look. "Would you like to be my guest at Ned's sister's coming-out? I can't avoid it."

"I don't think so," Venus demurred, not inclined to accompany Jack to a family occasion. "I'm sure the guest list is complete."

The marquis glanced at his friend. "Your maman surely has room for one more."

Ned looked up from buttering his bread. "I'll tell her."

"There. It's settled."

"I'm not sure," Venus dissented. "Really, I'd prefer you drop me off at home."

"Tell your maman not to expect us before eight," Jack informed Ned. He looked at Venus with narrowed eyes. "You're going, or I won't."

"Lily will cry her eyes out if you don't appear," Ned said, smiling at Venus.

"Don't make the poor girl cry," Jack gently prodded.

Venus pursed her mouth and shot him a heated glance. "Must you always have your own way?"

"He always does," Ned bluntly observed through a mouthful of bread and butter.

"Why don't we talk about this later," Venus quietly declared, her gaze squarely meeting Jack's.

"I'm not staying for the fight." Ned quickly came to his feet. "Hate women screaming, no offense. I'll see you tonight, Jack. It was a pleasure, Miss Duras." Grabbing the bowl with the remaining scrambled eggs, two slices of bread, and a fork, he made his escape.

"I don't want to argue about this," Venus asserted the minute Ned disappeared.

"Nor do I."

"The young girl is waiting for you to squire her tonight. I'd be very much in the way."

"Nonsense. Lily is my friend's baby sister. She looks on me as an uncle."

"I rather doubt that, when she's reserved her first dance for you."

"You're wrong. She's a tomboy who races horses and mucks out the stables. More often than not she has her hair in braids. So go with me and save me from an evening of boredom. We'll come back here afterward."

Venus traced a pattern on the weathered tabletop. "The *afterward* is tempting."

"Then come." He leaned across the table to touch her hand, enchanting appeal in his gaze. "You like to dance. How bad can it be? I promise we won't stay long."

"How long?"

"Dinner, Lily's first dance. Two or three others after that and we'll decamp."

"Lord, Jack, I don't know . . . I don't want to."

"I'll make it worth your while." A husky note underscored his words.

She smiled. "That's not fair."

"I'll buy out the supply of condoms in London."

"You know how to tempt a lady . . ." she whispered.

"We'll have to leave here by five. I'll dress at your house, or you can have your things brought to mine."

"Do I have a choice?"

He smiled at her. "None at all."

~~~

*H*E HAD HIS CLOTHES CONVEYED TO BELGRAVE Square. He didn't require a valet tonight, he told his batman, who delivered his wardrobe change; he was capable of tying his own cravat.

He dismissed Venus's maid as well, dropping into a gilded chair in the boudoir once she'd left. "Don't look at me like that," he cheerfully replied to Venus's questioning stare. "I'll help you."

"I'm not sure I care to know how adept you are at dressing ladies."

"I'm not adept at all, but I'm willing to learn if it means being alone with you."

"I hope you know what you're doing. We don't have much time."

He glanced at the clock. "How long can it take to dress?"

"You don't realize how much has to be laced and buttoned and hooked."

"Don't worry. We'll still have time."

She recognized his tone of voice. "No, absolutely not."

"I may pout." He thrust out his bottom lip.

"Pout away. If you want me to accompany you, you'll do this my way. And I still have to have my hair arranged. Are you accomplished with women's coiffeurs as well?"

They'd bathed at the cottage. Jack had had tanks installed in the attic that were supplied with water from the river and, ingeniously heated with coal, offered hot water for the shower-baths he favored.

"I am not. I'll fortify myself for the dull evening

ahead while your maid arranges your hair. Where's your liquor?"

"In the library. I'll have some brought up."

"Never mind. I'll fetch it. I liked your curls that night at Peggy's."

"Then I'll have Maude arrange curls. Your wish is my command, my lord."

He laughed. "If only it were true, my imperious young queen."

"And here I've been on my best behavior," she lightly mocked.

But she was on her best behavior, or Jack Fitz-James brought out the best in her, the level of her contentment extraordinary. And for a woman very much familiar with having her own way, she found herself willingly deferring to him in many instances. Such as this dinner and soiree, for example. She didn't relish appearing on his arm tonight. After the wagers staked and the inevitable gossip, she knew they'd be the cynosure of all eyes.

He seemed immune. She preferred a less conspicuous role.

But he returned shortly with some liquor and entertained her while Maude arranged her hair in ringlets, with fragrant white roses over both ears along with elaborate diamond clips. He knew every bit of scandalous gossip about town, and as he sipped his cognac, he regaled her with humorous stories of the fashionable world.

"And if Ned's maman quizzes you on Ned's future betrothed, I'll warn you now to plead ignorance. Ned told her a month ago he was about to become engaged, after she'd been hounding him unmercifully. Once Lily finds a beau, he expects the pressure on him will cease.

So he has only to survive the season, and his maman will have her hands full with Lily's marriage plans."

"I'll be pleased to tell her I know nothing. Now you're sure she won't take offense at an extra guest added at such late date?"

"Lady Darlington is flighty as a hummingbird. She won't even notice. Just smile and nod your head when she chatters on."

"How like a man," Venus rebuked, frowning into the mirror. "You don't even listen."

"She talks of nothing at great speed. There's no need to listen. You'll find out for yourself soon enough, so you needn't defend your sex with such a scowl. I like Frances. I just wouldn't want to be put into a carriage with her for more than a two-block ride."

"Her husband is deceased?"

"Killed riding to hounds, drunk as a lord. He died happy."

"Do you ride?" She knew so little of him.

"To hounds?"

She nodded and her maid frowned and reset a pin.

"Occasionally. I prefer steeplechase. My stable of jumpers has taken me a decade to bring up to scratch. We'll have to go riding at Castlereagh sometime. You ride, don't you?" She looked like a woman who would be fearless in the saddle.

"My parents' stable is primarily racers. I ride some."

"I just bought a new racer. The morning after I met you." He smiled at her in the mirror. "I should rename him for the occasion. He's going to take the Derby this year. Why don't you stay and see him run?"

"The Duras's horses are racing at Longchamps. You're welcome to come over if you like." She spoke as casually as he. "My brother rides in the amateur events. Do you have family?"

"A distant cousin in Devon, hoping to inherit, whom I've never liked because he's so damned malicious. My solicitor keeps him at bay with quarterly funds. Then there's my maternal aunt whom I seldom see. And Peggy. She's the closest I have to family."

"She's a wonderful surrogate family. You're very fortunate."

"I agree. She'll be there tonight."

"How very nice. Another person I know. Thank you, Maude, it's very nice. I can manage now."

A small hush descended on the room as the maid left.

"I find myself selfishly monopolistic of your company. I may have to learn how to do your hair."

"Anytime." She twirled around on the satin-covered stool and gazed at him lounging in her boudoir chair. "I'd much prefer you."

"While I prefer you to all else." He raised his glass in salute. She was an enchantress, an elegant Primavera with white roses in her hair. And his, he thought with a unprecedented possessiveness.

"Are you ready to begin tying and hooking?"

"In my current mood, it's going to require nerves of steel to keep you chaste until after the ball."

"There's always Maude."

He shook his head. "I can do it. And in three hours, we'll be away from London again."

"That makes even the inevitable stares endurable."

"Don't worry about stares," he said, rising from his chair. "No one will dare when you're with me."

Chapter 8

⸺⊷∞⊶⸺

$\mathscr{H}$E WELL KNEW HIS AUTHORITY. NOT A SINgle disparaging word, not an untoward glance was directed at her when they arrived at the Darlington soiree. And the anterooms were filled with guests waiting for dinner to be served. A string quartet supplied music for the milling crowd during the *quartre heure mauvais* and Lady Darlington was as bubbly and effervescent as Jack had warned. Taking his advice, Venus smiled and nodded her head and when their hostess fluttered away, she couldn't make sense of anything she'd heard.

But Lily was far from a tomboy with braids. She was a ravishing young red-haired beauty who took exception to Jack's companion with a pouty, sullen moue. Jack seemed not to notice, and once she was whisked away by her mother to meet other guests and Venus mentioned Lily's sulky response, he only said, "Nonsense. She's just jittery with all the commotion tonight."

When the next sulky beauty approached them, though, he was less obtuse. Lady Tallien, elegantly small and shapely, introduced herself with a haughty, assessing glance for Venus. "I understand you're the lady who dabbles in charity work. Did everything work out for you at Brookes, Jack, darling?" she snidely went on, her perfect brows rising in mockery. "I understand your interest in charity work garnered much interest."

"Then you understood wrong, Bella. Miss Duras and I are old acquaintances. Her father and my uncle were friends. So we're practically family."

"Will you be in London long, Miss Duras?" If looks could kill, murder charges could have been filed.

"I'm not sure." Jack's former lover had pale platinum hair and dark eyes like his. What a lovely couple they must have made, Venus resentfully thought.

"I'm hoping to convince Miss Duras to stay for the season," Jack interposed. "She hasn't seen Castlereagh, and I thought she'd enjoy the Derby as well."

"Really?" Icicles dripped from the gelid word.

"Lord Redvers has been the soul of hospitality," Venus silkily murmured, unable to resist a barb of her own.

"Sarah will be vastly disappointed, Jack." Lady Tallien spoke in punctilious rebuke.

"I can't imagine why."

"Really, Jack, you have to have been aware of her intense interest in you. Everyone says how well matched you are."

"Then everyone's wrong. You overreach, Bella. I dislike young maids. Ah, there's Ned. If you'll excuse us."

Lady Tallien was left seething with temper—always a danger.

"ONE OF YOUR LOVERS, NO DOUBT," VENUS REmarked as they strolled away. "She seemed quite willing to kill me on the spot."

"Ignore Bella, darling. She can be a bitch."

"An advantage at times, I'm sure. She seemed very familiar with you. How many more will I meet tonight?"

None as forward as Bella, he hoped, although an uncomfortable number of ladies in attendance tonight had been his lovers. "This is why I avoid society. I'm already inclined to leave, and dinner hasn't even been announced."

"Too many husbands glaring at you?"

He shot her a lowering glance. "You know better than that. How many aristocratic marriages do you know that are love matches? The husbands here tonight spend more time with their mistresses or in their clubs than with their wives."

"So we won't be disturbed by irate husbands, only irate lovers."

He grimaced. "You find this amusing, don't you?"

"Fascinating. Do you know how many women in this room are looking at you?"

"Could we change the subject? I can't imagine it will be productive in any way."

"Of course, my lord," she purred.

He sent her a sidelong glance. "I may have to spank you if you don't behave."

"Hardly an incentive to behave." She fluttered her eyelashes at him in flirtatious parody.

"I can see you're going to be difficult to control tonight."

"I tried to warn you to leave me at home."

"Maybe I should turn you over my knee and spank you right now."

His voice was much too calm for comfort. She quickly scanned his expression.

"You think I wouldn't?" His dark glance was audacious, his hand tightened on hers.

An unwonted thrill spiked through her senses at the thought of so salacious a spectacle. At the possibility that he actually meant what he said. "You wouldn't!" she whispered.

"Behave or you'll find out," he said, smiling faintly.

"Don't say that . . ." Her voice was low, tremulous. "Or we might have to leave precipitously."

"We *can't* leave yet." But he felt it, too—the irrepressible excitement, the shocking lust. His restless gaze swept the crowded room. "Come out on the terrace with me." His words were casual but a volatile impatience shaded the words. "It's cooler out there." He drew her toward the terrace doors open to the warm spring night. "And dark."

"Jack, don't," she protested, realizing what he meant, knowing all eyes were on them tonight. "Please." She kept her voice low, aware of the glances directed at them as they weaved through the throng. "Don't be reckless. We can't do this. Jack!"

Ignoring her, he pulled her along, crossing the threshold onto the terrace, taking them down a shallow flight of steps onto the lawn, and striding toward a vine-covered pergola as though he were familiar with the gardens, as though he'd been here before.

"How can you even think of this, damn you," she whispered, not daring to raise her voice in the night silence.

"Don't pretend you're not wet and ready, because I know better."

"Someone might walk out here!" She didn't have his cultivated disregard for the world.

"I'll have you back inside in a few minutes."

"You're mad!"

"Mad with lust." He forced her into the shadowed bower, quickly pushing her back against one of the carved uprights, impatiently brushing aside her skirt and petticoats.

"The scandal could be—"

He covered her mouth in a fierce kiss of domination and prerogative, not in the mood to discuss scandal or discretion, not willing to be reasonable, interested only in sating his sharp-set hunger. Swiftly unbuttoning his trousers, half lifting her for better egress, he bent his legs slightly and slid inside her, driving upward savagely, burying himself in her heated cleft, her liquid warmth melting around him, welcoming him.

She whimpered against his mouth, mortified, appalled, her skirts rucked up between them, his trousers chafing the tender flesh of her thighs, the slow rhythm of his strokes inciting her traitorous senses, a humiliating excitement shaking her.

He felt her shudder and nuzzled her ear. "See, I know what you want." Holding her bottom, he penetrated more deeply, forcibly, as if to verify his insight. A voluptuous dissipation began to move and swell, to convulse her with a mindless pleasure. Shivering, she took a deep breath as if she could contain the wild, dizzying flow of ravishment.

"I'm going to make sure you *stay* fucked." It was a low, deep growl, a primal warning.

She should resist; he couldn't impose his will on her, but her body responded to his force majeure without reservation or logic. She was insensible to all but the heightening rhythm of thrust and withdrawal, the powerful invasion that she felt in her brain and toes, blood and nerves, most desperately in the flame-hot core of her body.

"Wait," he said, when he knew she couldn't, when she was so frantic for release she was moaning, taut with the ache of it, when his soft command served only to spur her overflowing passions to a breathless, tumultuous orgasm.

With perfect timing, he withdrew in the wake of her climax, his ejaculation so explosive, so violent, so acute and shocking he gasped like a man coming up from near drowning. He was well disciplined, however, even in extremis, and his handkerchief served to save them both from inappropriate stains. Almost instantly, his mood altered, his wildness vanished. He began rearranging his clothes with a detached efficiency.

"I'm sorry," he gruffly said moments later, helping to straighten the skirt of her gown. "Jesus God, I need a drink."

A hint of anger resonated in his voice. Her own feelings were a maelstrom of uncertainty and tumult, the extent of her desire shocking to a woman who had always viewed men as expendable. "I'm not going back inside." She felt as though *wanton* were stamped on her forehead.

"We don't have a choice."

"*I* have a choice, and don't snap at me." How dare he exhibit resentment. "I wasn't the one who dragged you out here."

"Fuck yes, you did." Even in the shadowed moonlight, she could see his scowl.

"You're blaming me?" she asked incredulously.

"I'm blaming your hot fucking body."

"And you have no brain that functions?"

"Apparently not with you," he sullenly muttered.

"Screw you, Redvers."

"Not right now, although I'd love to later," he sarcastically noted, taking her hand in a harsh grip. "Let's go back in and get through this damnable evening."

"I'm not taking responsibility for this," she hotly said, trying to ease her fingers free.

"Fine."

"And if anyone dares say anything offensive to me, I'll crucify them on the spot."

"I'll help you," he brusquely said.

"And for *your* information," she went on, outraged by his presumptions of culpability, "I've never been fond of impersonal sex."

He snorted. He'd never been more consciously involved, disturbingly so. "I'll try to make it more personal next time," he said, perverse and contrary.

"Maybe there won't be a next time." She struggled to free her hand.

His fingers tightened their grip. "You can count on a next time." His voice was curt. "Just as soon as we get the hell out of here."

HE KEPT HER AT HIS SIDE, HIS COERCION SUBtle, a hand at the small of her back, at her waist or elbow, a swift warning look, a murmured comment that would pink her cheeks, his words, blunt and brutally earthy. He knew what she wanted from him, what he could give her, and he knew what he needed from her.

She should leave. She could if she wished. In such a public venue, he couldn't restrain her. But she desired him; he'd made certain of that, and overcome with shame, tortured with longing, she stayed, eating dinner, conversing with apparent calm, even making plans to pick out a hospital site with Peggy. But her body and brain, her senses and soul were awash with sexual desire, the world distant and hazy, the conversations around her and her own words real but unreal. Her entire awareness focused on Jack's powerful presence, on the pleasure he could give her.

When dinner was over and the marquis escorted Lily onto the floor for her first dance, a sudden silence filled the room, the contrast between the young girl's delicate innocence and Jack Fitz-James's unbridled sexuality so stark the audience was breathless with expectation.

Even the musicians were mesmerized by the sight, and Lady Darlington had to frantically signal them to begin. The first bars of the waltz broke the uneasy hush, but all eyes were still on the lone couple on the ball-room floor, the initial dance reserved for the honored debutante. The artless young girl gazed up at Jack with such unalloyed adoration, melted against his body with such terrifying lack of decorum, her mother found it prudent to quickly curtail the waltz in order to preserve her daughter's reputation.

Immediately shooing Ned out to dance with his sister, she waved all her guests out onto the floor, her pink marabou fan aflutter, and then took herself off to the retiring room for a moment of collapse. Much as she liked dear Jack, she reflected, letting the maid set a cool cloth on her forehead, he wasn't about to fall in love with Lily. Nor with any woman, she suspected, considering the reckless pace of his love life these many years past. Come morning, she would see that Lily was made aware of that incontestable reality.

"Ah, there you are, Frances!" a booming voice proclaimed.

Looking up, Lady Darlington saw the Countess of Belcher descending on her. Girding herself for the old harridan's inevitable, odious comments, she conjured up a polite smile.

WELL PLEASED WITH LADY DARLINGTON'S INtervention, Jack returned to Venus. "My duty's done, and not a moment too soon." It had taken all his considerable charm to keep the young chit from kissing him in sight of the entire ton.

"Do you still think you're viewed as an uncle?" Venus observed.

"You were right. I was wrong. Happy?"

"Happy about the state of your love life? I can't see that it concerns me."

Struck by such blatant hypocrisy when the heat of her anger was palpable, he said, "I refused her, by the way. Does that soothe your temper?"

"Not up to another stroll in the gardens tonight?" Biting sarcasm vibrated in every syllable.

"I explained to Lily my lust is exclusively centered on you," he silkily replied.

"I wouldn't be surprised at anything you said, after witnessing your gentlemanly manners earlier this evening."

"Is that a complaint? After such a conspicuously vocal climax?"

Her hand swung up to slap him, but he caught it just

short of his face. "Don't make a scene," he coolly enjoined, forcing her hand down with a casual strength.

"Am I interrupting?" The Duchess of Groveland had glided up in a cloud of scent, her brows raised.

"Not at all." His voice and gaze bland, the marquis released Venus's hand.

"I thought I might insist on my dance now," Peggy noted. "If you don't mind, Venus, my dear?"

"By all means, take him." Venus tamed her voice to politeness.

Bending low, the marquis brushed his mouth against Venus's ear. "Don't go away."

Her eyes flashed with impudence, unreassuring and volatile.

"I particularly like this song," the duchess interposed, ignoring their heated glances. "I won't keep him long."

"Take all the time you wish," Venus affably said. "I'll find myself some champagne, or perhaps a whiskey."

As if she needed liquor to be difficult, the marquis thought. But there was nothing for it but to be gracious to his godmother, despite the men hovering in the wings, watching Venus, waiting for him to leave. Before Jack and the duchess had moved into their first gliding twirl, a crowd of eager suitors had descended on Venus.

Familiar with admirers, she greeted the men with an added warmth that evening and, in her current high dudgeon, accepted their adulation with more than her usual casual disinterest. Two can play the game, she mutinously reflected, directing her full attention on the earnest, aspiring suitors, laughing and flirting with a playful élan. They all wanted to dance; they all wanted to hold her in their arms; and from the numerous, overly eager invitations, Venus chose a man she'd met at Peggy's.

"I was *hoping* to see you again," Lord Groten murmured, moving them out into the dancers in a great sweeping circle, readjusting his hold to draw her closer.

"I'll be in London for another week or so," she replied, agreeably aware of Jack's scowl from across the room, smiling up at her partner with a special cordiality.

Jack swore through his clenched teeth.

"For heaven's sake, show some restraint," Peggy remonstrated. "She's only dancing with Lord Groten."

Slowly exhaling, Jack gazed down on his godmother with a rueful smile. "You're right. It's only a dance. How can it matter?" His gaze returned to Venus and his nostrils flared. "But it bothers me. Damned if it doesn't."

"I'm pleased to see this departure from your normal indifference," the duchess cheerfully remarked. "I thought, perhaps, you had no feelings, like your father."

"Oh, the lady generates feelings, all right," he tautly said. "The out-of-control, devil-be-damned type."

"She's very lovely. Why shouldn't you be captivated?" She knew full well there was nothing casual about Jack's fierce, impassioned response.

"I hate feeling this way," he grumbled.

She smiled up at him. "It's about time you felt something. Do you want my advice?"

"Not particularly."

The duchess blandly met his scowl. "I'd say woo her, and marry her, if you can't live without her."

Horror instantly flared in the marquis's eyes. "What the hell kind of advice is that? I'm only twenty-four, for God's sake."

"Do you think there's a precise age when love strikes you?"

"I don't think there's ever an age when love strikes you."

We'll have to see, won't we."

"Save that knowing look, Peggy. I'm not interested in marriage. *Understood?*"

"Venus seems to be having a good time with Groten," the duchess calmly noted, as though her godson hadn't responded so brusquely. "He's making her laugh."

"He fancies himself a Don Juan, bloody insolent sod. I'm cutting in, Peggy," Jack growled. "I hope you don't mind."

"Heavens, no," she mildly replied, satisfied with her gentle guidance. "Groten's a marvelous dancer."

*M*Y TURN, GROTEN." JACK'S SHOULDER TAP WAS sure to leave a bruise.

"Not likely, Redvers." Thomas Manchester was also a large man, bulky and solid in contrast to Jack's lean strength, and he had no intention of giving up his partner. He danced away.

Jack followed without missing a beat. "You know that little redhead you have tucked away in Chelsea? Does she always giggle when she comes?"

His query brought Groten to a standstill, although he still held Venus.

"Now that I have your attention," Jack smoothly went on, "I believe Miss Duras would prefer dancing with me."

"I don't allow poaching, damn you." The Earl of Groten's face was flushed with anger.

"Nor do I," the marquis silkily replied, reaching out to take Venus's hand.

Groten's mouth went grim. "Stay clear, Redvers."

"How dare you both!" Venus exclaimed, wrenching away from her partner. "As if I don't have a mind of my own!" Her heated gaze swung from one man to the other. "Kindly leave me out of your battles!" Spinning away, she stalked off the floor, the duchess close behind.

Peggy caught up with Venus in the corridor outside the ballroom and offered her sympathy in slightly breathless accents.

Venus smiled at her and slowed her pace. "I'm not in the mood to be fought over. Not that I ever am. It's so childish."

The sound of running feet suddenly echoed down the corridor.

"Ignore him," Venus said, knowing who was behind her. Only the marquis would so disregard etiquette.

"He's rather hotheaded, my dear," the duchess warned, although she was delighted at the delicious turn of events. She'd never seen Jack so enthralled. "And young and impetuous, I'm afraid."

Venus pursed her lips. "That's hardly an excuse for his behavior."

"I understand. Jack shouldn't have made such a scene."

"He certainly should not."

"I admit I'm rather perplexed by his actions." And she was. Jack's conduct was incredible—but gratifying in the extreme.

"I refuse to be treated like a possession," Venus hotly said. "If he thinks he can just—"

Her sentence was abruptly curtailed as Jack scooped

her up into his arms without altering his stride. Swiftly passing the duchess, he said, "We'll be at the river, but don't come to visit."

He maintained his firm grip against Venus's struggles. "Now you can fight this, or you can pretend you've fainted." Jack's voice was brusque. "I'd suggest the latter. Here come the Duke and Duchess of Buccleigh."

Understanding the fashionable world's appearances-at-all-costs maxim, she shut her eyes and let her body go limp. If she was being carried away, the fiction of ill health would offer the requisite credible explanation. There would be gossip, of course.

But none that could be substantiated.

Reaching the staircase, Jack nodded to the duke and duchess. "The lady's fainted. The heat," he explained, his expression suitably concerned. And then he was past them and descending the stairs with quicksilver haste. They met another couple before reaching the entrance hall, and a handful more guests milling around waiting for their carriages, but the marquis was a consummate actor and no one risked a question should he take issue. He had a dangerous reputation for dueling.

Venus felt the cool night air on her face when they exited the Darlington mansion, but he said in an under-tone, "Not just yet," and then in a conversational voice, "Good evening, Countess Nottington. The lady's fainted from the heat. A shame, I know . . . such a crush upstairs." And for a time, only the click of his heels on the paved drive sounded in the night as he moved down the carriageway to his vehicle.

Moments later, he curtly said, "We're going to the river, Sam."

Venus's eyes snapped open. "You don't actually think I'm going there with you."

"I actually *know* you are," he replied, dismissing with a nod the servant who'd come forward to open the carriage door. Twisting the latch himself, he pulled the door open, leaned into the vehicle to deposit her on the seat, and climbed in behind her. He shut the door with a snap.

She stared at him mutinously. "It won't do you any good to take me there."

Dropping into the seat beside her, he calmly said, "Why don't we see."

"You're making a mistake, Jack. I won't be docile about being abducted. You're taking on a deal of trouble."

"Perhaps I can change your mind," he softly said.

"Save your seductive phrases for your adoring lady-loves." She moved into the farthest corner of the seat, although in the limited interior space, his body was still disturbingly close.

"We don't have to discuss it now."

"We don't have to discuss it at all. Take me home."

"I'll take you home tomorrow if you still wish to go."

"So sure of yourself, Redvers. This time you're wrong. I'm not interested in men with droit-du-seigneur mentalities. You'll be taking me home in the morning." And so saying, she closed her eyes, crossed her arms over her chest, and leaned back against the padded wall.

Self-assured and confident, he didn't attempt further argument, particularly since he was familiar with the lady's easily roused passions. They would be at the cottage within the hour, away from the inanity of the ton, from all the men wanting her as much as he, away from watchful eyes. He softly exhaled, relaxing in the wake of their highly visible escape, the rhythm of the carriage lulling his senses, the presence of the lady he coveted adding immeasurably to his contentment. Let her sulk now. There was plenty of time later to assuage her anger.

Within minutes, Venus had fallen asleep, exhausted after the previous sleepness night and the late hour, not in the habit of staying up for days like Jack. Even when they arrived at the cottage, she only briefly came out of her doze.

"Sleep," Jack whispered. "I'll wake you in the morning."

She mumbled an unintelligible reply as he lifted her into his arms. Carrying her in from the carriage, he put her to bed without waking her, taking off her ballgown and shoes before covering her. Then, pouring himself a cognac, he sat by the bed and watched her sleep in the glow of the grate.

He felt as though he'd been awarded a resplendent prize, having her here with him, having her alone in his hermit's cottage. He marveled at the rare sensibilities she triggered, basked in the singular pleasure she engendered, aware of the uniqueness of his feelings.

In those quiet hours of the night, he tried to come to terms with her curious hold on him, attempted to understand her special appeal. There was no single word or multitude of words that gave credence to his feelings. Rather it was an amorphous consciousness, both enticing and exhilarating. And it took no more than one of her smiles to make him feel that way—although he didn't discount the impress of her ravishing sexuality.

But he'd fucked for days on end before, and felt only

a weariness and vague disinterest afterward. So her allure wasn't exclusively sexual.

After a time, however, his musings seemed too much like the riddle of the universe, with no timely, facile answer, so he drained his glass of cognac, undressed, and climbed into bed next to the woman who consumed his thoughts.

Lying beside her, he listened to the night sounds, the crickets and frogs, the small fish owls, the rippling flow of the river, and smiled into the darkness.

This must be happiness, he thought, with a degree of wonder.

Strange.

Distinct from amusement.

Satisfying, like a glorious rainbow after the rain.

Chapter 9

W AKING EARLY, THE SUN STILL A PEACH-GOLD gleam on the horizon, he rose and went for a swim as though he needed exercise to calm the agitation of his thoughts.

For with morning had come cooler reason.

With morning had come the necessity of setting some limits on what he was willing to offer.

With morning, he'd become Jack Fitz-James again, with a woman in his bed and a life of independence in his future.

He made breakfast because he was famished and he liked to cook at his river cottage, and he thought perhaps the scent of food would soothe the wild beast in his houseguest.

An unerring truth, as it turned out.

When he brought in her breakfast tray, he found her stretching lazily, her gaze bereft of anger, a faint smile on her face.

"I offer you breakfast and a thousand apologies. I could say I was drunk, if you wish," he added, placing the tray on her lap.

"But you weren't, of course, only wanting what you wanted."

"Groten's an ass."

"I agree. Now what did you bring me for breakfast?" she queried, lifting the linen napkin from her plate.

"You're impressively agreeable this morning."

"And you're impressively talented with poached eggs and ham, or do you have a chef hidden in the closet?" Setting the napkin aside, she began cutting her ham.

Beginning to feel a niggling unease, he moved to a chair by the window and sat down at a safe distance. Did she have some ulterior motive? Had he stepped into some devious female trap?

"Aren't you going to eat?"

"I already have."

"Don't look so apprehensive. I don't have a priest hidden in my reticule." She smiled. "See, I can read your mind."

He slid into a comfortable sprawl, his mood lightened. "I'm continually astonished at your sense of situation."

"Unlike your usual paramours who all want your money and title and perhaps you as well. Now there's a thought, eh, my lord?"

"You mean if I were penniless, I'd be less appealing?"

She surveyed him over her coffee cup for several moments. "Perhaps you're an exception to the rule. I believe you'd be appealing without a farthing. Now don't become excessively prideful. I dislike conceited men in my bed."

She could have stripped naked and struck a licentious pose in terms of the shocking impact of her words. Instantly aroused, he shifted in his lounging pose to accommodate his swelling erection. "Then I'll endeavor to remain humble."

"You don't have a humble bone in your body, darling.

But I'll overlook your shameless self-confidence for self-ish reasons of my own. Did you bring condoms?"

"And if I said no?"

"I'd say go and get some and hurry back."

He smiled. "My valet bought and packed a sufficient number."

"Are you planning on staying here long?"

Talk of the future, however innocuous, brought him sitting straighter. His gaze took on a new gravity. "We need some ground rules," he quietly said.

"Meaning?" she said as quietly, her toast arrested halfway to her mouth.

"I'm not interested in love. Forgive me if that's too blunt."

"Nor am I," she succinctly replied, taking a bite of her toast. "And blunt is fine. Is there more?"

"Perhaps we should agree on some time limit to this . . ."

"Holiday?" she suggested. "I'm afraid I really do have a limited number of days I can allocate to dissipation." Her smile was delectable, like that perfect sunrise rarely seen.

He visibly relaxed, his answering smile full of charm. "Then you must tell me what I can do to make your holiday enjoyable."

"Oh, I think we both know what that is."

"Do you do this often?" he abruptly asked, though he shouldn't. A man who deliberately made known his preference for amour over love didn't have the right to ask.

"I'm not sure I care to tell you." She knew, too, he had no right to ask; perhaps wisely, she didn't wish for him to know he was the first.

"Fair enough," he neutrally said, but a touch of pique simmered in him. How many men had she been with? How many other mornings had she woken with that dazzling smile for the man beside her? As if to test the level of her profligacy or flaunting of convention, he said, "Am I forgiven for my abduction of you from Darlington House?"

"You mean you're not going to marry me, now that you've compromised my reputation?"

He sat bolt upright, looking stricken, and she laughed.

"Very funny," he muttered.

"Rest assured, I'll expect some penance for that gross faux pas. You understand some very fine walking-of-the-line will be required to carry off our pretense of fainting. Not that I had a choice." She frowned at him. "You really should learn to control your temper."

"My apologies, my most profound apologies," he said with a small sigh. "In the cold light of day, my actions appear exceedingly rash."

"I've had plenty of time since last night to deal with the practicalities of the situation, and I've come to the conclusion that since I'm leaving England shortly and am not apt to return any time soon, the scandal should die away quietly." She shrugged. "My grandpère says decisions are made on the battlefield. We can't always live life by neatly defined rules."

His dark brows rose in commendation. "You're very remarkable."

"My family's remarkable. I was fortunate."

"My family was detestable." He grimaced. "But I survived."

"Reason for gratitude, then," she said, smiling, then

removed her tray from her lap. "And speaking of grati- tude, I'd be extremely grateful if you'd join me in bed and do what you do so well."

"My pleasure." The words were too tame for what he was feeling. His pleasure was the kind he could sweetly taste and hear like joyful music. He could feel it in his gut like a kick.

"We can argue about whose pleasure it is later," she softly said. Leaning over, she placed the tray on the floor, displaying the supple perfection of her back and hip and thigh, lush pale flesh and womanly allure.

He didn't know if it was possible to fuck oneself to death, he thought, unbuttoning his shirt, but he was willing to try.

𝒯HAT SAME MORNING, SARAH PALMER AND HER aunt Bella were in wrathful moods over their chocolate pot and sugared strawberries, dissecting the events of the previous night, more viciously dissecting Miss Duras with their acid tongues.

"I don't see what all the men find so fascinating," young Sarah pettishly said. "She's much too tall."

"And large-breasted, like a peasant woman." Bella sniffed, her own delicate form not in the least buxom.

"I doubt very much whether that hair is natural. More likely from a bottle." And Sarah should know, considering her own blondness had been enhanced by Bella's hairdresser.

"The bitch has money, though. Always a factor," Bella complained, her own financial state less than ideal, with her husband's penchant for gambling.

"You don't think Jack is interested in her money?"

Wide-eyed, the younger woman considered how her hero could be so crass as to think of gross lucre.

"Don't be a ninny. He doesn't need her money—but some of the other men swarming around her like the idea of a rich wife."

"What *does* he see in her, then?" Sarah gazed at her aunt with a perplexed crook of her brows.

"Knowing Jack, she must please him in bed. And save that shocked look for your mother. I know what you've been doing with your dancing master. Not that I blame you. Vincenzo is quite lovely." If her niece hadn't been so recently sleeping with him, she would have considered offering the Palmer hospitality to the dancing master herself.

Sarah wrinkled her nose. "Jack never seemed interested in me like that."

"He's not partial to young girls, he tells me."

"Well, how will he ever marry? It's always young girls in the marriage mart."

"Now that's where we put our heads together, darling, and come up with a plan to change his mind."

Sarah smiled for the first time that morning. "Can we really? Tell me, Bella, and I'll do whatever need be to bring Jack to the altar. I want him ever so desperately."

"As does every woman who sees him, sweetheart. But don't despair," she quickly added at her niece's doleful look. "I'm sure if we put our heads together, we can come up with a way to *make* Jack marry you." She wasn't naive; she realized numerous women had tried to become his wife, but she liked to think she was more devious than most. Hadn't she brought her husband to the altar after he'd been a confirmed bachelor for twenty years?

She smiled. "First, perhaps, we should call on the Duchess of Groveland. Jack adores his godmother. It never hurts to become more friendly with his family."

"But she's so *old*. What can I possibly say to her?"

Bella cast a tolerant smile on her niece. "What does anyone say to someone one wishes to charm? Something flattering, of course. The old woman likes horses, as does her godson. We'll talk about the Derby." She gave Sarah a warning look. "And not an unkind word about Miss Duras. Is that understood?"

The young girl turned sullen. "I despise that French-woman."

"You may despise her all you like in private, but in public, you will remember to be polite. You can be sure the marquis is sleeping with her even as we speak."

"Bite your tongue, Bella!"

Lady Tallien had never revealed her own interest in Jack, nor their shared amours. There was no need for her niece to know. "One has to face reality, darling. As women, we only survive in this man's world if we view life with extreme clarity. Do you think I ask Charles where he spends his nights?"

"When I marry Jack, I won't let him be gone at night," Sarah firmly declared.

"How very sweet. I wish you good fortune." As if anyone could restrain Jack's lascivious sensibilities. In fact, she looked forward to continuing her liaison with the marquis once the Frenchwoman was gone. And if he was married to Sarah, that would matter not a whit to her. Or to him, she suspected.

"He just needs someone to love," Sarah romantically said with a sigh.

"Perhaps you're right, my dear." Lady Tallien wasn't

about to mention he had all the ladies he wanted to love. "Which gives us added incentive to see that he marries you." The marquis had to capitulate someday, and his title and fortune might as well be aligned with the Palmers. Also, how pleasant it would be to have Jack in close proximity. How very pleasant indeed.

$\mathcal{T}$HAT AFTERNOON, THE DUCHESS OF GROVE-land received two unexpected visitors, and while she concealed her surprise, her other guests were less reserved.

"Well, if it isn't young Sarah come calling, Peggy," the duchess's oldest friend, Lady Hester Stanley, exclaimed. "And Bella, too. Jack's not here, if you're looking for him."

The duchess repressed a smile at Hester's bluntness and at Lady Tallien's instant vexation.

"We hardly expected to find Jack at tea, Lady Hester," Bella tartly replied. "Unless he's changed his ways."

"You'd know his ways better than most, my dear," Lady Hester silkily murmured.

Bella looked down her nose at her elderly antagonist. "While we're friends, I hardly know his daily schedule."

"Nor do any of us," the duchess graciously interposed, wishing to avoid a distasteful scene. "Jack's very much his own man. How pretty you look, Sarah," she went on. "That shade of rose is perfect with your fair coloring."

Sarah prettily responded, and Bella curbed her testiness and offered the duchess a smile.

Casting a warning glance at her old friend, 'Peggy

offered her new visitors a seat at the tea table with a wave of her hand. "Please join us," she said, smiling an actress's smile. "It's been an age since we've had an opportunity to chat."

Groveland House appeared to be the preferred destination that afternoon of several more visitors. Everyone's curiosity was piqued after the scene in the Darlingtons' ballroom, for Jack's precipitous leavetaking with Miss Duras in his arms was far too titillating to ignore.

No one actually came out and asked where the marquis and Miss Duras had gone, but the question hovered in the air like potential lightning on a sultry summer night. And everything short of that question was discussed.

"I hear the lovely Miss Duras has a family connection with the marquis," one visitor coyly said.

"She's also very wealthy," another supplied.

A plump matron smiled archly. "I thought for a moment Redvers and Groten were going to come to blows."

"And no wonder. The marquis made mention of Groten's mistress," an elderly lady said in a hushed voice. "I heard the words clearly."

"What did he *say*?"

The question brought several of the ladies forward on their chairs, their eyes wide with curiosity.

"I really can't repeat it, but suffice to say, the marquis has more than a nodding acquaintance with Groten's mistress in Chelsea."

"Chelsea?" The sibilant word exploded into the air, uttered in piquant unison.

"Apparently Groten has set up his mistress there," their informant supplied.

"I dare say, the ways of bachelors are much the same the world over," the duchess calmly remarked. "And rivalries occur, no doubt. Would anyone like more tea?"

"For a certainty, the marquis was protecting Miss Duras," the lady with firsthand information declared, ignoring Peggy's attempt to change the focus of the conversation. "He told Groten he don't allow poaching."

"How ridiculous this all is," Bella snapped. "Jack's ears must be burning."

"I quite agree," the duchess said. "Does anyone care to wager a pony on my Derby racer? He's been setting some fine records in training."

"If you don't wish us to discuss your godson, Peggy, may we gossip a bit about the lovely Frenchwoman?" Lady Hester teasingly inquired.

"We know even less of her, so all would be the grossest speculation."

"You've become prudish today, Peggy. What of Lily, then?" Lady Hester went on, clearly alive with curiosity. "Frances will have to give that gel a talking-to if she wants her married off properly. She afforded quite an ill-timed display of affection last night."

Giving in with good grace to the burning interest in the events of the previous night, the duchess fielded those questions directed at her, disclosing as little as possible, claiming ignorance of Jack's motives or plans. At the last, interested in attaching a modicum of propriety to the relationship of such breathless concern to everyone, she said, "I do know that the lady's father and Jack's uncle were very good friends. So there *is* a family connection, you see." She smiled. "I'm sure they have much in common."

$\mathcal{F}$AMILY FRIENDS, INDEED," BELLA SPUTTERED, as she and Sarah exited the drawing room some time later. "Much in common, indeed." Chagrined to find her interest in Jack's activities mirrored by what seemed the entire ton, she was in high dudgeon over Jack's unseemly regard for Miss Duras. "She's nothing but a French tart!"

"They *could* be friends, Bella. The duchess seemed to think they were," Sarah cheerfully remarked. She was a simple girl, unaware of the artful subtleties. "And we didn't have to discuss horses once. It was quite a relief, since I don't know one racer from another."

Lady Tallien looked at her niece, momentarily dumbfounded at her naïveté.

"You don't know about racers, either," the young girl pointedly observed, "so you needn't look at me like that."

"I'm not concerned with horses or racing or anything remotely connected with them. I'm interested in putting Jack Fitz-James's ring on your finger, so pay attention. Jack and the Frenchwoman aren't friends, no matter what Peggy Hexton says. They're lovers. Do you understand?"

"I don't know how you can be so sure when his godmother, who knows him much much better, disagrees." Sarah's mouth was stubbornly set. "How do you know so much anyway?"

"I just do."

"Well, maybe you're wrong. Maybe they're not even together."

"If you don't believe me, what of all of the duchess's guests who were almost salivating, hoping to glean some tidbit of information from Lady Groveland?"

"I didn't hear anyone say they were lovers."

Bella blew air through her clenched teeth in a very unladylike fashion, forcibly tamping down her rising temper. "Do I have to show you?"

"I hardly think that necessary." Sarah's temper was beginning to heat up as well. "And even if they *are* together, you already said the Frenchwoman was a tart, so he'll not marry her anyway. Men don't marry co-cottes. Mama said."

"Despite what your mother said, if a lady's wealthy enough, society overlooks her indiscretions."

"Do you think he might *marry* her?" Suddenly Sarah was giving her aunt her full attention.

"I'd just as soon not wait to find out," Bella snapped, motivated by her own jealousies and resentments.

"Can we *do* something?" The young girl's cheeks flushed with her sudden perturbation. "I want him for *me!*" she declared with childlike fervor.

"We might travel to Gloucestershire and pay a visit to Castlereagh."

"Oh, my God!" Sarah's blue eyes opened wide in horror, the implications of Jack's bringing a lady to his home of great import. "Do you think he's there with *her?*"

"There's a very good possibility."

"He *can't* be there with her. That might mean—"

"He was more serious than any of us would wish," Bella coolly finished. "We'll leave in the morning."

ANOTHER CONVERSATION IN THE CITY WAS proceeding along a similar vein, Jack's cousin discussing the same concern with his solicitor.

"Since Redvers has never shown any serious interest in a lady before, last night was highly disturbing. At the Darlington ball, he almost fought with Groten over the Frenchwoman." Small and dark, Trevor Mitchell pursed his lips, his annoyance plain. "Should Fitz-James marry, my expectations are destroyed."

The solicitor steepled his fingers beneath his many chins, surveying his most promising client. "How is it you were invited?" The man sitting opposite him didn't move in the first circles of society.

"The advantage of being a member of Redvers family, no doubt."

"Lady Darlington was being complaisant in the extreme."

"Maybe she wants Redvers for her daughter and thought it prudent to include those few existing relatives of the marquis."

"Apparently," the lawyer bluntly agreed. "As to your expectations, could Redvers simply be pursuing another of his ladyloves with a degree more attention than usual?"

"Had you seen him last night, Percy, you'd not be so calm. I tell you, I could see my chances for his title and fortune going up in the smoke of his passion for this woman."

"You're sure?" The lawyer's gaze scrutinized more closely.

Taut with nerves, Trevor shifted in his chair, his

knuckles white on the chair arms. "As sure as I was before last night that my cousin would die from dissipation before he turned thirty."

"Hmmm." Mr. Percy regarded his agitated client with a less tranquil regard. The Honorable Mr. Mitchell would need considerable financial and legal expertise should he suddenly become a marquis; Mr. Percy had much to lose in terms of fees and commissions. "Perhaps Redvers could do with a bit of surveillance."

"In case of an accident?" Trevor softly interjected, a flash of a smile showing teeth yellowed from his penchant for Turkish cigarettes.

"No need for offensive measures just yet." Harold Percy specialized in family trusts and guardianships of a more disreputable nature. "Perhaps you could pay your cousin a visit first."

"*If* I knew his whereabouts. He left the ball rather hurriedly last night, carrying the Frenchwoman."

"Really?" the lawyer murmured, as familiar with the marquis's casual disregard for women as anyone with an ear to the fashionable world's indiscretions. "In sight of everyone?"

"He took her down the main staircase and out the door as bold as you please."

"Why don't I see what I can find out in terms of his destination? Provided he's in residence where a social call's possible, you could arrive at his door and see for yourself exactly how serious his preoccupation is with this lady."

"I have no intention of giving up my expectations, Percy. Not in the least."

"I understand. Perhaps Redvers will resort to type and the lady will be gone ere long."

"Or she can be persuaded to leave," Trevor ominously intoned.

"Let's not anticipate problems." Percy's large nostrils flared, as though he were sniffing the air for possibilities. "First things first. I'll put some men on the case, and once we've run the marquis to ground, you can go and survey the situation for yourself."

"With all due speed, if you please." Trevor's dour face further soured. "I don't care to wait until his wedding."

WHILE JACK AND VENUS WERE THE OBJECT OF much conversation that afternoon, the two lovers were already en route to Castlereagh, as if anticipating their most assiduous pursuers.

Jack lounged in the corner of the seat, Venus lying between his sprawled legs, his foot braced on the floor to hold them in place, the rhythm of the carriage delicious adjunct to their warm contentment.

The feel of her in his arms was like holding heaven, he thought.

"You're sure I won't be disrupting anything at your country home?" she murmured, half turning to gaze up at him.

"No more than you've disrupted my life completely." He bent his head to drop a kiss on her forehead.

"As you've vastly altered my life."

"We were meant for each other, it seems."

"At least for now," she said, smiling.

"Hmmm." He kissed her smile, not inclined to relinquish her for a prolonged time. "I have a feeling you'll bring me luck in the Derby."

"If I stay."

But the message in her voice offered more certainty and he pleasantly said, "I'll have to think of some incentive for you to stay."

"And I'll have to decide if it appeals."

"We can discuss it at Castlereagh," he lightly replied. "I'll have you a day's journey from London and in my clutches."

Her eyes shone with mischief. "It's more appealing already."

"Cheeky little wanton."

"Would you wish me different?"

He grinned. "God, no. I think I've gone to heaven."

"You offer glimpses of paradise as well, my lord," she playfully returned.

"It almost makes one reconsider the nature of religion." His arms tightened around her waist and his gypsy eyes looked thoughtful for a moment. "Hell and damnation," he whispered, disconcerted but unwavering in his intent. "You're staying for the Derby."

"Perhaps—if I can ride your black."

"They won't let you. Jockey Club rules."

"I meant in training."

"That's all?" He wasn't used to women asking for so little.

"Should I ask for more?"

"Ask for whatever you like. So long as you stay."

"You're that enamored of me?"

He hesitated for the merest moment, such an admission unparalleled in his life. But she was smiling up at him and he'd never felt such pleasure. "I'm that enamored, darling. What I have is yours."

She liked his open-handed largesse as much as she liked the warmth of his smile. And while she didn't wish for anything beyond his company, it was pleasant to know her feelings were reciprocated. "I'm looking forward to our holiday in the country."

He understood the significance of her words, the layers and texture, the anticipation. "I'll show you everything at Castlereagh, show you off to everyone."

"After I send for my clothes." She lifted the wrinkled fabric of her ballgown.

"There are local dressmakers. We'll summon one in the morning to make you something until your luggage arrives."

"Discounting my behavior to date, I'm not sure I'm that brazen. What will your neighbors say when they hear the inevitable gossip?"

"I see no reason I can't have my spinster cousin out to visit."

"Thank you very much. I'm a year older than you."

"But quite on the shelf, darling, in terms of the marriage mart," he playfully noted. "Think how amusing the pretense. When I'd refer to you as my spinster cousin, anyone with eyes would have to swallow their cavil."

"Because you're the mighty lord of the county."

"Of course, but what an enticing role you could play, dear cuz."

She laughed. "I'd prefer less drama. Can't we be in hermitage at Castlereagh?"

"Whatever you like," he said, entirely serious once again. "You decide."

"I'm allowed carte blanche?"

"You're allowed anything for the pleasure you bring me."

"Now I know why all the ladies adore you."

He shook his head. "Not for that," he bluntly said. "You're the first." And abruptly he spoke of his Derby horse, as though he'd talked out of turn.

Equally uncomfortable with ardent emotion, fully aware of the transience of their relationship, Venus immediately responded to the new topic, which was less fraught with earnestness. They compared notes on their thoroughbreds, stables, and jockeys with a casual politesse, and in the course of their journey that sunny afternoon, both were careful to keep the discussions entirely urbane.

Chapter 10

$\sim\!\!\!\infty\!\!\!\sim$

$\mathcal{M}$EANWHILE, A FLURRY OF ACTIVITY WAS
taking place in London. Both Bella and Harold Percy
had servants and servitors out on the street, talking to
the staff at Lord Redvers's and Miss Duras's establish-
ments. The investigation was done with discretion in
the case of Lady Tallien, her lady's maid having connec-
tions with both houses. For his part, Percy's men were
skilled at their craft; over drinks in the neighborhood
pubs, they discovered the necessary information from
the footmen at both homes.

Come morning a day hence, two carriages left London bound for Cheltenham. The inhabitants were noticeably distrait, Jack's cousin partaking of considerable
rum on his journey to allay his nerves. The marquis had
indeed taken the lady to Castlereagh, an ominous por-
tend, considering Lord Redvers had always punctiliously
avoided having his paramours anywhere near his country home.

Inherited directly from Jack's grandfather, Castlereagh was a place of solitude, without undue taint of his
father's memory; a place of refuge, Trevor knew. And
now Jack had taken Miss Duras there.

Bella understood less of the marquis's family issues,

but she knew perfectly well it boded no good that Jack had brought that woman to his favorite abode.

"He never brings anyone to Castlereagh," she heatedly remarked to her niece. "Never!"

"Then we must stop her by all means!" Sarah exclaimed, wringing her handkerchief into a twisted wreckage. A second later, her perplexed gaze fixed itself on her aunt, sitting opposite in the fast-moving carriage. "But how?"

It wasn't as though the topic hadn't been discussed at some length already, but young Sarah couldn't retain facts beyond the color and cut of a gown. Everything other than fashionable attire and gossip was quite outside her capacity to recall.

"We'll decide for certain once we arrive at Castlereagh and see what's transpired in the past two days."

"What if he's procured a special license!" Sarah wailed.

"That news would have reached London within hours." Bella drew in a calming breath. "Apparently he hasn't entirely lost his senses—yet." However, Lady Tallien's personal concern was more that Jack Fitz-James might have fallen in love. Marriage itself wasn't of concern to her. Men were never faithful to their wives in the beau monde unless . . . That dreadful word *love* again came to mind.

"I might still be able to marry him after he tires of that Frenchwoman." Sarah pronounced the last word as though she had something distasteful in her mouth. "He *will* tire of her, won't he?" Sarah looked to her aunt as ultimate social arbiter; her mother's passion for whist left little time for maternal duties.

"We'll have to see what we can do to facilitate that

process," Bella firmly said. "But first, we must call on Lord Redvers in the most benign fashion. Remember, we're abroad on a spur-of-the-minute excursion to escape the frenzy of the Season for a few days. You're too fatigued to go on a moment more, and Farleigh House is only in the next county."

"Oh, Bella, you're ever so smart. How do you think of such cleverness? Farleigh House, indeed. How perfect, and I shall display the most dreadful ennui and weariness. You'll be exceedingly proud. Look." She half-swooned in her seat, gazing up at her aunt from beneath lowered lashes.

"A little less drama, my sweet," her aunt cautioned. "We mustn't put Jack on his guard. Perhaps a small sigh on occasion will suffice."

"Oh, I can sigh ever so well."

"And you must be exquisitely polite to the Frenchwoman."

Lady Sarah's mouth turned down in an instant pout.

"If you don't give me your word, I'll leave you in the carriage and go in alone." Lady Tallien's voice was determined.

"Oh, very well." Sullen and moody, her niece agreed.

"If you want Jack, you must conduct yourself without petulance or any other adverse behavior that might be construed as discourteous. He won't tolerate it, I assure you. And our visit will be highly suspect, so we must behave."

The young girl smoothed her skirt briskly, clearly agitated by the necessity of being civil to her rival.

"You'll have time tonight to ready yourself, since we'll arrive in Cheltenham too late to call. We'll stay at the inn near Castlereagh tonight and visit on the morrow."

"I shall behave, of course," Sarah grumbled. "Lord Redvers is surely the very greatest catch in the ton, so I suppose I can be polite to a light-skirt doxy if it will serve my purpose."

"Wisely concluded, my sweet, but don't deceive yourself in terms of the Frenchwoman. She's no light-skirt. Her family is powerful, wealthy, and assured of their position in the world. And now that Jack has shown his preference, she must be treated with the greatest deference."

*T*HE BARSET ARMS HAD GUESTS FOR CASTLEreagh in both of their front suites that night, and by the merest happenstance, the maid delivering supper made mention of it to the two ladies in the superior rooms nearest the garden.

"Whatever is Jack's cousin doing here?" Bella speculated as the door closed on the serving girl, who had divulged the name of the other guest. Although she had a very good notion.

"Why not ask him?" Sarah said with childlike candor.

Not sure such artlessness would serve her purposes, Bella debated how best to approach Mr. Mitchell, and decided ultimately to invite him for an after-dinner port—as a friendly gesture between two acquaintances far from home.

When Trevor received his invitation, his first reaction was alarm. Were others on a similar journey? Lady Tallien had no interest in the country unless a man was somehow involved; she was licentious in the extreme.

And at such close quarters to Castlereagh, her target, of course, would be no other than his cousin Jack.

He swore and gnawed at his lower lip and wished Percy were near for counsel. But there was no possibility of refusing her invitation without suspicion falling on him. Indeed, they were both far from home, such an invitation wasn't out of place. So he fortified himself with additional rum and arrived at their door some minutes later, disconcerted and wary.

"Do come in, Mr. Mitchell," Bella purred on opening the door, and Trevor's apprehension mounted.

But she spoke of banalities and he relaxed. In addition, the port was excellent; furthermore, Bella's bosom was conspicuously displayed above her corseted bodice, and while it wouldn't be described as sumptuous, it was more than a delectable handful.

Leaning over a short time later, allowing him a better view, she quietly said, "I have a question for you, once Miss Sarah retires."

No man alive could refuse such a flagrant invitation, not even Mr. Mitchell, for all his dourness and rough manners. Filling his own glass that time, he proceeded to drink it down with one eye on the young lady's imminent retiring and the other on the expanse of Bella's pale bosom.

When it came time for Sarah to retire, he unsteadily rose to his feet and attempted a bow, eliciting a frown from his hostess. Mumbling an apology, he straightened his red vest, flushing a similar bright shade.

"Sit down," Bella sharply said the moment Sarah closed the door into the adjoining bedchamber. All pretense of courtesy was gone, her voice and expression severe. "And that's enough for you tonight," she curtly added, lifting away the port decanter. "I need you to be in your wits for this discussion." With a swish of her skirts, she sat down across the table from him and directed her stern gaze on him. "Now tell me why you're here."

Feeling as though he were at his last judgment, he stammered and stumbled over what he hoped was a bland explanation, the large amount of liquor he'd drunk not conducive to clear thinking.

"Now, the truth if you please," Bella charged, once he'd finished. "You never visit Jack, and everyone knows it. He despises you."

Having regained a modicum of his composure and had his hackles raised by her rudeness, he found the courage to say, "I don't answer to you or anyone concerning my plans. And don't think I don't know what you're about, either. It's the middle of the Season and you have a marriageable chit on the block. A trip to the country won't help your niece get a husband."

He realized the significance of his words as soon as he'd uttered them, and had he not, the tight smile appearing on Lady Tallien's face would have jogged his understanding.

"If you could stay sober, perhaps we could help each other." Bella's tone was heavy with insinuation.

"Partners are dangerous." Although there was a faint slur in his words, his eyes no longer looked befuddled, and his gaze turned piercing.

Bella smiled, a superficial conspirator's smile. "We're not partners, only brief allies. Surely you're here because of the woman."

"And if I were?" Trevor hedged.

"I'd say you're sensible. She poses a danger to your future."

"I don't need you."

"You do if I were inclined to drop a hint to Jack about your motives."

"I'm not sure he'd believe you, and even if he did, he's not unaware of my motives."

"I think he might be, shall we say, not entirely clear how determined you are, with a solicitor like Harold Percy."

"How do you know Percy?"

"My husband is twenty years older than I, and given to drink and . . . other amusements. Who better than Percy to protect my financial interests." Her brows rose in exaggerated innocence. "He happened to mention one day that you were one of his clients."

"Happened to mention, damn his hide. I'll give him—"

"Don't become alarmed, Mitchell. Percy and I are old friends. I'm sure he's not in the practice of disclosing such information to the general public."

"What else did he tell you, damn him?"

"Nothing to become alarmed about. There's no need to be bristly. I just feel it more useful for us to cooperate on our venture at Castlereagh. Think how odd it will seem when we both appear on Jack's doorstep tomorrow. We really have to agree on some plausible explanation."

"There ain't a plausible explanation. And he's apt to shut us out, anyway."

"If we put our heads together, perhaps we can come up with a reason he might care to see us."

Trevor grimly laughed. "Has he addled your brains? He don't care if he sees any of us."

"Now there's a thought," Bella softly murmured. "Who could he not turn away?"

"Jack? Are you jesting? He'd turn away the Queen herself if it pleased him."

"But would he turn away the Mayor of Cheltenham if the man was bringing him news of a donation for the local racecourse?"

"Naturally not. He's mad for racing and the local heats. But that don't get us in."

"I'm not surprised you haven't found a way to improve your living from Jack. You have no imagination. The donation will be compliments of an anonymous donor, and you and I will just happen to arrive on the heels of the mayor's coach. Now how much should this anonymous donor give?"

"Don't look at me. His nibs keeps me too close to the wind to have any extra guineas."

Bella pursed her lips for a moment and then said, "I'll sell one of Sarah's necklaces. She has plenty enough not to miss one or two. You can find a jeweler for me, I presume, seeing how you aren't able to contribute anything."

"You're not contributing anything, either, so don't take on airs with me."

"Never mind, I'll find my own jeweler," she heatedly said. "You're not averse, I take it, to following the mayor into Castlereagh?"

"I'll go."

"Well, then." She placed her palms on the table and rose from her chair. "Should some measures be required to hasten Miss Duras's departure from England, I assume you wouldn't be averse to those plans either?"

He started in his chair, wondering if Percy had disclosed more than he would have wished to Lady Tallien, wondering if he was putting himself into jeopardy even talking to her. "What do you mean?" he cautiously inquired.

"I mean, what would it be worth to you to have the Frenchwoman gone?"

"Not much if you're going to marry your niece to him two shakes later. We really can't be partners," he brusquely said, rising, hoping he'd not compromised himself.

"It makes no difference to me if she marries him or not. Her marriage to whomever offers me no advantages. On the other hand, should Jack remain single, that might be worthwhile to you. I'm bargaining for money, you dolt. Are you interested?"

"I'm not sure you can do anything for me I can't do for myself."

"I can keep Sarah away from him."

"He ain't going to marry her, anyway."

"He might if necessity requires it," she smoothly replied. "If Sarah's father requires it."

"Now that sounds like a scheming woman."

"I don't care what it sounds like. It might just work, and if it does, you'll never be a marquis. Sarah wants lots and lots of babies."

He looked squarely at her as though he could see behind the bland mask of her expression. "Maybe we could talk about it."

"Talk away."

"Tomorrow, when I'm sober." Her machinations would require a keen mind.

"In the morning, before I go to the jeweler and the mayor. You have until then to decide if you wish to invest in some insurance, as it were." She smiled. Percy had been useful, although all the men she conferred her favors on had to be profitable in one way or another.

It required ingenuity to make one's way in the world without a wealthy family or a generous husband. She could always use additional money.

Wɪᴛʜ ᴍᴏʀɴɪɴɢ, ᴛʀᴇᴠᴏʀ ꜰᴏᴜɴᴅ ʜᴇ ʜᴀᴅ ᴀɴ aching head, but even through the twinges of pain, he understood that he might have something to gain from a partnership with Lady Tallien—and he had nothing to lose. He needn't disclose his plans, only go along with hers. And if she could keep Redvers single, well, that *would* be worthwhile.

They agreed on a price swiftly. He had only to give her a small down payment now, and she'd accept monthly sums. It unnerved him slightly that she handed him a short agreement to sign, but the wording was ambiguous enough to wiggle free of, should that be required. Two devious, mistrustful people in partnership. But then they were both hard-pressed for cash.

Lady Tallien handled the mayor beautifully; he was ablush and chivalrous at the same time. London belles weren't common in his country world, and Bella had had much practice in tantalizing men. When they parted, she pledged him to secrecy about her part as messenger in the racetrack donation. "The benefactor fears disclosure and wishes her love of racing to remain secret. You understand, kind sir," she murmured, taking his hand in hers and squeezing it lightly. "We ladies must put our faith in gentlemen like you to retain our reputations."

"Never fear, Lady Tallien," he said, coloring furiously when she looked up at him from under her lashes. "Your secret is safe with me. Lord Redvers will learn nothing from me save the news of the wonderful, generous donation for our track."

"I can't thank you enough, Lord Mayor, and should you ever be in London, you must by all means call on me . . . and your wife too, of course," she coyly added so he understood perfectly what she meant.

" 'Pon my word, that is . . . most generous of you, my lady, most kind, most wonderfully kind—"

"We may meet again later, dear sir," Bella interposed, curtailing his stammering amazement. "My niece and I may stop to call on Lord Redvers. I do hope you'll not disclose that we've met before."

"No, no, of course not, my lady, my lips are sealed, my lady. You may count on it—absolutely!"

$\mathcal{B}$UT HE TURNED A BRIGHT PINK AND SLOSHED a bit of brandy over the rim of his glass when Bella and Sarah were announced at Castlereagh that afternoon.

"I told you we shouldn't have been home to the mayor," Jack murmured near Venus's ear, disgruntled at seeing the Palmer ladies in his doorway—a damned long way from their normal haunts.

"They can all be dismissed soon," Venus whispered. "You have that appointment with the bishop."

He chuckled. Was she ever discomposed? And in a more cheerful frame of mind, he looked up at the two ladies approaching across the large expanse of Savonnerie carpet, and decided he would give their afternoon callers another ten minutes before putting an end to this absurdity.

When making introductions to the mayor, Jack wondered at the man's unease, but put it down to country manners in the presence of two fashionable ladies. Venus, on the other hand, he noted with affection, outshone them both despite her plain muslin frock, borrowed from the recently departed dressmaker. Tomorrow, they'd been promised three finished gowns of more splendor.

"What a surprise to find you at Castlereagh, Miss Duras," Bella lightly remarked.

"What a surprise to find you so far from London, Lady Tallien," Venus replied, aware of Jack's thigh brushing hers as he sat beside her on the settee.

The hard scrutiny of their two new visitors brought an added sense of intimacy to the lovers, a heightened consciousness of each other.

"Miss Duras has promised to advise me on a new infirmary for Castlereagh," Jack said, leaning slightly into Venus's shoulder.

The butler was pouring the ladies tea, but they seemed not to notice, so intent was their surveillance.

"How charming." Bella's tone was barely civil, despite all her admonitions to her niece. The damned woman was practically in Jack's lap, and every form of jealousy burned in her breast.

A small silence ensued and the mayor quickly jumped into the breach. "I've come to give Lord Redvers some very good news," he nervously declared. "Very good news, indeed . . . extremely, that is—"

Taking pity on the mayor's obvious discomfort, Venus intervened. "A donor has given generously to the local track. The mayor was kind enough to bring the news to Jack."

"How very nice," Bella said, ignoring the mayor's agitation.

"What track?" Sarah asked, since she'd not been privy to the scheme—for good reason.

"The local downs," Jack supplied.

"The race meets are well attended, very well, very well indeed," the mayor said.

Bella sent him a scathing look that caused his mouth to clamp shut, and Jack was contemplating curtailing his ten-minute allowance by eight minutes when Venus graciously inquired, "Have you enjoyed your first Season so far, Miss Palmer? I remember my own with fondness."

"It's ever so much more fun than staying in the schoolroom or practicing the piano, although I love my dancing lessons, and all my new gowns are—"

"Sarah has been feeling a certain ennui of late," her aunt interposed, "so we decided to repair to Farleigh House for a few short days of peace and quiet."

In her enthusiasm, Sarah had forgotten to dislike Venus, who seemed rather nice, and her part in the plan. With her aunt's reminder, she immediately lounged back on her chair and said in a faint voice, "I've felt ever so weary, I fear. Farleigh House will be a calm haven."

Jack's mouth twitched into a smile, quickly repressed, and with remarkable serenity, Venus noted, "I recall moments of enervation as well in my first Season. The pace of entertainments is wicked."

"Is it not? I mean with balls every night, and dinners, not to mention all those afternoon teas and musicals,

I'm changing gowns five times a day, and—" A sharp glance from her aunt brought her words to a standstill.

"You see how agitated the poor girl is. Quite unlike her usual calm." Bella's smile was fixed and stiff.

"I perfectly understand. You know, Jack, how dizzying the social schedule for all the debutantes." Venus offered her companion on the settee a warm smile.

"I can sympathize," he said with a feigned gravity. He was thinking that the visit had to end very soon or he would burst into laughter, when another visitor was announced who erased any contemplation of smiling from his thoughts.

"You're a long way from Devon," the marquis brusquely said, before his cousin had fully entered the room.

"I'm going north to the Lake Country for a walking tour."

"Really."

"I feel the need for exercise," Trevor mendaciously replied, deciding the Frenchwoman was even more splendid in daylight. His pulse rate quickened with apprehension. "And since I was in the neighborhood . . ."

"Out of money so soon?" Jack softly murmured.

"No, as a matter of fact, although I'm not one to refuse additional funds."

"You'll have to talk to my bankers."

"They do what you tell them to do," Trevor churlishly retorted.

The marquis didn't care to haggle with Trevor over his stipend. "Is there another reason for this visit, then?"

"Can't I come to call without a reason?"

"What do you hope to see on your walking tour?"

Venus politely asked, conscious of the antagonism in the air.

"I don't have a planned itinerary." Trevor's voice was gruff. "Will you be leaving England soon?"

Perturbed by his cousin's tactlessness as well as by the transparent excuse for a visit given by Bella, Jack decided one uncharitable turn deserved another. "Darling, should we divulge our joyful news to everyone?" The gaze he turned on Venus was studiously bland.

"It's up to you, dear." Improvising with grace, she smiled at him.

Taking Venus's hand, he gave her an affectionate glance before turning back to his guests. "I'm pleased to announce Miss Duras and I are engaged." The proverbial pin-dropping phrase had just entered Jack's mind, and the shock on his guests' faces was gratifying.

Stepping into the stifled hush with aplomb, Jack's announcement too outré to be anything but farce, Venus mildly said, "I was as astonished as you. Lord Redvers proposed after such a short acquaintance, but what a delightful surprise." She offered the marquis a demure smile, but her green eyes were wickedly speculative.

"I was completely overwhelmed by love," Jack dramatically declared, while Bella and Trevor wondered whether he could be drunk so early in the day.

"It's impossible!" Sarah's high-pitched squeal soared upward, reverberating against the coffered ceiling. "Bella!" she exclaimed, swiveling toward her aunt, "you said Lord Redvers would be m—"

"—The very last bachelor in the ton to be married," her aunt smoothly interjected. "I stand corrected, Lord

Redvers. You've stunned us all." Suspicious by nature, she quietly challenged, "Have you set a date?"

"Miss Duras and I are debating suitable times . . . and places."

"Lord Redvers is intent on a speedy timetable, aren't you, darling?" Venus offered him a tender look.

"Under the circumstances," he said, audacious to the bone, "the sooner the better, my sweet, don't you think?" His unabashed grin was cheeky.

Lady Tallien gasped.

"What?" Sarah cried, watching the color drain from her aunt's face.

"Nothing, my dear," Bella returned, her mouth grimly set. "Our congratulations, of course," she went on, although her expression and tone suggested a desire for bodily harm more than good wishes. She rose in a swish of silk, her petite form rigid with fury. "Come, Sarah, we've still some considerable distance to travel."

"Could I beg a ride with you?" Trevor inquired, swiftly coming to his feet, maintaining his fiction of a walking tour. "At least for a few miles."

"Very well." Lady Tallien's voice was brisk, her gloved hands clenched into fists. "Good day, Lord Redvers, Miss Duras." She could barely contain the wrath in her voice.

In moments the drawing room was bereft of the unwelcome guests, leaving only the mayor to entertain. Relaxed once again, Jack discussed the coming race meets with him for a courteous interval before making his excuses, pleading an appointment.

Jack escorted the mayor to his carriage, genuinely fond of the local magistrate who, like so many country squires, embraced the simple life of the hunt, races, and convivial drinking. Once free of all their guests, the marquis's good spirits returned, and he was whistling when he entered the drawing room.

"That certainly was a surprise," Venus noted, lifting her glass of sherry to him in salute. "Couldn't you have resorted to something less inflammable than an engagement announcement?"

He paused for a moment, then shrugged away her concern. "If they're desperate enough to drive all the way out here and invade our privacy to discover the status of our relationship, they deserve a bloody scare."

"You're shamelessly wicked." She watched him move toward her with a delicious sense of expectation. He exuded a male strength and virility so potent and intense, her body responded at the mere sight of him.

"But you like me nonetheless—or perhaps because of it." His voice was low and teasing as he dropped into a sprawl beside her, gently stroking her thigh in a proprietary gesture.

"Are you saying I'm not entirely proper?" Setting her glass down, she half turned and twined her arms around his neck, her smile flirtatious.

"Luckily," he whispered, brushing a finger over the fullness of her bottom lip. "And since I haven't made love to you for—" his brows rose in brief contemplation "—thirty minutes at least, could I interest you in this small but comfortable settee?"

"What of the servants?" The drawing room was large and open, and while the double doors to the hallway were closed, there was little chance of concealment should someone come in.

"Would you like them to watch?" His eyes were amused.

"I *meant*, will we be disturbed?"

"Not unless you scream so loudly they think you need assistance."

"Otherwise, they're well trained?" A hint of pique entered her voice.

"Don't look at me like that. I don't bring women here. A fact you may have noted when first we arrived and the staff stood gap-mouthed at the sight of you."

"That was rather sweet." Appeased, she lightly kissed his cheek.

"You enjoyed that, did you?"

"Of course, darling. Why would I not? To have brought the notorious Lord Redvers to his knees is a mark of consequence, I'm told."

His startled gaze held hers for a moment. "By whom, pray tell?"

"By the lady's maid you provided me. Hattie knows every scrap of gossip attached to your illustrious person. All the housemaids are in love with you, by the way."

He rolled his eyes. "Don't believe everything you hear."

"It's quite true." Her grin was mischievous. "Hattie tells me your sexual exploits are the cause of great sighing and hopeful longing. You could have a virtual harem here if you wished."

Genuinely uncomfortable with adulation, he grimaced. "Hattie's making it up, you can be sure. I never even look at the housemaids." His father's scandalous behavior toward the maids had caused him to make a vow of abstinence apropos his female staff. Such virtue set him apart from most of his aristocratic counterparts, who viewed chambermaids as fair game.

"So I have your undivided attention here at Castlereagh."

He gently stroked her back. "Undivided, complete, and total."

"What a charming pledge from a man of your repute."

"You, no doubt, will make it worth my while."

"Ah . . . ulterior motives." Her mouth quirked into a slow smile, her fingers tangling in the dark curls at the nape of his neck.

"Always, with you," he murmured. "Obsessed as I am, you never need wonder what I want."

"Do you think it as strange as I to have these overwhelming desires?"

"Of course. But I'm not stupid enough to question the pleasure."

"A hedonist of the first water . . ."

"I've been practicing for years."

"Lucky me."

"Lucky us."

"At least until the next group of curiosity-seekers arrives, wondering if Lady Tallien has lost her mind."

He grunted in displeasure. "We won't be home to any more visitors. I don't care if Christ himself appears on the doorstep."

She traced a finger down his cheek. "You realize your little subterfuge won't last. I'll have to throw you over soon."

"Not too soon, I hope," he said, grinning. "I need some respite from the Bellas of the world."

"Or the young Sarahs. She was distraught at hearing her aspirations for marriage thwarted."

"Spare me the young Sarahs," he said with disgust. "They're all empty-headed ciphers. Unlike you."

"My parents believe in education."

"How quaint. That must be why I adore you."

She fluttered her lashes in flirtatious parody. "Men have always been attracted to me for my conversation."

Nonplussed at the realization that her allure wasn't exclusively sexual, he briefly struggled with the discordant thought; sex had always been his sole criterion for female company. Unnerved by such unacceptable feelings, he safely reverted to type. After all, the beautiful woman in his arms was warm, willing, and deliciously wanton; there were more pleasant things to do than speculate on what had been, to date in his life, very trustworthy standards. "So tell me," he lazily drawled, beginning to unbutton the neckline of her spring frock, "do you think Lord Russell's cabinet will put any reform bills on the floor this session?"

"I think I shall put *you* on the floor," she whispered. "This sofa's too small."

"You *are* an enchanting conversationalist." His grin was roguish.

"We try, my lord. Would you like me to talk you into an orgasm?"

He laughed. "I'd rather feel my way to an orgasm. And if this settee is too small, I'd be more than happy to accommodate you on the carpet . . ."

Chapter 11

❧❧❧

$\mathcal{M}$ARRIED? CAN YOU BELIEVE HE'S ACTUALLY going to marry that bitch after knowing her for such a short time? Not if I have anything to say about it," Bella darkly said, answering her own question with chill purpose. She surveyed her carriage companions with a furious glare.

"It's a bloody alarming thought." Jack's cousin chewed on his bottom lip. "There may not be much time to wait, if you know what I mean."

"How can we stop him if he wishes to marry her?" Sarah gazed at her aunt, a worry line creasing her pale brow.

"I'll think of something," Bella murmured, intent on reclaiming Jack Fitz-James. "He may talk of love now, but I rather doubt his feelings will last long. He doesn't have a record of constancy with women."

"If you can get him to marry me, Bella, I'll give you all my jewelry." Sarah's voice held a pleading note, all her girlish dreams wrapped up in visions of marriage to the handsome Lord Redvers.

Not that Bella needed added incentive with her own selfish motives in the fore, but such a lucrative offer could hardly be refused. "What a darling child you are. I'll have to see what I can do. And once you're Lady

Redvers, married to one of the richest men in England, you'll have all the jewelry you want." And she'd have her lover back.

"I will, won't I." Sarah sighed, visualizing her fairy-tale life of wealth and splendor.

Trevor cleared his throat loudly, his annoyance plain. "I believe we have a small matter of business, if you recall, Lady Tallien."

"I haven't forgotten, Mr. Mitchell," she cryptically replied, casting him a silencing glance. "We can discuss the matter once we're back in London."

"Aren't we going to Farleigh House?" Sarah inquired.

"We were never going to Farleigh House."

The young girl clapped her hand over her mouth and giggled. "I forgot."

"I shall remember such things for us both."

"And I shall rely on you to bring me Lord Redvers," Sarah cheerfully declared, her confidence in her aunt complete.

While Bella wasn't quite as confident in her ability to bring Jack to the altar, she did have a delectable scheme already forming in her mind. It meant she might have to renege on her agreement with Jack's cousin—although the financial merits of each proposal would have to be carefully weighed. In the meantime, she needed Trevor's cooperation—at least until her decision was reached. "Why don't we meet at Percy's in a few days," she suggested. "To discuss our mutual concerns."

Now Trevor Mitchell wasn't so obtuse as to think Bella Palmer was looking after his interests, and he, too, was considering various other ways to thwart his cousin's marriage plans. But like his female cohort, he wasn't in any rush to disclose his methods. Time enough after the meeting at Percy's to see if he still needed her.

And so two grasping, nefarious souls contemplated the future of Jack Fitz-James and themselves.

*U*NDISTURBED BY THE SELFISH SCHEMES BEING hatched, the two lovers at Castlereagh spent the following days in blissful companionship. They made love in unending measure as though both were conscious of the limits of time, wanting to capture each moment of delight, each joyful sensation. When, on occasion, they emerged from the marquis's suite and sat in the sun on the terrace or walked through the gardens or took a picnic down to the lake, splashing and swimming in the warm water like frolicking children, the servants would look at one another and nod their heads in agreement. The Marquis of Redvers had found himself a wife.

In the days of their hermitage at Castlereagh, the lovers also set about planning an infirmary on each of the marquis's estates. Jack's steward met with them several times, carefully listening while Venus described the style of buildings required and enumerated in detail the essential supplies needed. They toured the site selected for Jack's first clinic at Castlereagh, interviewed women who could serve as nurses and midwives, and hired two local doctors to deliver services to the staff and tenants.

Astonished by the breadth of Venus's knowledge, the extraordinary technical expertise and medical competence she possessed, Jack found himself further charmed and delighted. She was a source of continuing wonder and fascination. They often sat on the terrace after dinner, savoring one of Jack's special cognacs, and talked—

of politics, finance, farming, travel, or any number of varied subjects.

Venus had seen much of the world in the Duras's vessels. Her father's political interests had often placed her in the midst of history-making occasions, and they exchanged anecdotes on the tumultuous events that had transpired during their lifetimes. They agreed, too, on favorite sites of interest in the world—the pyramids, and the Parthenon in moonlight.

With a common interest in the stock market, they compared their growth stocks in railroads and manufacturing and debated the declining state of Turkey and China as world powers. Venus even understood the finer points of agriculture, her close contact with the life of the peasantry on the Duras estates bringing her a wealth of knowledge not common to women of her class.

And of course, their mutual fascination with racing was a constant source of discussion.

"You talk like a man," Jack said one night, his voice half musing.

"No, darling, I talk like a woman," she replied with a smile.

He exhaled softly and gazed at her over the rim of his glass. "Not any of the women I know."

"Perhaps you should expand your horizons." Her voice was lightly teasing.

"I prefer the very narrow focus of my horizon at the moment." He leaned over to refill her glass, his smile so warm and affectionate, she felt a wistful rush of longing. How beautiful he looked in the moonlight, the purity of his face and form illuminated in muted chiaroscuro.

Damping her threatening emotions—it would never do to become involved with a man like Jack—she murmured, "I shall always remember these days at Castle-reagh with fondness."

He instantly scowled and set the decanter down as though readying himself to move. "I'm not letting you leave just yet."

"Nor am I planning to, when you offer such pleasure."

"Good," he said in a restrained growl, his taut posture relaxing.

"I'll stay until the Derby, but then I *must* return home. All the new equipment I purchased isn't doing the new hospital in Paris any good stored in the hold of my ship." There were limits to a liaison with Jack Fitz-James, she knew, and she preferred leaving to being discarded. A matter of pride perhaps, but there it was. "I expect your black to win, though," she said with a smile. "I'm placing a sizable bet on him."

The marquis smiled back, content once again. "I'm beginning to feel the *pressure*."

"Keep in mind the pressure of gossip as well. Our engagement should make us the center of attention at the Derby."

His chuckle rumbled in his throat. "Now *that* I'm looking forward to."

She grinned. "Shameless provocateur."

"But think, darling, how much fun it will be. All those wagging tongues and sidelong glances, not to mention the direct questions of those brave enough to confront us."

"I warn you," she softly admonished, "I intend to be a silent bystander. Acquit me of adding fuel to your brazen conflagration."

"Now that'll be a first. You silent? I'm almost inclined to offer you odds on that one."

"You think I can't be silent?"

"I *know* you can't be silent. I'll give you five to one— hell, ten to one you can't curb your need to speak out when all the busybodies approach us with their pointed queries."

She quirked her brow. "I should make you face them alone."

"And miss all the entertainment?"

When she chuckled, her diamond eardrops sparkled in the moonlight. "It should be interesting, at least, I'll give you that."

"Interesting is too tame a word, darling. An assault of bloodthirsty Goths and Vandals, more like."

She wagged her finger at him, her eyes bright with humor. "You're going to owe me for this, Jack Fitz-James."

He lifted his glass to her. "I already owe you for the best days of my life."

THE STARTLING ANNOUNCEMENT OF THE MAR-quis's engagement had taken the ton by storm, the tittle-tattle reaching shrill proportions as each matron with a daughter to marry off cried out in indignation, each renounced lover loudly lamented the loss of the marquis's astonishing sexual prowess, each eligible peer of the realm howled with fear and amazement. If Jack Fitz-James, the bellwether for predatory male instincts, could be struck by Cupid's arrow, there was no hope of escape for lesser men.

⁓

𝒯N CONTRAST TO THE VULGAR CURIOSITY OF the beau monde, the schemers with more personal antipathy for the marquis's engagement assembled in Percy's office one afternoon. "Do you actually think Redvers intends to go through with this?" the solicitor asked.

Lady Tallien and Trevor Mitchell both gave him cool stares as though questioning his judgment and intellect.

"You're certain?" he challenged. "I'm simply concerned with preemptive measures, should this be a sham."

"Damnit, man, how do we dare *not* take measures," Trevor growled. "Think of what we stand to lose. Although I'd like some reassurance from you," he added, nodding curtly in Bella's direction. "Do you intend to cooperate with us or not? Your niece seems to think you can deliver Redvers to her."

"She's young and foolish. Do you actually think I can make Jack marry her?"

"Very well. We agree then," Percy interceded, playing the conciliator between the two resentful clients in his office. "And we all consider Lord Redvers difficult to control. I suggest we concentrate on the Frenchwoman."

"How?" Bella scrutinized the lawyer's placid face with critical regard. Her dearest wish was for Venus Duras to disappear from the face of the earth.

"We deprive the marquis of her company."

"Abduct her?"

"Or simply suggest she'd be safer in France. She might be easily persuaded."

"Since when did you take the high road, Percy?" Bella queried.

"The Duras family is powerful, their reach long." The solicitor tipped his head in emphasis. "A sensible reason to handle her carefully."

"Just kill her and dispose of the body." Trevor's face was as grim as his voice.

"Unless you wish to do the deed yourself," the lawyer pointed out, "which I seriously doubt, I remind you it's difficult to find trustworthy assassins. Persuasion is by far the better method."

"I'm not so sure you can frighten her. The woman has a rare confidence," Bella grudgingly conceded.

"Let me take care of it." Harold Percy was a master at his craft. Threats and intimidation were his specialty.

"I don't care what you do, so long as you do it quickly," Trevor declared. "What if Fitz-James marries her at Castlereagh before he returns to London?"

"The marquis hasn't taken out a marriage license. I had my men check."

"Maybe there actually is a God," Trevor muttered, his relief apparent. "Just do something, damnit, and do it soon."

Bella rose from her chair and straightened her bonnet bow with cool deliberation. "Do let me know if there's anything I can do to help. Although I'm sure we can put this all in your capable hands, Percy." Her smile was devoid of feeling. "If you'll excuse me, I have an appointment at a musicale this afternoon."

After the door closed on Lady Tallien, Trevor harshly said, "I don't trust that bitch. She doesn't seem particularly helpful."

"Don't worry about Bella," Percy replied. "She and I have managed similar arrangements before."

"Have you now . . ." Mistrust gleamed in Trevor's eyes.

"We have. I'll handle her, and nothing more need be said. This should take a week, two at the most. Relax, Mr. Mitchell. Redvers won't be marrying this woman."

$\mathscr{B}$ELLA WAS AS CERTAIN OF THAT PRONOUNCE-ment as Percy, but for reasons that had nothing to do with the discussion in the lawyer's office.

She had designs of her own to marry Jack to her niece.

And they were almost sure to be successful.

So she didn't need Percy or Mitchell, but it never hurt to know a competitor's plans.

Chapter 12

ONLY ONE INTRUDER WAS ALLOWED TO breach the gates of Castlereagh and she was brought in against Venus's protests.

"Mrs. Prichett is already in the south parlor, so you might as well see her," Jack insisted, their argument an ongoing one for the past few days. Venus remained opposed to Jack's largesse—or more precisely, to the gossipy dressmaker who couldn't restrain her look of breathless scandal.

"Jack, I'm not going to deal with someone so—" she searched for the appropriate word "—provincial. You know a Parisian modiste wouldn't spare a glance for a man and his lover."

"And you know if there'd been time, I would have summoned one for you from Paris or London. But, darling, indulge me, please. You'll never see Mrs. Prichett again. She's had the gowns finished for days, and I want to buy you something."

"I can buy my own gowns."

"Let's not argue about money. I know you can buy your own, but it pleases me to give you them."

"She's too righteous," Venus muttered. "I intensely dislike righteous people."

"If I promise you she'll be amiable in the extreme,

will you see her? She's brought several gowns for fitting—one is a luscious cherry red perfect with your coloring."

"You want me to look like a tart?"

"As long as you're *my* cherry tart," he replied with a flashing grin. "Come now, see her."

"I'm tired, too tired to take on a tradeswoman who provokes me."

"She won't provoke you. My word on it." Placing his hands on her shoulders, he bent his head so their eyes met. "Do this for me?"

"I do everything for you," she murmured with a pettish moue.

Contemplating her greedy sexual desires, not only of the night past but of all the days of their acquaintance, he rather thought he did his share for her as well. But in the interests of harmony, he diplomatically said, "I know, darling. You're absolutely unselfish."

"You're an incorrigible liar," she said with a grin, "but adorable." She sighed. "Very well, show her in and I'll suffer her sniffs of outrage."

"I promise it won't take long." He kissed her pouty mouth. "Don't move. I'll be right back."

*H*IS CONVERSATION WITH MRS. PRICHETT IN the south parlor took only a few moments. It had to do with money, a generous sum of money; always an antidote for righteousness and principle, he'd found. When the dressmaker was shown into the sitting room of Jack's bedroom suite, she was all smiles and cordiality to his guest, regardless that she viewed Frenchwomen as seductresses.

But Venus looked very unlike a seductress that morning, rosy-cheeked and sleepy-eyed, the past night of passion telling. She wore a simple blue-and-white striped robe borrowed from the housekeeper, her tawny curls tied back with a white silk ribbon. Even three cups of coffee had failed to bring her fully awake. She looked drowsy, curled up on the window seat, the spring sun highlighting the gold of her hair.

Mrs. Prichett bid Venus good morning without a taint of censure or discourtesy. In fact, her cheery greeting was so different from her previous demeanor, Venus surveyed her more closely, wondering if it was the same woman.

Jack smiled reassuringly over the dressmaker's shoulder. "Mrs. Prichett tells me the fitting shouldn't take more than twenty minutes."

"Come, girls," Mrs. Prichett ordered, clapping her hands for the maids who had followed her into the room carrying the gowns. "We must hurry. If you would please stand right here, my lady," she deferentially said to Venus. Taking note that the marquis was pulling up a chair, she reacted without forethought and frowned.

"I'm interested in fashion too, Mrs. Prichett," he murmured, sitting down despite her censorious look. "I mentioned that downstairs, if you recall." His smile was replete with charm. "Miss Duras won't mind, will you, dear?"

Venus hesitated for the merest fraction of a moment, not sure whether she cared to be onstage before so many strangers. But Jack was looking at her with such an easy smile, she relaxed, responding to his casual disregard for propriety. He was right, of course, to overlook decorum.

She'd never set eyes on Mrs. Prichett again. "Stay if you wish," she agreed.

Realizing she'd come close to antagonizing the marquis and losing the large gratuity he'd offered, the dressmaker immediately altered her tone to one of utmost cordiality. "If Miss Duras would care to select a gown—"

"The red gown first," the marquis said.

"I'd prefer the green," Venus noted with a studied politeness, rarely tractable to orders, however softly put.

Jack dipped his head in acquiescence, first to Venus and then to Mrs. Prichett, who knew better than to ignore the marquis's commands after her near brush with disaster.

As the maids bustled about, taking the selected gown from its wrappings and removing Venus's robe, Jack conversed with the dressmaker about the weather, fashion, the botanical fair scheduled at Cheltenham. Hattie and the other maids exchanged astonished glances at the marquis's shocking familiarity, his manner that of a man who regularly lounged before his staff, exchanging gossip with tradesmen. The marquis usually spent his time at Castlereagh in seclusion.

Docile under the maids' ministrations, turning when asked, lifting her arms or putting them down as needed, Venus listened with half an ear to the easy flow of conversation, the idle chatter lulling her senses. It seemed very natural to be here with Jack, trying on gowns to please him, and for a brief moment she considered the extent of her involvement. She'd never consciously set out to please a man before. But too happy to debate such useless nuances, she dismissed questions of self-awareness in favor of the very pleasant present.

The green gown, a printed dimity with cascading ruffles on the skirt and tiny sprigged ribbon rosettes at the neckline and elbows, needed only a minimum of fitting, a tuck or two at the waist, a moment of debate over the depth of the neckline—Venus allowed Jack his way—and the light summer dress was whisked off to be replaced by a white muslin morning gown with a lace jacket.

"This isn't me, darling," Venus said, gazing at herself in a cheval glass. The gown was awash in ruffled lace and flounces.

"I like that look of innocence. Wear it for me some morning and I'll forget you speak ten languages and have sailed around the world twice."

"You may change the packaging, darling," she said with a faint smile, "but innocence isn't my forte."

"We'll keep it, Mrs. Prichett," he said. "You can give it away if you don't like it," he quietly added, smiling at Venus.

The next few gowns were quickly fitted, the two maids and Hattie kept busy, hooking hooks, buttoning buttons, and then undoing them as swiftly.

A sense of delight pervaded the marquis's mind, a feeling of contentment previously unknown to him, and he questioned his sanity. He'd known Venus such a short time, and yet he felt as though he'd been here before, watching her dress, feeling this way. Feeling as though she was more than an inamorata, as if she were family—when he'd never had a family.

It was strange and curious but enchanting, too, and companionable. He half smiled at the incongruous word, never previously considered in relation to a woman. But he liked the association and he liked the feeling, and he decided coming to Castlereagh had been one of his better ideas.

The cherry red silk was unwrapped at last, shaken out, buttoned and hooked into place. The resulting vision brought Jack to full attention.

"It's stunning," he murmured, a palpable heat in his voice, the distinctive nuance enough to swivel heads around.

Venus frowned.

"Forgive me," he apologized, smiling at the maids and Mrs. Prichett with an open boyishness. "I like the color."

It was a gross falsehood; everyone understood perfectly what he liked. Even the temperature in the room seemed to have risen several degrees.

The cherry red silk was a flamboyant gypsy dress that conjured up images of a decidedly sensual nature, a blatantly outré garment for a dressmaker of Mrs. Prichett's disposition.

"It's the latest fashion from Paris," Mrs. Prichett nervously declared, as though the sudden carnal implications hovering in the air required a hasty explanation. "The fashion prints show it in any number of bright colors, in polka dots, too, and black lace. There's one in a fuschia silk, and—"

"No need to explain, Mrs. Prichett. Do you like it, darling?"

"If you do, my sweet," Venus dulcetly murmured, amused by the dressmaker's sudden discomposure and the maids' breathless titters. "Are you satisfied with the décolletage?" The neckline was so low there was a distinct possibility her breasts would tumble out.

"Definitely satisfied." The marquis quickly rose from

his chair. "Thank you, Mrs. Prichett, Hattie." He nodded in a general way to the other maids. "That will be
all. See Mr. Longford on your way out, Mrs. Prichett.
He'll settle your account." And with more deference
than was required to servants and tradeswomen, he
showed them out of the room.

"You're not going out in public in that gown," he
murmured, leaning against the closed door a moment
later, reaching over to turn the key in the lock. "But it's
damned enticing for what I have in mind."

"*I'm* even shocked. This was meant for a courtesan.
Mrs. Prichett must have misunderstood the illustration."

"You heard her, darling. It's all the rage in Paris."

"I just came from Paris, and outside of the dance halls
and brothels, I doubt this lurid number is worn."

"In terms of fit, it's absolutely made for you."

"It's almost *not* made for me." She tried to adjust the
extremely low V neckline to better cover her breasts.

"Leave it," he softly ordered. "I like the sense of
breathless expectation."

She looked up at him, her brows quirked. "It's not as
though you haven't seen me nude."

"But the display is so tantalizing." He grinned. "The
sense of availability striking."

"What makes you think I'm available?" She offered
him a coy glance from under her lashes.

"Considering how well I've come to know you,
there's no question in my mind."

"You're insinuating I can't control my urges?"

"Not with me." His half-smile was impertinent.

She pursed her lips. "Is this a contest?"

"If it were, you'd lose."

"Or win, depending on your point of view."

"That's what I was thinking." He pushed away from the door. "Now, since you can't actually wear that gown in public, I think I'll just lift the skirt on that hot red confection and make love to you in all that silken splendor."

"You may have to pay for your impertinence first," she said, mildly piqued at his suggesting she was captive to his sexuality.

"Are you charging now?"

"In a dress like this, why shouldn't I? And you're much too smug, in any case. I may make you beg before . . ."

"I fuck you?"

The base words were uttered in the softest of whispers, and they both felt the heated implication, the carnal expectation resonating in the air.

"Before you do anything at all," she corrected with delicate precision.

"Tell me how much this will cost. I don't care to wait." Blunt and curt, the marquis wasn't in the habit of begging for anything.

"I don't need your money."

"But I have something you do need. Perhaps you'll have to beg me."

Suddenly the game had turned.

"We'll have to see, then, won't we," she replied, untying the black silk bow at the very top of the lacing that held the risqué décolletage together. "Why don't I take this courtesan gown off and see how you manage."

"I'll manage just fine." Walking away, he stopped at the liquor table, poured himself a brandy, drank it down, and refilled his glass.

"Isn't it a bit early for drinking?"

When he turned to her, the twitch over his cheek-bone was evident. "Some women drive a man to drink."

"While some men are entirely too familiar with having their own way."

"It's always worked just fine for me."

"Perhaps you'll learn something new today. Broaden your horizons, as it were."

"From you? I don't think so."

"What insolence. I suppose it's all those women fawning over you who have contributed to your overweening arrogance."

"I suppose it is." He emptied the second glass of brandy, pouring it down his throat like a shot of medicine that had to be quickly dispensed with.

"While I've been obliged to settle for what—only fifty or so men, each willing to give me his heart, fortune, and name. I suppose I'll have to give you points in that regard."

Fifty, he thought, rancor rising in his throat like bile. How dare fifty men offer for her, touch her . . . kiss her. His temper wouldn't allow consideration of anything more intimate than a kiss or he'd lose control. "I'm sure you have a legion of suitors," he crisply said. "But count me out. I don't marry."

The words left unsaid spiked her already heated temper. "Women like me, you mean?"

"No. Don't accuse me of morality. I mean I don't marry. Period."

"Well, neither do I. I thought we were clear on that point."

"Fine. We're clear. Now are you going to take that dress off and fuck me or not?"

"That doesn't sound like begging to me."

"And you're not going to hear it."

"Well, then, I might have to find some other means of satisfaction. You don't have any dildoes. Hmmm . . ." She surveyed the sitting room.

"Very funny." He turned to pour himself another drink, and when he swiveled back around, his fingers clenched on his glass.

Venus was holding a polished wooden object, an elongated ovoid atop a beautifully turned handle. "Hattie left her sewing kit behind," she said with a smile. "How fortunate."

"What the hell's that?"

"I suppose you don't darn much."

"I suppose I don't," he snapped.

"Well, I don't either, but I can think of another charming use for this lovely smooth object."

"And I'm supposed to watch?"

"Feel free to go. I really don't need you for this."

"You do this often?"

"I don't have to. So many suitors, you see," she pointedly noted.

If he wasn't averse to capitulating, he would have taken her that instant, without preliminaries. If he wasn't so in rut, he would have had sense enough to leave. Instead, he said, "How much do you charge for *that* display? Courtesans generally know the value of their cunts."

"Who better than you to understand the trade."

"You're damned irritating."

"Leave if you wish."

He couldn't; the vision of female pulchritude before him was irresistible. The gown's laced bodice was open to the navel, held in place only by the black silk ribbon, the fabric over Venus's breasts barely enough to cover the outer fleshy curves. Constrained by the tight lacing, her breasts were mounded, half exposed between the inadequate red silk. The ruffled skirt opened in front in a flaring curve that displayed a portion of her legs almost to the thigh. The sleeves, in contrast, were long and tight, covering her arms to the wrist, where a fall of black lace draped over her fingers.

Her sumptuous body was most tantalizingly offered for view.

And she had the audacity to tell him to leave.

Grabbing the brandy bottle, he pulled up a chair into the center of the room, sat down, and said, "Show me what you can do. Name your price—as long as it's money."

"Maybe I can make you beg."

"Why don't we see." He lifted one brow and gazed at her. Shrugging out of one coat sleeve, he switched the bottle to his other hand and eased his coat off. He ran his hand over the obvious bulge in his trousers. "Then again, maybe you'll be interested in pleasing me."

"Or we can just please ourselves," she softly said, beginning to unlace the black silk ribbon. "This really is tight."

A hush descended on the room, the sound of the silk lacing sliding through the embroidered grommets unusually loud, the sight of her breasts slowly being unveiled bringing Jack's erection to a new taut dimension. He drank directly from the bottle as he watched her, and when Venus smiled at him as though knowing the degree of his need, he slowly inhaled and forced himself to restraint. He'd once outlasted everyone in a brothel when the prize was the exquisite whore on display, and if he could outlast a dozen men, he could outlast one easily aroused woman.

"Let me suck on your nipples," he murmured, gratified to see her pink crests further elongate, aware as well of Venus's arrested breathing.

It took her a moment to speak, but when she did, her voice was seductive, not a scintilla of nerves evident. "You can only look, you can't touch."

"If I pay enough, I can."

"You don't have enough money, darling." The last bit of black ribbon slipped through the lacings and she tossed it away. Slipping her hands under her barely covered breasts, she lifted the heavy globes, the ostentatious exhibition inviting to the touch. "Whenever you want to ask me nicely, I'll consider any proposal."

"I can outlast you."

"Really. When I thought you were the catchword for fornication."

"I think unbridled better fits you." But it took effort to speak in a normal tone, her showy breasts a spectacular lure to the eye.

"Since I have such lurid desires, perhaps they should be assuaged." Letting her hands fall, she reached for the darning device.

"I have something more satisfying."

"But not so manageable."

"You like to be in control?"

"Not necessarily. Do you?" When he didn't answer, she said, "I thought so," and sliding the polished wood instrument between her legs, she eased it into her vagina. Her eyes closed briefly at the rush of pleasure and Jack gritted his teeth.

It was a contest of wills, self-indulgent, confrontational between two headstrong people who had always had the world at their feet.

He was utterly still while she used the instrument, his gaze on her hand as it moved in and out, his fingers white-knuckled on the chair arms. He took note when she became so absorbed in the pleasure she was no longer aware of his presence. He counted the rhythmic undulations, observed how far the sculpted wood disappeared, contemplated her bounteous breasts suspended like ripe fruit as she leaned forward to press the object home. When she began climaxing, his self-restraint broke, and lunging up, he took no notice of the chair toppling over, or of the rippling sound of his trouser buttons being torn away. He just knew he was going to bury himself inside her.

Sweeping her up into his arms, he carried her through the connecting doorway into his bedroom, oblivious to her keening orgasmic cry, acutely aware of her hot scent, like an animal tracking a female in heat.

He dropped her on the bed, jerked the makeshift dildo from between her legs, climbed on top of her fully clothed, and oblivious of his shoes smudging the coverlet, guided his erection to its destination with single-minded purpose. He would have her, now, later, and often, he thought, plunging in with an ungovernable violence. "Don't fuck with me," he growled, driving in with a savage frenzy. "You'll always lose."

"Can't control yourself, can you?" she murmured, lying motionless beneath him.

"You should talk."

"I didn't pounce on you."

"You're telling me you're not interested?"

"Not in this."

"Really . . ." He hitched her closer, his hands crushing the ruffled red silk bunched over her hips. "We both know how much you like to fuck." He held himself motionless for a moment so she could feel the full extent of his penetration, so she could experience the exquisite totality of his size and length. So every tingling nerve and suffused tissue in contact with his rigid plenitude was blissfully overcome.

No, she thought, I won't—as the first ripple of arousal registered in her brain.

But he seemed to know, or perhaps had felt it, and he moved in a gentle undulation that delicately touched every interior surface. And what had been sleek became sleeker, what had been heated became hotter, what had been a ripple swelled.

She bit her lip, tensed against the unwanted pleasure, tried to withstand the rapturous feeling.

"Neither one of us can," he whispered, as if reading her thoughts. "Call truce?" he murmured, his mouth brushing hers. "I will if you will . . ."

It was impossible to ignore the throbbing ache between her legs; she recognized how little control she had against the inevitable explosive ecstasy—or at least with him. And he knew, too. "Truce," she whispered. "You insolent libertine."

His wink was shamelessly wicked. "Truce, my darling wanton."

"Lost to all reason, aren't we?" she murmured, a smile in her words.

"Utterly lost," he softly agreed.

Before they were sated or replete or momentarily quenched that morning, the cherry red dress was ruinously wrinkled and rumpled and creased.

"A testament to love," the marquis said, holding it at arm's length before tossing it on a chair.

"A testament to obsession," Venus noted with a slow, sensual stretch, gazing at him from the shambles of the bed.

"One and the same, are they not?"

"Don't ask me. I'm not qualified on the subject."

"Then perhaps we should explore the possibilities," he said, climbing back in bed.

"Now?"

"Whenever you're ready." Infinitely courteous, he might have been asking for a walk in the park.

She looked at him from under her lashes. "I'm beginning to think this is a match made in heaven."

"In many ways, it is."

"In what ways?"

"In the only ways that matter," he murmured, bending to kiss her.

⟨⟨⟨⟩⟩⟩

Chapter 13

*V*INCENZO, DON'T BE RUDE," SARAH PETTISHLY said. "You know I must marry someday. My papa's rich, and I can have anyone in the ton." She lay beside him on his bed in a small room over a baker's shop, her pale brows drawn together in a faint frown.

"I thought you loved me." Ill-tempered and moody, he scowled back at her.

"Of course I love you. But I'm going to marry the Marquis of Redvers because he's ever so wealthy and well connected and every deb wants him."

"I'll challenge him." Vincenzo was patently young, or he'd have known better than to trust a girl like Sarah, who viewed the world through opportunistic eyes.

Sarah's father and mother had never minced words about her duty to marry well. With the Palmers' peerage of recent origin—the first baron a beer magnate only one generation removed—she understood it was up to her to elevate the status of the family. "You'll do no such thing. Good heavens, Vincenzo, I'll be ruined if you implicate me in your life."

"I'm good enough to make love to, but not to acknowledge." A hot-blooded young Italian, Vincenzo took issue with society's rigid caste system.

"Of course, silly. Everyone knows that. You're a dancing master, for heaven's sake." Her voice turned cajoling. "Come now, darling, give me a little kiss and forget all this fuss." Rolling over, she slid an arm around his neck and smiled up at him. "Just because I'm married doesn't mean I can't see you anymore."

He hadn't been in England long, but he understood the ways of the aristocracy in his own country, and fidelity wasn't a requirement in marriage—although generally an heir was required before a wife could take lovers. "What if you have my child?"

"But I won't."

"But what if you did?"

"Then your child would be a very wealthy Fitz-James."

"It won't look like him."

"Really, darling, this is all irrelevant. I can't think of having your child. And if you'd stop talking, we could find something much more pleasant to do. See, you still want to play," she whispered, reaching out to languidly stroke his erection.

He drew in a sharp breath against the carnal rush spiking through his body. "I should beat you, *cara mia,* for being a wanton minx."

"I never said you *couldn't* beat me, darling." Moving over him, she lay atop his heated body, her seductive smile close and suggestive.

"I may not let you marry him," he whispered, swiftly rolling over, pinning her beneath him. "What do you think of that?"

"I think you have to stop talking and make love to me instead. I have to be back home in two hours."

"We'll talk later, then."

"Vincenzo . . ." she whispered, spreading her thighs wide and arching her pelvis upward. "No more talk."

He couldn't resist—but then, what man in his position could?

$\mathcal{A}$LL SPECULATION AND DISCUSSION IN THE next fortnight were concentrated on the Derby—in London, in the country, in every pub, and on every village green, all of England in readiness for the great national event.[5] Horse racing pervaded every grade of society, every walk of life, every age. No business appointments were made for the Wednesday of Epsom Week. The House of Commons adjourned. All of London deserted for the sacred hill of Epsom.

Why the Derby was more important than other races could be accounted for by the enormous amount of stakes and bets. And while the major part of the denizens of "the sporting world" had never seen a race or a racehorse, they knew all the horses' names and pedigrees, their public performances, their private trials, the state of their health and of their temper.

While the favorite horses had nominal owners, in reality they were public property.

Jack and Venus had come down to his racing stud, Lawley Mill, the previous day, although the marquis hadn't entered any of his horses in the Tuesday races. He and Venus had kept to themselves, ignoring the several dozen invitations that had come from his friends who were at Epsom for the races. While Venus hadn't again mentioned leaving after the Derby, both were aware of the unspoken stipulation.

As a concession to the occasion, Venus had had her

maid bring down some suitable gowns from London. The style of the Derby, unlike the easy country manners at Castlereagh, was *haute monde*, and she had no intention of being seen in one of Mrs. Pritchett's creations. Always dressed by the best Parisian couturiers, Venus selected a jonquil silk walking dress ornamented with jet beading and black braid for the festivities.

Since Jack's recent purchase, Fortune, was the hot favorite, the moment he and Venus arrived at the track that Derby Wednesday, they were thronged with well-wishers. Jack accepted all the goodwill with a smile and a pleasant response, his progress through the crowd slowed by dint of the great number of people who wanted to speak to him.

"You're almost as great a celebrity as your colt," Venus remarked, smiling as they approached the parade ring where Fortune was showing signs of temperament.

Jack shook his head. "It's not about me. A lot of money is riding on this race. Two hundred thousand pounds, last I heard from my friendly bookmaker. And from the looks of it," he murmured, glancing at his colt who was beginning to sweat up, "Fortune is feeling the pressure."

Greeting his jockey and trainer, the marquis exchanged a few casual words, nothing that couldn't be overheard by the press of onlookers and handicappers. The men had already discussed their strategy that morning; short of Fortune coming up lame, he wasn't the favorite without good reason. If Woods, the marquis's jockey, could keep off the rail and not get boxed in by the very large field, it was only a matter of giving Fortune his head and letting him gallop away.

The morning sky had been overcast, but the rain seemed to be holding off and on that cloudy day, Venus's bright-hued gown struck a dramatic chord. Not that her gown alone drew the eye. She was as much the center of attention for her beauty. And those in society who had heard the latest *on dits* concerning the marquis's new liaison were piqued by Lord Redvers's continuing attention to the lovely Frenchwoman.

He wasn't a man who had ever shown undue regard for a woman.

And it had been upwards of three weeks now since society had last seen him.

With the flood of foreign visitors to the Great Exhibition, the course that day was graced by more than the usual number of aristocrats. Among the more distinguished were the Duke and Duchess of Nemours, Prince Henry of the Netherlands, the Duke of Cambridge, the Prince of Saxe-Weimar, Lord Waterford, Lord Worcester, Lord Stanley, Lord Eglinton, Lord Zetland, Lord Granville, Lord Glasgow, and Lord Enfield March; Sir J. Hawley, Sir W. Codrington, Sir H. Campbell, Sir R. Peel, Colonel Peel. Everyone had come out to see one of the premier races of the season.

Including Lady Tallien and the entire Palmer family.

And Trevor, too.

Both of whom were well aware of the marquis's unusual attention to Miss Duras, and each of whom had individual plans to see that their own aims were achieved.

THE RACE GROUNDS WERE FILLED WITH SPECTATORS; the betting was spirited, the number of horses

running a record thirty-one and, although there were
distinct favorites, the race was still considered an
"open" one. On the other hand, Fortune was still stead-
ily in the lead, leaving off at very short odds, in some
few cases backed at evens.

It was a full, high-class field of three-year-old colts
that day, all bred for stamina and speed to go the mile
and a half. Some said Derby thoroughbreds were freak
horses; racers were generally bred for speed or distance,
but not both. And while the best jockeys were up when
the stakes were so high, the incalculable and unpredictable were always a factor on a course as tough as Epsom.

The pressure on Jack's jockey was immense. Woods
was riding a horse who had been built up as all but
unbeatable, and that kind of report always made the
other jockeys resentful. There was a possibility they
might try to keep him from winning. To cap it all, some
days before, an offer of ten thousand pounds to stop
Fortune had been making the rounds.

As was usually the case, Fortune had settled by the
time he reached the starting gate. There was no delay;
the moment the tapes went up, all thirty-one mounts
surged forward. Woods had to literally fight his way
through the crowded field to get out on the course. Lord
Enfield's racer, Hernandez, immediately took the lead,
and Woods tracked him, holding his own against the
rough riding and gamesmanship of the other jockeys.

At Tattenham Corner the order hadn't changed. A
press of six or eight horses raced down the descent in
tandem behind Hernandez, the rest of the field strung
out behind. Then, as so often happened, the race
shifted. Hernandez began to hang out distress signals,

and as Woods shifted his weight to take Fortune past him, he found himself suddenly boxed in by a wall of horses.

Someone had paid off somebody, he thought; there was nothing to do but sit and suffer until he could pull out and make his run on the outside. But he understood it was more desirable in the Derby than in any other major race of the same distance to be well placed throughout, and usually of paramount importance to hold a good position on the steep descent to Tattenham Corner. Shut in behind the leaders, Fortune was going to be put to the test once he had a chance to break free.

Woods also knew that very few horses won the Derby after being among the back-markers at Tattenham Corner, and he intently watched for his chance to escape. The instant the opportunity arose, he took it, but Fortune, unbalanced for a few strides after being switched sharply for a clear run on the wide outside, briefly floundered. Woods eased up on the reins; Fortune rallied, regained his balance, and answered him with tremendous courage. The big chestnut slipped by one horse and then another, coming around that wall of thundering beasts with great fighting spirit. The cheers went up the minute Fortune swung over for his run, increasing in volume as he passed one racer after another, each powerful stride bringing him closer to the lead. Woods did his best, but there was no holding Fortune once he was given his head, and he galloped right away from his field, ears pricked, nostrils distended, his great, powerful frame and limbs moving with the rhythm and force of an express train.

He won by twenty lengths.

The roar of the crowd rang out across the downs, through the grandstand and private boxes. The best horse had won the best race of the season.

"Fortune has made me a very tidy sum," Venus cheerfully said, her face wreathed in smiles, her color still high after cheering on the huge chestnut in his valiant victory.

"Both of us," Jack replied, bending to kiss her rosy cheek. Gossip later had it that Lord Redvers had won seventy thousand pounds in those two minutes fifty-one seconds.[6] "Now, come," he urged, taking her hand. "And we'll give our congratulations to Woods and Fortune."

Epsom was like a huge picnic on Derby Day, and it took a deal of shouldering through the crowds before the marquis and his companion could reach the winner's circle.

"Well done." Jack's voice was neutral as he offered his praise to Woods's fine riding. "Under the circumstances," he casually added.

"A bit rough out there today, sir."

"You and Fortune slammed your way through nicely."

"He's a right prime stallion—a smasher, sure enough," Woods proudly said. "And I had a bob or two riding on his shoulders, too."

"Always an incentive," Jack pleasantly said. "Here come the Jockey Club stewards. It won't be much longer now, Fortune." He stroked the stallion's lathered neck. "Soon we'll have you away from this throng."

"And me, too," Venus whispered.

The marquis glanced down at Venus and winked.

"You more than anyone." His voice was low, insinuating. "We'll have to celebrate this Derby win tonight."

"Alone?"

"Definitely alone."

"Then you're going to have to be rude to a great many of your friends." She nodded her head in the direction of the royal box, its occupants bearing down on them as they spoke.

"Watch me and learn." His grin crinkled the corners of his eyes.

Jack was inexpressibly charming to all the dignitaries who came to offer him their congratulations, his manners without reproach. And to those of his friends who wished for his company as well, he refused with grace. The ladies pouted at being denied Jack at their entertainments after the race, but the men understood. If they had the delectable Miss Duras on their arm, they wouldn't be in the mood for fashionable society, either.

Ned Darlington spoke for them all when he quietly said to his friend, "I won't ask you to our party tonight. It sounds as though you're better entertained at home."

Jack dipped his head in acknowledgment. "Come and see me in town next week instead."

Within the hour, Jack and Venus were returning to Lawley Mill. The sun had come out from behind the clouds, bathing the green countryside in a warm glow. The landau moved slowly in the narrow hedge-lined country lane, its top down, the coachman trained to ignore the sounds behind him of the marquis and his lady kissing and laughing and kissing some more on the drive back.

"I feel giddy and I haven't even drunk any wine." Venus giggled, quickly covering her mouth in embarrassment. "My apologies." And then she giggled again.

Jack smiled, tolerant of giggles this afternoon, tolerant of anything the beautiful woman in his arms might do. "Perhaps you're enjoying your win."

"Do you think so?" She quirked a lacy brow. "I think my extreme good humor has much to do with you."

"I'll gladly accept responsibility for that," he facetiously said.

"You're to blame for everything. Absolutely everything," she added, sticking her tongue out at him.

This time he laughed. "Now *that* kind of censure I recognize."

"I expect you do."

"I have a certain reputation to maintain," he lightly said.

"I hope you can maintain it tonight," she whispered.

"I don't expect a problem, mademoiselle," he replied in a conversational tone. "Now tell me what you want the chef to make for dinner," he went on, considering it best to divert the conversation with company so near.

"You decide. I eat anything," she answered, clearly in a frolicsome mood.

After a quick glance at his driver, Jack mouthed the question *Anything?* with a cheeky lift of his brow.

She playfully slapped him. "Mind your manners." Her gaze was provocative.

"Now?"

She cast a significant look at the servant only mere feet away and nodded her head.

Touching his mouth to her ear, he whispered, "And afterward?"

"Manners are no longer required, my lord," she softly murmured, her smile so close he could almost taste the pleasure.

His head came up and his voice was brisk. "Drive faster, Sam." As the horses moved into a canter, he debated the delectable merits of obsession.

Chapter 14

❦

$\mathcal{I}$T WAS AFTER TEN WHEN A RAP ON THE bedroom door interrupted the activities in Jack's bedchamber.

He stopped in midstroke, glanced at the door, looked back down at Venus, and said, "Someone must have died," because his servants knew better than to disregard his orders for privacy. Brushing Venus's cheek with a kiss, he eased away and shouted, "What is it?"

"An urgent message, my lord, from Baron Darlington."

Springing from the bed, he quickly strode to the door and opened it marginally so Venus wouldn't be seen. "It had better be important."

His majordomo, aware of the flagrant intrusion, stood at attention and thrust the note at the marquis. "The groom from the Sutton Inn insisted I wake you, sir."

"Never mind," Jack gruffly said, ripping open the sealed envelope, pulling out the single sheet, and beginning to scan the sprawling script. "I'm not blaming you. Knowing Ned, he's probably half into his cups and thought of some way to—" He softly swore. The note wasn't from Ned but from Charles Burnham; Ned had been badly wounded in a duel. "Have my horse saddled," Jack crisply ordered. "I'll be down in five minutes."

Shutting the door, he swung around, already moving toward his dressing room in long strides. "Ned's been severely wounded," he brusquely explained. "I'll be back as soon as I can."

Scrambling from the bed, Venus followed him into the small paneled room. "Let me come with you. I have some competence in nursing."

Pulling a pair of trousers from the wardrobe, Jack shook his head. "He's at the Sutton Inn, in the midst of some lechery, no doubt. Things must have gotten out of hand—not unusual, with Ned's temper. Burnham didn't give any details, but I'm sure it's no place for a lady."

"I've treated bullet wounds before. I might be able to help."

"No," he muttered as he plunged his foot into the khaki twill trouser leg. "We'll find a doctor."

"Maybe you will and maybe you won't, considering the hour of the night and the fact that duels are illegal. I'm no missish young woman who faints at the sight of blood," she said, walking to the armoire where her gowns had been placed. "I work with the doctors in our charity hospital every day."

"I'd prefer you not be exposed to the scandal." The marquis was tugging on his riding boots.

Venus snorted. "A bit late for such concern, after a fortnight in the country with you."

He swore, clearly discomposed. "It could be a rowdy tumult there. Really, darling, I'd rather you didn't come." Frowning, he took note of her buttoning up the skirt of her riding habit.

"What if Ned needs assistance?"

Jack stood for a moment, his indecision plain, then, grabbing his shirt and coat, he moved toward the door. "I'll wait five minutes," he growled. "Then I'm leaving."

She ran downstairs in three minutes and smiled as she saw the horse saddled for her beside the black thoroughbred Jack favored for riding. A host of servants were attending to Jack's instructions. He planned on bringing Ned back to Lawley Mill in a wagon being readied.

A groom gave her a leg up and she waited in the saddle while Jack relayed the last of his orders.

Once he was mounted, he acknowledged her with a nod. "Keep up. I can't wait for you."

THE SUTTON INN WAS FILLED WITH A RAUCOUS crowd celebrating the Derby race, no one apparently distracted by the circumstances of Ned's duel. But considering the act was illegal and secrecy a necessity, Jack hadn't expected his friend's activities to be public knowledge. Guiding Venus up the stairs, he scanned the doors, looking for number twenty-three, the room mentioned in Burnham's note.

As they reached a small alcove, Jack led Venus over to a chair. "Wait here for a minute." His voice was polite but detached, his thoughts predominantly of Ned, who had been his best friend since childhood. "There could be people in there—unruly types. I'll be back for you if it's safe."

She understood, though convention wasn't her first motive in life, that there were degrees of scandal best avoided. "I'll wait," she agreed. "Come for me if I can be of help."

He was gone almost before she'd finished speaking, striding down the dimly lit hall in search of Ned's room.

It was oddly quiet when he reached the door and for a moment, his stomach sank in apprehension. Had he come too late? Was Ned already dead and carried away? Taking a sustaining breath, he reached for the latch, turned it, and pushed the door open.

The room was deserted, although he recognized Ned's brilliant bottle green coat and embroidered waistcoat tossed on a chair. Moving forward, Jack wondered at the pristine condition of the garments, considering Ned had been shot. It was rare to fire below the waist in a duel.

Picking up the yellow silk waistcoat adorned with racing motifs, he turned it over, looking for bullet holes, finding none. Next, the coat received his scrutiny, and when it revealed no untoward damage, he was just beginning to consider the possibility that Ned was embarked on some practical joke when the sound of a door opening spun him around.

Ready to lash out at his friend for luring him out in the middle of the night and bringing him into town riding hell-for-leather, Jack stood arrested, his gaze on Sarah Palmer entering the bedchamber through an adjoining door.

She was smiling.

She was nude.

And he felt the jaws of a trap closing around him.

Without a word, he turned away to make his escape. He was halfway across the room, only yards from the door, when he heard a harsh male voice exclaim, "What the hell's the meaning of this?"

Jack kept walking, the smell of ambush so powerful now it was choking him.

"Stand or I'll shoot you for the knave you are." The low growl was accompanied by the metallic click of a pistol hammer echoing in the silence. Even then Jack debated taking his chances with a pistol at ten yards in a poorly lit room.

But suddenly the hall door opened and Bella stood there, a small pearl-handled pistol directed at him. He knew she'd shoot him gladly.

He stopped, his dark eyes hot with temper, his voice like ice when he spoke. "What do you want—as if I don't know."

"Then there's no need to waste any unnecessary words. Do move back so I don't have to mar that perfect body of yours," she softly murmured.

"You won't get away with this."

"But then we have a great many witnesses," Bella sweetly replied. "Turn around and see for yourself."

He did, and counted five, three of whom he didn't recognize. Servants, no doubt, who could be paid to say anything in court. The other two were the Palmers, mère and père, scowling at him with what he thought was superb acting considering the stage-managed scene. Meanwhile, the deceitful little baggage Sarah was slowly putting on a robe, as though being nude before a crowd wasn't in the least embarrassing.

"I can pay for witnesses, too." His voice was chill.

"Our daughter is having your child," Sarah's mother peevishly said, "and you'll be made to do your duty by her."

"It's not mine."

"She says it's yours." Baron Palmer bridled, always stung by what he perceived as aristocratic arrogance.

"Then she's lying." Jack gave Sarah a cold stare. "You're not my type."

"But then you're my type, dear Jack, and I have your baby to prove it." Sarah well understood the powerful incentives to stand firm against the marquis's opposition—wealth, position, and a title for her child. Bella hadn't had to explain that twice.

"Then prove it." Each word was bitten off, the tight line of the marquis's jaw indication of his barely suppressed rage.

"We don't have to," Baron Palmer retorted. "The court will give due relevance to these witnesses—and to others, too. You were seen together often, Sarah tells me."

"Are we done?" Lord Redvers voice was infinitely mild, like the calm in the eye of a storm.

"My barrister will call on you in London with the marriage settlement."

"If you'll excuse me, then," the marquis said with the fine hauteur of twenty generations of noble lineage. "You interrupted my evening plans."

"Don't think your blue blood will see you clear of this, Redvers," Lord Palmer rebuked, stung by the insolence in the marquis's tone. "I intend to win."

"My antecedents have nothing to do with this, Palmer. I can fight as low and dirty as you. How do you think my ancestors got where they are today?"

"By fucking the king," Lord Palmer snarled.

"And a good number of others, too. Keep it in mind when you get too greedy." Brushing past Bella, he stalked from the room, furious and wrathful, wanting to inflict damage on someone.

"It was a hoax," he brusquely said when he reached

Venus. "Ned wasn't here. Let's go home," he added with a small weariness, knowing the grotesque farce he'd just been privy to was the prelude to a distasteful litigation.

"I'm sorry." Responding to the annoyance she saw in his face, she said, "At least Ned isn't hurt."

"True." He forced himself to smile. "And we'll be back home in fifteen minutes."

"The night air was pleasant."

He chuckled. "You're much too understanding." He put out his hand. "Let's get the hell out of here."

They'd almost reached the stairs when a female voice called out. "Don't forget to tell your solicitor about the marriage settlement." Bella's malice echoed down the hall. "Sleep well, darling."

Venus's gaze came up and held Jack's for a moment before she turned around. The voice was sickeningly familiar. Even with the considerable distance and indistinct lighting, Lady Tallien was recognizable.

"Don't answer," Jack said, taking Venus's hand and pulling her back.

"I have no intention of speaking to her." Venus tugged her hand free and started down the stairs.

"She's delusional," he bitterly said, following her. "All of them are."

"I'm sure none of this is any of my business." Venus kept her voice deliberately mild.

"Or mine," Jack grumbled. "Damn them all."

"There seems to be some dispute over your marriage."

"You might say that," Jack testily replied. "Although it's going to cost me to buy them off."

"Now why would you have to buy them off? Never mind," she quickly interposed. "Really, I don't want to know."

"And I don't want to think about it. Leave it to the lawyers to haggle over the lies."

But Venus was noticeably cool on the ride home, and he didn't blame her, although his temper, already heated, wasn't improved by the prospect of pacifying her for something he hadn't done.

"You needn't pacify me," she said though, when he expressed his recalcitrant feelings once they were back at Lawley Mill. "With the Derby over, I really should be on my way home anyway." Her smile was insincere and mannered, the kind one offered acquaintances when making excuses.

"I don't want you to go."

"I never intended to stay long. You knew that."

"You needn't return right away."

She sighed faintly. "I'd just as soon avoid people like Lady Tallien. You may have to deal with her, but I don't."

"You won't have to. I promise."

"Jack, I *have* to go home. Come and see me in Paris sometime."

"You'd just leave like that?"

"I have responsibilities in my life, people who depend on me for their support, a charitable organization that requires enormous funding. I've worked hard for years to bring these services to the less fortunate. And I've been on holiday too long."

"It's because of Bella, isn't it?"

"Honestly, no. Although, certainly, being reminded of your *colorful* way of life puts me in mind of the realities."

"What can I do to change your mind?"

"I don't want you to do anything, Jack. We both understood there was a time limit to this diversion."

"Diversion?" A moody edge came into his voice.

"Surely you're not telling me your feelings are more involved." She knew better than to allow herself the fantasy. Realistic to the core, she'd always been rigorously objective.

"I don't know what I feel," he bluntly said, which didn't help her objectivity.

"Then I'll tell you. You don't wish to marry. I don't wish to marry. We both have very busy lives. And this was a most pleasant, gratifying, and ardent interlude we'll both remember with great pleasure. Now don't be difficult, darling. You know you aren't inclined to offer me more."

He sighed. "What if I wish to be selfish?"

"But then I'm selfish as well."

"Can we negotiate some delay in your departure?"

She smiled. "Maybe."

"Another fortnight."

"Two days."

"Ten days."

"Four."

"Six, and I'll swear you'll never have to see any of the Palmers again."

"Five, if we don't go back to London until the day I sail. Lady Tallien is much too resolute for even your promises of protection."

He grimaced at the truth of her observation. "Done. We stay in the country."

Chapter 15

~~~~~

*T*HE RAIN THAT HAD BEEN THREATENING
finally began falling, and Jack and Venus didn't venture
outside the next day. All too aware of the end of their
holiday, they kept to Jack's bedroom, only coming out
to sit over drinks in the study in the evening. But the
following day would require they reenter the world, for
the Oaks was being run. It was one of the classic races of
the Season, and Jack had Fortune entered.

They arrived at the track late, wanting to avoid the
necessity of socializing, and after cheering Fortune on to
victory, they quickly slipped away, leaving the marquis's
trainer to receive the prize. With their time together so
limited, even minutes seemed to matter, and while neither was ready to acknowledge how deeply they would
feel the loss of parting, they were sensitive to a chafing
disquiet.

Dispensing with servants in their increasing need for
seclusion, Jack drove the cabriolet back to Lawley Mill.
Neither was in a talkative mood, both distracted by a
sense of urgency—insistent and claustrophobic—as
though the world were coming to an end. In the silence
of the country lane, the soft thud of the horse's hooves
the only sound, the sudden snapping of underbrush was
conspicuous.

The horse pricked its ears. Jack looked in the direction of the noise and alarm spiked through his senses. "Get down!" he shouted.

A gunshot exploded.

Venus dived for the floor of the carriage.

"Stay down!" Jack cried, whipping the horse to greater speed, not sure if more assailants might be in ambush ahead, his gaze scanning the road and surrounding hedges for danger, his mind struggling to understand who would want to kill Venus.

The bullet had torn a ragged hole in the carriage seat, exactly where she'd been sitting.

He didn't slow the carriage until they reached the safety of Lawley Mill, where he had the gates closed and locked behind them. After carrying Venus in, he made her comfortable in a room that safely faced a walled garden. Calling in his grooms, he immediately arranged for an armed patrol of the estate.

Still in a state of mild shock, Venus half listened to Jack give his men instructions. Although she'd spent enough time in remote locales to understand the risks of being shot, to be attacked in the pastoral English countryside, short miles from the busy racetrack at Epsom, seemed astonishing. Much as she racked her brain, she couldn't think of anyone who would want to harm her.

Jack had clearly seen the man behind the gun, however, and once they were alone, he asked Venus if she had any enemies.

"I can't think of anyone. Could the shot have been aimed at you? Could it have been someone out hunting?"

"Perhaps," he evasively said, sitting down beside her on the sofa and taking her hand in his. But the gun barrel he'd seen was resting firmly on a tree branch. The tall man visible through the underbrush had had a solid mount for his weapon, and plenty of time to take aim. And the only hunting that took place in these well-populated counties was for fox and grouse, neither found at the same level as a carriage seat. "Under the circumstances, it might be wise if we left for London early."

"Why not go directly to Dover?"

"Dover's fine, if you prefer. But you can't leave me yet," he said, squeezing her hand. "We still have three days left."

She smiled. "You *are* persistent. Why don't we stay aboard my vessel then? In the interests of safety."

"I'm having my men scour the neighborhood for information. Strangers are obvious in the country. Someone may have seen the man who shot at us. In the meantime, I'd suggest we stay indoors, and leave for Dover once it's dark."

"Could it have been some accident?"

He shrugged. "Who knows." But the Palmers' recent bid for his title and wealth reminded him too vividly of the deviousness of greed. "But why take a chance?"

"Agreed. So what are we going to do until dark?" she murmured, smiling faintly.

He turned to her with a lazy grin, more pleasant possibilities in the air. "Insatiable, are we?"

"Only with you."

"That must be why I adore you."

Lounging against the heavy sofa, designed for a man's larger dimensions, she looked delicate and pale, her tawny hair aglow in the shadows of the paneled room. "How charming you are." Her head was resting against the brown velvet upholstery, the transient flutter of her lashes the only movement in her languid pose. Until she gathered the skirt of her indigo silk gown in her hands and pulled it up in crushed folds. "Why don't you lock the door," she said, shifting slightly, moving against the sofa arm and spreading her thighs invitingly.

"My pleasure," he replied, quickly rising. "Although I'd rather lock *you* up."

"Can't." She playfully thrust out her bottom lip like a pouty child.

He glanced back at her. "We'll see about that."

"If you do, my father and brother will come to my rescue."

He turned the key in the lock and stood with his back against the door. "If they can find you."

WHAT DO YOU MEAN, YOU MISSED HER! HOW could you have missed? There couldn't have been another soul on that country road!" Trevor Mitchell was almost apoplectic, his face crimson, his prominent Adam's apple jerking up and down like a puppet on a string.

"Redvers saw me, damned if he didn't, and it threw me aim." The large man didn't often miss his target, which was why he'd been recommended by one of Trevor's more unsavory friends, but he wasn't apologetic so much as blunt in his statement. Unrattled, he sat at the table in the back parlor of the country inn, one beefy fist wrapped around the handle of his ale mug, his expression impassive.

"Well, you'll have to try again, damnit! I paid for results and I want them!"

"I'm telling you, he saw me. Find someone else. I'm

not about to put myself in his path again. The man has a reputation with weapons. He's one of the best shots in England. Berty Wells might be able to help you, though. He's looking for some scratch."

"You're telling me you're out? Who the hell do you think you are?"

"I'm someone who can beat you to a bloody pulp and dump your body where no one will ever find it." The brawny man took a last draught of ale, set the mug down, and rose from the table. "Any questions?"

Trevor seemed to have shrunk in his skin, all his blustering swagger silenced.

"Good night, mate." The man put a finger to his cap.

"Tell Berty—" Trevor cleared his throat against his trembling croak. "Tell him to call on me in London."

Trevor received a nod in acknowledgment, and the door quietly shut on his hired killer.

THE NEXT DAY LONDON WAS THE SCENE OF much activity on the part of those trying to separate Jack from his money. Lord Palmer was spending the afternoon with his barrister, drawing up a marriage contract that served his affronted notions of vengeance. Bella and Lady Palmer were discussing the marriage details over tea. Sarah, who chose to indulge herself more pleasurably, was lying beside her young lover, Vincenzo, in the aftermath of an orgasm.

"Do I care whether I have orange blossoms or roses in my hair?" Sarah airily said, crinkling her nose in aversion. "Or whether we have Lord and Lady Balliol at the head table at the wedding breakfast? You can't imagine, darling, how tedious this entire business will be."

"You put a knife to my heart, *cara mia*," her companion dolefully grumbled.

"I'll hire you all for myself," Sarah promised. "And you won't have to work for any more of those parvenu chits with their fat, ugly daughters."

"Your husband won't allow it." Downcast by his lover's imminent nuptials, Vincenzo was fretful and moody.

"My papa will make Lord Redvers do whatever he tells him. Papa is ever so furious with him."

"Why?" Vincenzo tipped Sarah's chin up and looked directly into her eyes with an intense scrutiny. Young but not gullible, he'd been making his own way in the world for many years. "Why would Lord Redvers listen to your papa?"

"He just will, and don't look at me like that, Vincenzo. This marriage will work just perfectly for everyone, you included. Don't you want your own nice apartment? Don't you want to give up having to instruct silly girls? I'll take care of you. Bella says it's perfectly fine for me to have my own lover."

"You still haven't told me why Lord Redvers, who doesn't do anything for anyone, will listen to your papa, who is only a beer baron." His voice had taken on an inquisitorial tone.

"How very rude you are," she pettishly declared, rolling away from him and sitting up against the pillows.

"Is it because of the baby?" His voice was cool.

Her face turned pink and wide-eyed. "How did you know?"

"You haven't had your courses, *cara mia*." His gaze focused on her stomach. "Not for months."

"Well, then, why ask if you already know?"

"I wasn't sure what you told your papa, or what he said to Lord Redvers."

"I can't see that it's any of your business," she huffily retorted.

"I'm a man, *cara mia*, before I'm a dancing master or your lover. I care about my child."

"It's not your child."

"Then whose is it, when you were an untried maid not long ago?" His dark eyes were piercing. "Are you going to lie to me about that as well?"

"You know I can't marry you, darling." Cajoling, she reached out to touch his cheek. "Wouldn't you rather have your child born into a title?"

"Your papa has a title, and my family is as acceptable as a beer baron's. My father was court physician to the Austrian governor of Verona."

"I don't care about any of that." Piqued her lover wasn't easily persuaded, Sarah reverted to a pout. "Papa says he will make Lord Redvers marry me, and I want to be a marchioness. I don't know how you can be so self-ish and not let me have what I want."

"Even if you don't love him?"

"Vincenzo, please." Her pale brows came together in a frown. "Love has nothing to do with aristocratic marriages. And that's why I need you," she added, smiling again. "We can love each other all we want."

"I think you're overestimating the marquis's toler-ance."

"Pooh on that. Bella says you just have to know how to handle a husband."

"She's one to talk. Her husband gambles away what little money they have."

"Well, my husband won't, because he has more

money than almost anyone in England. And I refuse to argue about this anymore. If you don't love me, just say so."

"You know I do, *cara mia*. Even though your mama and papa are making you sacrifice yourself."

"It's not a sacrifice! I'll live in a grand house in London and have my own carriage and lots and lots of estates in the country—and don't you dare try to make me feel bad for wanting to marry a rich man."

Vincenzo fell silent.

"And don't think you can make me feel sorry for you. You're ever so handsome and talented and I won't feel sorry for you, no matter how you look at me with those sad eyes."

"Maybe I don't want to be your lover once you're married."

"Of course you do."

"I may not."

"Vincenzo, don't you dare leave me."

"Maybe I'll find some young lady who doesn't want riches alone."

"Of course I don't just want riches. You make it sound so crass."

"It is."

"Then any number of other young ladies this season are also similarly inclined."

"It doesn't make it right." The slender young man rose from the bed and padded across the shabby carpet in his bedchamber. "I'm going for a walk." Lifting his trousers from the chair, he began dressing.

"You are *not* going for a walk. I forbid it. Vincenzo!"

"I wish you good fortune with your wealthy husband." Slipping into his shoes, he grabbed his shirt from the floor where it had been dropped in his haste earlier that afternoon. Walking to the door, he heard her jump from the bed and run across the floor. With his hand on the door latch, he hesitated, and when she threw her arms around his waist and pressed her warm, nude body against his, he forgot his anger in the bliss of knowing she cared.

LORD PALMER'S MEETING WITH HIS BARRISTER wasn't going well. Familiar with commanding a large business, he'd expected to simply dictate the terms of the marriage settlement. He discovered, instead, that the marquis would not only be difficult to coerce, but perhaps impossible.

"Even with witnesses, my lord, the judge may not agree with your viewpoint," the barrister was saying for the tenth time, trying to make his wealthy client understand there were entirely different standards for peers of lesser rank and those of ancient lineage and prominence.

"But Redvers has ruined my daughter, damn him."

"He will contest that. I can't make that more incontrovertible. The Marquis of Redvers is entirely without conscience, or so rumor implies. A man of his stamp and wealth and influence can bring as many witnesses as you, or more, to refute your charge. And he will."

"Is the judge necessitous?"

"What are you implying, sir?" The barrister put on his most affronted pose. While he had been in Lord Palmer's employ on numerous occasions and taken his money without scruple, he was offended by men who thought they could buy anything they wanted because of their financial successes.

"The obvious, of course," Lord Palmer bluntly answered. "Is the judge financially needy—or better yet, greedy?"

"I'm sure I wouldn't know."

"Well, make it a point to find out. And then maybe Lord Redvers will stop looking down his nose at me."

"Lord Redvers's arrogance is democratically accorded to all, if that is any consolation to you, my lord."

"The only consolation to me, Symington, will be seeing my daughter made the Marchioness of Redvers. See that you take care of that situation for me. I don't care what it costs."

"I can't guarantee anything, my lord, with a man of the marquis's determination and arrogance."

"If you can't do it, tell me now, and I'll find someone who will."

George Symington understood his capabilities, and without undue vanity knew he was the equal of any barrister in London. "I will do my best, sir, but should you wish to find someone better qualified to act as sycophant, please do so."

Lord Palmer also knew that George Symington was one of the best, which was why he retained him as his primary barrister. "Very well, George," he conceded, "no need to take issue. Do what you can. But should you see your way to giving me what I want, there's a sizable bonus in it for you."

"I hope I can earn it, sir, but Redvers will fight this tooth and nail."

*J*ACK STOPPED BRIEFLY IN LONDON TO SEE HIS barrister on the way to Dover. He'd given Venus an edited version of the incident at the Sutton Inn as explanation for their detour. But cautious should Redvers House be under surveillance, he arranged for the meeting to be held at Austin Watts's home.

While Austin's wife, Helen, and Venus had tea, he spoke to his barrister alone, giving him a more graphic account of his meeting with the Palmers. "You know the drill," he said at the end of his narrative. "Keep me out of court if you can. But the Palmers' trap was more blatant than most, so in my current mood let them take me to court if they dare. Their daughter's reputation is the one at stake. Mine is long past the need for protection."

"Lord Palmer retains Symington for most of his legal work."

"It that a problem?"

"Not particularly, but he'll know how to drag this out in the legal system if he chooses."

"Let him. What is this, the third time now that some family has thought to force my hand? When I never even look at young misses," the marquis added in disgust. "It was a mistake in the past to settle quietly out of court."

"But you preferred not facing the tedium of litigation, as I recall. Dare I say, I told you so?" Austin smiled, his friendship with the marquis of long standing.

"Yes, of course you may." Jack's expression was tolerant. "Tell me, though, is there a possibility we can deal with this promptly?"

"I hate to make promises with Symington as an adversary."

"Do what you can to exert pressure on them. I have

complete faith in your ability to get me out of this mess with all due speed."

"Where will you be should I need you?"

"In Dover for the next few days, although my whereabouts are confidential, for obvious reasons. After that I'll be back in London."

"Would you like protection for your journey to Dover?" Jack had briefly discussed their near-fatal incident near Epsom.

"I've plenty of my own, but thanks."

"So I have carte blanche with the Palmers in terms of discomfort."

"No holds barred. Make that clear with Symington from the start."

Austin adjusted his shirt cuffs under his velvet smoking jacket, his grin one of satisfaction. "I look forward to taking the offensive this time."

"Good." Jack's smile was relaxed. "Let me know if you need anything. Should you require my presence before I return from Dover, my valet generally knows how to reach me."

"You're not taking him with you?"

"No." Jack looked amused. "Do you care?"

"You've been incommunicado this past month. Tongues are wagging."

"Would you like to ask me something?" the marquis drawled, looking at his friend with a heavy-lidded gaze.

"The entire ton would." Austin dipped his head minutely in a small gesture of tactful deference. "How serious is this affair?"

"Serious enough to keep me interested for a month."

"Miss Duras is very lovely."

"Only one of her many assets."

"But she's leaving?"

"I'm trying to talk her into staying, but Venus actually works—there's a new concept for a wealthy woman—and with the attack on her, I'd be a brute to put her in further danger."

"Will you pine?" Only newly married, Austin was aware of the intensity of love.

"Good question. Ask me in a few weeks."

"So casual, Jack?"

"I doubt I'll change my mind about my freedom, if that's what you're waiting to hear."

"If you're in love, freedom isn't an issue."

"Then I must not be in love, because it's still high on my list of priorities."

"In that case, have a pleasant sojourn in Dover."

"I intend to."

"And I'll inform the Palmers that they won't be entering the Fitz-James family anytime soon."

"My thanks, Austin." Jack rose.

"Why don't we see if the ladies are finished with their tea," his friend replied, coming to his feet.

It was another hour before Jack and Venus left the Watts home, the conversation over tea having turned into a heated discussion of the latest reform bills in Parliament. Helen Watts was active in a group promoting ragged schools for the poor in London, and while Jack didn't publicize his charitable interests, he was a generous donor to the day schools.

But the marquis kept an eye on the clock, and before long he suggested they leave. Once Venus was settled into the carriage again, she looked at Jack with a new degree of curiosity. "I didn't realize you were involved in reform issues."

"My secretary handles most of the arrangements, but he briefs me from time to time on the successes we've achieved. Harry likes to remind me that a man of my wealth should return some of his fortune to those less fortunate."

"I doubt it's his urging alone that prompts your generosity."

"I have more money than I need. Why not do some good with it?"

"You're not at all what you seem," Venus murmured.

"You know me as well as anyone, darling. This is it."

Her gaze was speculative. "Why do you cultivate your profligate persona?"

"I don't. But I don't deny it, either. A man can have more than one interest."

"Most think yours is exclusively vice."

"While you know now how domestic I can be," he replied with a grin.

"Don't tease. You do have a great number of domestic virtues—outside the bedchamber as well. You're a generous landlord to your tenants, a benefactor to the poor, a donor to the churches in your parish."

"Don't forget my racehorses," he lightly said. "I'm indulgent to them as well."

"You're uncomfortable with praise."

"Just realistic. I'm no paragon of virtue."

"Let me change the subject to something less fraught. Come visit me in Paris sometime and see my new hospital. No commitment required, darling," she quickly added, taking note of his sudden guarded look.

"I'd be pleased to." He didn't elaborate further, and

she took her cue from his evasion. For the remainder of their journey she took care to talk in the most casual terms of society and their mutual acquaintances, and within a short time Jack's dégagé manner returned.

Venus didn't realize she'd been the topic of conversation between Austin and Jack, nor did she know that conversation had stirred up a great many issues the Marquis of Redvers had never before considered. And much as Jack wished to disregard the ambiguity of his feelings for Venus, even the fact that he was ambiguous was alarming to his peace of mind.

IN HASTE TO SPEAK TO BERTY WELLS, TREVOR Mitchell had reached London the morning before Jack and Venus came into town. Fortunately, Berty was in immediate need of funds for his bookmakers and open to most anything Trevor had in mind. With each passing day of Jack's liaison with Venus, Trevor felt his expectations slipping further away, and he was becoming increasingly frantic. He couldn't afford for Jack to marry and sire children.

Trevor's financial affairs had worsened, and his creditors were exerting more pressure on him. There was a very real possibility he might be thrown into debtor's prison, and it rankled that his cousin should live in such luxury while he suffered.

Trevor never took responsibility for his ineptitude and lack of industry. Had he been less unwise, he could have lived at ease with the money Jack gave him, but such sober assessment never entered his thoughts. Jealousy and rage drove him, and he'd nurtured a warped resentment of his cousin to a savage hatred over the years.

So Berty Wells was sent out to be the instrument of Trevor's vengeance, while he anxiously waited in his rooms in Chelsea for favorable news.

Chapter 16

◦◦◦◦◦

WHEN JACK AND VENUS ARRIVED IN DOVER late that night, they were rowed out to the *Morea* where it lay offshore. With a guard no longer required and the risks aboard ship minimal, Jack's men found accommodations at one of the seaside inns. And after introductions and the necessary courtesies to the captain, Venus showed Jack to their quarters.

Lamps had been lit, the luxury of the large stateroom immediately visible even in the muted light. The waxed teak deck was covered with Turkish carpets in vivid shades of crimson and blue, the Chinese furniture bolted to the floor with polished brass brackets, the trellised bed in one corner suitably elaborate for an Oriental potentate.

"You travel in comfort," Jack murmured, a touch of censure in his voice.

"Peggy mentioned your yacht has some of the finer amenities as well," Venus replied, moving into the room. "I think she spoke of a sunken tub and a cooled wine cellar. I make do with a copper bath and a few bottles of rum."

"Touché," Jack agreed, following her. "Still, this cabin looks like one designed for entertainments."

"And I'm sure it's seen its share." Venus dropped into

a large cushioned chair. "My brother prefers the *Morea* when he travels. I travel for business, not pleasure."

"Do you now." Leaning against a large ebony desk, Jack scrutinized her as though the truth of her words would be apparent with close inspection.

"Feel better now?"

He shrugged, his emotional equivocation not noticeably improved. "How do people deal with jealousy? It's appalling."

"Something new for you, dear?"

"I dislike it intensely."

"Soon you can go back to your normal life of dissipation and forget the word exists."

"Somehow I'm not comforted at the thought."

"I'm sure you'll acclimatize. Old habits don't die."

"And what will you do?"

"Work and then work and work some more." She smiled. "Don't look so astonished. I like what I do. There's genuine pleasure in helping people who wouldn't otherwise survive."

"I'll come to see you soon." Surprised to hear himself make the offer, he debated some added caveat should he require an escape clause, but he decided against it. He said instead, "I'll take you to the races at Longchamps."

"Or I'll take you," she suggested. "And you needn't meet my family if you prefer. We can rent a box."

"Do I look as if I'm afraid to meet your family?"

"Yes."

He grinned. "Is it so obvious?"

"I don't expect you to alter your customary habits."

"Although I have the last month and willingly."

"So I needn't get all teary-eyed at the thought of never seeing you again."

"Nor I of you."

"Which means we can thoroughly enjoy our last two days together."

"Are you tired?"

"It depends."

"On?"

"What you have in mind."

"Nothing too strenuous. I'll do all the work."

"So I just have to lie there and enjoy myself."

"That's all."

Her smile was inviting. "How can a girl refuse?"

He began by undressing her, taking off each item of clothing without haste, her gown and petticoats, her chemise, her pale blue silk stockings that matched the pearl blue leather of her shoes. And sliding pillows behind her, he made her comfortable before bringing her a glass of cognac.

"If you ever need a recommendation as a footman," she playfully murmured, lifting her glass to him in salute.

"Thank you, mademoiselle," he said with feigned deference, his eyes beneath his dark lashes roguish. "I look forward to serving you."

"In what capacity?" A sportive quality had entered her voice. "Tell me your name. I haven't seen you before."

His mouth lifted in a wicked grin. "John Thomas, and I'm here to serve you in whatever capacity you wish."

"I see." She looked down her fine nose. "That's plain enough."

"I've found ladies prefer coming directly to the point."

Her brows rose in delicate rebuff. "They like that kind of frankness?"

"So I've been told. Some have called me unbridled as well, mademoiselle. I believe it was meant as a compliment."

"How interesting. What can I expect, should I decide to use you?" She took a sip of her drink.

"I have recommendations if you wish."

Her eyes narrowed, disapproval in the set of her mouth. "I do not."

"Pardon me, mademoiselle. Some ladies prefer a man with letters of recommendation."

"Letters?"

"French *lettres*, ma'am. I could supply them."

"In that case, John Thomas, I accept."

"Very good, my lady." Putting his hand into his coat pocket, he drew out four packets of condoms and, walking to the bed, placed them on the bedside table.

"I'm not sure I like such brazenness, Thomas. Did I ask you to put them there?"

"Should I remove them?"

An infinitesimal moment of contention transpired. "I'll overlook your impertinence this once," Venus said, a fine condescension in her tone.

"Thank you, my lady. I won't presume again."

"In my household, I expect obedience."

It took enormous effort not to smile. "Yes, mademoiselle, I understand."

"You may disrobe for me and we'll select a livery for you."

"Do you want everything off, mademoiselle? Some ladies want me to take off only enough to—"

"I don't wish to hear about other ladies. And yes,

everything. How do I know what size you wear if I don't see you unclothed?"

He discarded his clothing slowly, enjoying the game, taking pleasure in the play after the past days of concern and caution. Wanting her, as he always did, with unrestrained lust.

"Ummm, very nice," Venus murmured, looking him over from head to toe, focusing for a lengthy time on his blatant erection. He stood casually before her as if he'd done this before, as though women had often been rapt at the sight of him, and she could feel herself open as though his virility were an instant trigger to her body's desires. "Your credentials are superb, Thomas," she noted, trying to maintain some control over her impatience. Restless, her desire quickening, she drank the remaining cognac in a single large swallow.

"Thank you, my lady." Her nipples were jewel hard; he could almost smell her arousal. "I'm glad you approve."

"I need another drink," she imperiously said, feeling a need to equalize the dynamic.

There was the familiar moment of hesitation she'd come to know with Jack. And then he said, "Yes, ma'am," with a small nod and went to get the cognac bottle.

She held out her glass when he arrived at the bedside, and after pulling out the cork, he poured a small amount of cognac into her glass.

"More, please." The throbbing between her legs intensified at his closeness, at the pungent spice of his cologne and the palpable heat of his body.

"It might spill."

"Of course it won't spill."

"It could, and you don't have any clothes on."

"I assure you, Thomas, I have no intention of spilling."

"You might not want a full glass—" he held up the bottle cork "—when I put this in." Leaning over, he quickly slipped the cork up her vagina.

Her eyes went shut against the sudden feverish rush, the cork pressed exquisitely high, Jack's fingers filling her.

He plucked the glass from her fingers just in time.

Setting it on the table, he bent to kiss the taut crest of one nipple, his mouth closing, gently suckling, and he felt a reciprocal reaction in the rippling flesh of her vagina. His fingers were drenched, the cork pressed to the farthest depth. And when he lightly bit the turgid, sensitive tip of her nipple, she writhed against his hand.

"You need more, don't you," he whispered.

She slid her fingers into the ruffled silk of his hair, pulled his head up, and looked into his eyes with a smoldering gaze. "I don't want to wait."

"Mademoiselle is overzealous. Most of my employers prefer a more leisurely encounter."

"Do as you're told."

The smallest tick appeared over his cheekbone. He didn't respond well, play or not, to direct commands. "Mademoiselle is too hasty." He eased his fingers out.

"Jack! Don't—"

His mouth covered hers, his hands hard on her shoulders, pressing her back on the pillows, his kiss intrusive, forceful, impassioned, and when his mouth lifted, she was reminded of the merits in pleasing him.

"If mademoiselle would refrain from giving orders, we'd get along better."

The violence, the burning urgency of her desires generated a more tractable sensibility. "Forgive me," she breathlessly intoned.

"Certainly, my lady."

Her gaze drifted downward to his erection, rising splendidly from the dark, luxuriant hair at his crotch. "May I touch you?"

The hesitation in her tone brought a surge of blood to his erection. "Of course. And later, when I feel you're fully aroused, you may have this."

"Don't make me wait long," she whispered, reaching out to run her fingers down the distended veins.

"Just long enough." His hand closed over hers and then deliberately lifted it away. "We have to see that you're ready . . ."

"But I am." The pulsing between her legs was intense, the slightest motion stirring the lodged cork with riveting consequences, its presence like a captivating prelude to the full glory of Jack's monstrous erection.

"Just a few minutes longer . . . It always feels better—if you wait." He reached for the cognac bottle, emptied the remaining liquor into her glass on the bedside table, and spreading her thighs wider, stroked her throbbing labia with the mouth of the bottle.

The sudden realization of what he was about to do sent a racy thrill through her senses.

"Don't move. It's glass," he softly warned, easing the neck of the bottle inside her sleek flesh.

As her labia gave way, she felt a delectable shudder deep inside her, the hard coolness slowly forced upward, a glowing heat in stark contrast flowing outward in its wake. An intoxicating delirium grew like fever in her blood as she was stretched, filled, engorged, and when at last the bottle mouth met the lodged cork, she shivered with insatiable longing.

"It's not in very far," he whispered. "I'm not sure you can take me."

She didn't respond, transported to a level of sensual ecstasy that overwhelmed speech.

"Do you think you can?" He gently moved the bottle in a delicate rhythm of thrust and withdrawal that made it impossible to concentrate on anything but delirious sensation.

Running his warm palm over her breasts, he stroked the soft fullness, slid his fingers down the deep valley between the quivering flesh, lightly squeezed each nipple as though estimating her degree of readiness. "You have to answer me, mademoiselle, or I won't know whether you want my services."

She looked up, understanding an answer was required but unsure of the question, lust dominating her senses.

Lifting his hand, he slid his fingers under her chin and tipped her face up, forcing her to look at him. "Will you be able to take me?"

"Yes, yes . . ."

He smiled. "How kind of you, mademoiselle."

She smiled back, beautiful, compliant, welcoming.

Perhaps too compliant, he suddenly thought, wondering if she'd actually done this before. "Have you ever let a footman service you?"

The fine edge in his voice stripped through her heated insensibility, his words clear, his implication clearer still, and her independence abruptly reasserted itself. "Now why would I want to do that?" she murmured in a normal tone of voice, gazing at him from under the curve of her lashes.

He softly laughed. "You're back. Would you tell me if you had?"

"Of course not."

"Do I have to beat the truth out of you?"

"I'm not sure you dare."

"I could try."

"That might be interesting. But I think I'll climax first."

"Or maybe not," he softly countered, pulling the bottle out.

"I can do this without you." She reached for the bottle.

He moved it out of her reach.

When she lunged for it, he caught her hands and held her at arm's length. "Now tell me about your servants."

"There are so many," she said with dulcet sweetness. "I'm not sure I can remember them all."

"Just recall those likely to have fucked you."

"Why should I do that?"

"If you want to come tonight, you might wish to comply." Shoving her back on the bed, he quickly extracted the cork and tossed it away.

"You're altogether too domineering."

"Just answer the question."

"Maybe I can't remember."

"Try."

"You may not like the answer."

He inhaled, not sure how he'd respond, his dragooning need inexplicable. "I just want to know."

"And then I'll have what I want?"

He nodded.

"None, none at all, my whimsical John Thomas. You're the only one."

"Liar."

"You wanted an answer."

"It's not satisfactory."

"Really, darling, what do you want me to say? If I tell you I've slept with some of my servants, you'll be angry."

"Some?" he growled.

She shrugged, as willful as he, not about to tell him her sexual experiences had never included servants. "Why don't we dispense with these irrelevancies and spend an enjoyable evening. I want you very much—as usual, as always." She smiled. "I'm thoroughly besotted. And at the risk of inflating your considerable ego, you're the only man to so inspire me. So make love to me." She lifted her arms to him. "Please, please, please . . ."

"The only one?"

"Without exception—bar none. Consider yourself the ultimate delight of my life." Sitting up, she reached out, grasped his erection firmly and, lying back down, tugged at him.

"No question of what you want," he teased, easing down atop her.

"Sometimes you're very hard to convince."

"Just jealous."

"I know. Are we fortunate or unfortunate to feel that way?"

"Fortunate to be here together. Fuck the rest."

"Yes," she whispered, "and me too. Now kiss me, darling Jack, because I'm going through withdrawal and I need you."

"I'm yours," he said without hesitation or thought, without all the normal misgivings and dread.

She touched his cheek. "I like the sound of that."

"And oddly, it doesn't strike terror in my soul," he replied, grinning.

"Definitely progress. Now about another kind of progress. Do you think you could get just a little bit closer?" She slid her legs around his hips and pulled his head down for a kiss. "You know what I mean."

He did, of course, much better than most. "I think I'm going to like this job, mademoiselle," he whispered, his mouth brushing hers.

"I'll see that you're kept busy, Thomas. I don't believe in idleness for my servants."

"I'm a very hard worker, ma'am," he impudently replied, sliding into her heated warmth. "You won't be sorry you hired me."

THE SUN WAS HIGH IN THE SKY WHEN THEY woke, neither having slept until almost dawn. And it was warm, almost hot in the cabin in the late forenoon.

"I have to eat," Jack mumbled, rolling over on his back and rubbing his eyes. Pushing himself up on his elbows, he glanced at Venus, who was stretching awake. "I think we forgot dinner last night." He surveyed the stateroom. "Are those grapes over there?"

Still half asleep, Venus murmured, "I'll call the cook in a minute."

"I'll eat the grapes while I wait." Swinging his legs over the side of the bed, he rose and walked to the table. "Should I call the cook?" he inquired, bringing the bowl of fruit back to the bed.

"I'd better. He's temperamental."

"He only listens to you?"

"Something like that. My brother complains, but I told him it's a matter of rapport."

"Hmmm . . ." Seated on the edge of the bed, Jack sent her a discerning look. "I'll *bet* your rapport with the cook is better than your brother's. The man's no idiot."

"Why do males always see relationships in terms of sex?"

"The same reason women like to talk about their feelings."

"If you wish to be argumentative, darling, I don't have to call the cook."

"A thousand apologies for my crassness, ten thousand. Just call the cook before I faint." He held up the bowl, his smile disarming. "The grapes are gone, and I absolutely adore you for your mind."

She grinned. "Now, that's better. Don't confuse me with reality so early in the morning."

"Late in the morning, sweet. The sun's damn near midpoint in the sky. Let me find your robe for you."

"Are you always so pushy?" She watched him rummage through the armoire.

"Only when I'm on the verge of starvation. If you recall, breakfast at Castlereagh was ten minutes after I woke. Ah, here we go." Turning, he tossed the robe at her.

"I think Alexander would prefer you were clothed as well."

"Then Alexander will see me clothed." Snatching up his trousers, he began dressing.

"I'm going to remember to let you go hungry, should I ever need you to acquiesce without argument," Venus cheerfully remarked, slipping into a white piqué robe.

"While I know how to make you agree as well. There are certain things you don't like to wait for."

Her voice was playful. "Would you be so cruel?"

"It depends on how fast I get my breakfast," he said with a grin. "We still have another day that I can make very pleasant for you, if you give me some cooperation."

"Consider it done." Venus quickly moved to the door and, throwing it open, shouted for her cook.

Alexander was much too young, Jack disgruntledly thought when the cook appeared on the run. And much too eager to please his mistress. Furthermore, he glared at the marquis as if he were some intruder.

"I hope you don't mind Greek cooking," Venus noted, after Alexander had nodded in agreement to each of the items she'd suggested.

"Not at all. I'd like my coffee immediately, though."

Alexander spoke rapidly in his mother tongue, his voice low and gruff, his expression resentful.

Venus responded in a diplomatic tone. Jack's school Greek was not sufficiently fluent to catch all of the words, but the meaning was clear. She was soothing the young man.

But their coffee appeared shortly with honey buns and lemon marmalade and Jack could overlook the young cook's pique because his talents in the kitchen were so superb.

"I've died and gone to heaven." Jack sighed, his mouth full of the light, rich pastry. "And this coffee . . . Even if he poisoned it, I'll die happy."

"Alex hasn't seen me with a man before."

"That was pretty obvious. I thought he might challenge my place in your bed."

"Really, dear, you misunderstand. It's just that on some of my journeys, we spend time together."

"Reading?"

"How did you know?"

"How old is he? Seventeen, eighteen?"

"Eighteen."

"And you are?"

"You know how old I am."

"And so does Alexander. So you see, my dear, he's not quite sure how to approach you sexually. But he's damned well not going to give up your company."

"Impossible."

"Fine. I'm wrong. But I'm not going to fight a duel with him, so I'm counting on you to keep him under control."

"Since you're wrong, it won't be a problem."

"Good. Push the sugar a little closer, will you?" he blandly said.

Jack kept an eye on Alexander, though, when he returned, and the young man behaved with such constrained courtesy Jack decided Venus had spoken to him. The young Greek would have her back to himself soon enough anyway, he disgruntledly thought. She was sailing home tomorrow.

*T*HE NEXT MORNING, JACK HAD GONE ON DECK to see if the boat to take him ashore was ready. On returning to the stateroom a few minutes later, he stepped over the threshold and stopped at the sight of a visitor.

Sitting across the table from Venus, drinking coffee

from Jack's cup, was a small, grizzled man clearly out of place in such sumptuous surroundings.

"Jack, come and meet Mr. Berty Wells. We've just come to a very satisfactory business arrangement. Tell Lord Redvers why you're here," she pleasantly said.

"You sure, ma'am?" A nervous tick appeared along Berty's jaw, and he quickly set the coffee cup down.

"I assure you, you're safe," Venus prompted.

"Safe?" Jack closed the door behind him without taking his eyes off the man.

"Don't be alarmed, dear. Mr. Wells is quite willing to change employers for a sum agreeable to us both."

"What the hell's going on?" Jack growled, moving to place himself between the man and Venus.

"I tol you the gov'nor'd be right sore." Berty Wells visibly cringed.

"Relax, Jack, everything is under control. Mr. Wells was sent here by your cousin to scare me off."

"That weren't exactly the words, ma'am."

"Never mind, Mr. Wells, I'm sure Lord Redvers understands the gist of your task."

"Were you supposed to kill Miss Duras?" Jack inquired, watching the wiry old man closely. "I suggest you don't lie to me."

"If'n it were necessary, your ludship, Mitchell hisself said she were to be finished off."

He should have suspected, Jack thought, cursing his witlessness. Trevor, of course, damn him. "Were you involved in the shooting at Epsom?"

"No, sair, that weren't me."

"Did my cousin commission that business as well?"

"I don't rightly know, but I were recommended by a

friend o'mine who comes from that line o'work, if'n you know what I mean."

"A large fellow, sandy hair."

"Might be, sair. I wouldn't want to get on the wrong side o' my particular friend and say yes, fur sure."

"Did Mr. Mitchell tell you why he wanted Miss Duras finished off, as you say?"

"I don't ask no questions. Best that way."

Jack was relieved that Venus was about to sail and distance herself from Trevor's dangerous schemes. "You should weigh anchor immediately," he suggested to her. "I'll take care of this man."

"We're on schedule," Venus replied. "I've sent someone to bring Mr. Wells his fee and once that's settled, the captain is only waiting my orders."

"I'll pay him. Trevor's my problem, not yours." Astonished at Venus's composure, Jack was less serene, finding himself hard-pressed not to beat the man into a pulp. Or better yet, his cousin.

"Why don't I have some of the crew detain Mr. Wells until you're ready to leave," Venus proposed.

"I will. Come, Wells," the marquis curtly said. "You can wait elsewhere for your money."

ONCE THE SCOUNDREL WAS UNDER GUARD ON deck, Jack returned, his feelings still in turmoil. "Now tell me what the hell happened in here?" he said, moving toward Venus. "How did he get in?"

"Your guess is as good as mine on how he managed to get on board. As for what happened, I managed to reach my pistol, and once we both had weapons, my assailant was ready to deal. Men like Mr. Wells come rather cheap, as you no doubt know. Although I don't understand why I was the target, and not you. Wouldn't it be more profitable for your cousin if you were dead?"

"He probably knows I'd come back from hell and kill him. Which I intend to do the moment I return to London." Drawing her into his arms, he quietly said, "Forgive me for involving you in this. Trevor will pay, I promise." A rueful half-smile flickered across his mouth. "This is a helluva way to end our holiday."

"Exciting to the last." Venus's voice was teasing.

"You're taking this much too calmly. The man was serious."

"As children, we were taught never to show fear, and considering some of the outlands of the world in which we lived, it was a good maxim. I think Wells was more frightened than I, once I had my weapon in hand. I'm a very good shot, by the way."

"You constantly amaze me. What can't you do?"

"I embroider poorly and can't paint watercolor flowers at all. My governesses were quite distraught."

"But you can hold killers at bay and make me miss you before you're even gone. What am I going to do once you leave?"

"Forget my name in a week?"

"Not likely."

"Come and see me for the races, and then we won't have to say more than au revoir. I dislike good-byes."

He sighed. "I'd better not linger, anyway. The sooner you leave, the sooner you're safe. Au revoir, darling." He bent to kiss her, the touch of his lips delicate, already bittersweet with memory. "I'll think of you. And of Castlereagh and Epsom—"

"And the river house . . ."

A touch of mischief shone in his eyes. "Sure you won't stay?"

She shook her head, knowing she had to be resolute and sensible even as the weight of tears filled her eyes. Jack Fitz-James wasn't a man a woman would ever be able to hold.

His smile was gracious, touched with affection. "I know you have to go." He touched the tip of her nose with his finger. "Thank you, for . . . everything."

She nodded, unable to speak with the same equanimity.

He kissed her one last time, and with a touch of sadness in his eyes he turned to go.

The door shut without a sound.

She dropped into a chair, her legs suddenly weak, and she felt a deep sadness she'd never felt before. The noises of the longboat heaving away came to her as though through a great distance. Even the first shudder of movement barely registered on her consciousness.

He was gone.

How was she going to live without him?

Chapter 17

———❦———

$\mathcal{T}$REVOR MITCHELL JERKED OUT OF A DEAD sleep, terror flooding his mind. Someone was racing up the stairs; considering the location of his rooms in Chelsea was secret, the intrusion signaled danger, especially at this hour of the night. Leaping out of bed, he snatched up the loaded pistol on the nightstand just as something crashed into the door so hard the hinges squealed. Sweat broke out on his brow, and he pointed his weapon at the door with trembling hands.

Jack's boot slammed into the solid oak again, and then again a moment later, the rhythm of his murderous intent settling into a steady, determined battering that gradually forced the latch and hinges from their moorings. Driven by rage and a need for vengeance, he meant to see that Trevor paid for his treachery. Swinging his foot back again, he slammed his spurred boot into the door once more, and this time the lock shattered in a shower of splintered wood.

Trevor's worst nightmare came through the smashed portal like a vision from hell, Jack's wrathful strength and power exploding into the room. Ignoring the pistol aimed at him, homicidal impulse burning in his brain, he surged forward, oblivious to Trevor's shouted threat, heedless of the click of the pistol trigger. He scarcely noticed the shot grazing his temple, shaking his head minutely as though flicking off a fly. A second later, he was on top of Trevor, chopping the pistol from his hand with such force the weapon left a gaping hole as it smashed into the wall. He lunged for Trevor's neck, shoving him into the wall with a rampaging fury. Trevor's shriek filled the room.

Jack's breathing was labored after his strenuous exertions at gaining access to the room, but he fought off Trevor's desperate resistance, forcing him hard against the wall, his hands reaching, searching for purchase around Trevor's neck until finally he twisted past the flailing arms and kicking feet and locked onto his prey. His fingers tightened around Trevor's throat, squeezed with fatal determination. "It's just you . . . and me now," he rasped, his strong hands closing off the air to Trevor's lungs, every muscle in his body taut as he maintained the slow, measured pressure. "How does it feel . . . you bastard . . . without . . . hired killers . . . to protect you?"

Trevor's face was blue, his eyes bulging, as he struggled to breathe, his frantic efforts to push away Jack's hands leaving bloody scratches.

"You shouldn't have tried . . . to kill her." Teeth bared like a wolf on the attack, Jack stared into Trevor's terror-filled eyes with a pitiless gaze. Leaning into the dying man with all his strength, he sank his fingers deep into Trevor's flesh. "She matters . . . to me."

The inexorable pressure of Jack's hands took its deadly toll a second at a time, slowly strangling breath and life, deliberately destroying the man who'd tried to harm Venus. Until, at last, Trevor's struggles ceased and his body went limp.

Relaxing his grip, Jack watched the lifeless body crumple to the floor.

Don't fuck with me, he brutally thought, or with the woman I love. In the heat of his madness, he didn't notice the simple truth of his reflection, retribution still overwhelming his senses. And when his gaze came up from the dead man and swept the room, he didn't know for a moment where he was; the hideous wallpaper design jumped out at him, startling his visual receptors. It took a second for reason to reassert itself, for the room to register as reality.

He felt no remorse, and he wondered at his lack of humanity, at his capacity to kill a man in cold blood. But he shook his head, not wanting a conscience just yet, and at the sudden movement droplets of blood sprayed outward in a perfect arc. Following their trajectory, he watched them fall to the floor in a pattern of crimson splotches, and conscious of pain for the first time, he raised his hand and gingerly touched the torn flesh at his temple.

Tracing the blood seeping down his cheek, he swore.

An echoing moan answered.

Searching out the sound, he scrutinized the body of his cousin, the mottled purple of his face altered now to a lighter shade of blue. As he watched, a faint movement of Trevor's chest became visible.

Brief disappointment washed over him, but a niggling relief also insinuated itself into his brain. He hadn't killed a man in cold blood, after all.

Perhaps someday there would be satisfaction in that.

He immediately walked from the room. With Trevor alive, limitations had to be speedily imposed on his freedom. Quickly riding to Austin's home, Jack pounded on

the door until he woke the servants. Short moments
later, when Austin appeared at the top of the stairs tying
his robe, the marquis said, "I need a man transported
tonight."

"Tonight?"

Jack nodded and blood struck the marble floor.

"Good God, you're bleeding." Austin came down the
stairs in a run, calling for the housekeeper.

"It's nothing serious, but thank you for your concern," Jack said, taking a cloth from a servant and holding it against his wound.

"In here." Austin gestured toward his office. "Bring
coffee," he ordered a servant, "and see that the housekeeper brings some bandages and hot water. This way,
Jack."

He listened while the marquis quickly related the
pertinent events. "I need the police to go to the apartment before Trevor has a chance to recover. Although I
don't think he'll be moving any time soon. Send the
message now," he ordered. "The rest of the story will
wait." And while Austin went to make the necessary
arrangements to have Trevor detained, the housekeeper
cleaned and bandaged Jack's wound.

"You *should* see a doctor," Austin suggested on his
return.

"I will. As soon as my cousin is in custody. I *can* have
him transported, can't I?"

"It shouldn't be a problem. He tried to kill you, from
the looks of it."

"Actually, I was hoping I'd killed him. The bastard
sent a second man to kill Venus."

"Is she hurt?" Austin's concern was evident.

Jack smiled faintly. "She managed to outmaneuver

her assailant, and then convince him to change allegiance."

Austin's brows rose in approval. "A resourceful woman,"

"Very." Jack glanced at the clock. "She should be in Paris by now, out of range of Trevor's malevolence. Call in any necessary favors, but I want my cousin gone immediately. He can keep his damned stipend, but on some distant shore where he won't do any more harm. Van Diemen's Land would suit."

"I'll see that someone drives you home, and rest assured, Trevor will leave England."

"I'm still not sure I shouldn't have killed him."

"I'm glad you didn't. There's scandal enough in your life now without that."

Jack's gaze sharpened. "Meaning?"

"The Palmers. I'll explain when you're feeling better."

Jack gestured away his concern. "Give me a brandy and then tell me the bad news. Once I leave here, I'm planning on sleeping for days."

Soon each men had a brandy in his hand, and Austin explained the most recent events. "I'm afraid Lord Palmer insists on going to court. Apparently, he believes his daughter and insists the child is yours."

"I never touched her."

"Unfortunately, she doesn't agree, and with your reputation there's a substantial element of doubt."

"Palmer won't consider a settlement?"

"He has money. He's interested in your title."

"So what's next?"

"I'm going to have my people try to interview some of the Palmer servants and see what we can discover—

in terms of possible liaisons, other than the alleged one with you. I'll continue discussions with Palmer as well, point out to him the influence your name will have in court, the risks he has of losing, et cetera, et cetera."

"But it looks as though we're going to court on this one."

"It seems so. I wish I had better news."

"Never mind. Knowing Venus is safe is good news enough. The Palmers will just be a minor disturbance for a time, but they can't really coerce me into marrying their daughter."

"I don't know what they expect. Symington is careful to give away nothing."

"Perhaps I should speak to Sarah myself."

"Please, don't. Have no contact with her at all—nothing that could later be construed as an assignation."

"You don't think I could intimidate her?"

"You told me of her attitude that night at the Sutton Inn. What do you think?"

Jack frowned, then winced at the shooting pain that resulted. "You're right. She's beyond intimidation. Send me a message once Trevor has sailed. I'm going home to sleep. My holiday, while glorious, was exhausting," he said with a faint smile.

"Will you be seeing Miss Duras again? Helen liked her, and I thought her stunning and intelligent. Not your usual combination."

"I told her I'd come to Paris for the races."

His tone was so equivocal, Austin's brows rose in query. "Will you?"

Jack shrugged. "Probably not."

"Does she know that?"

He shrugged again. "I don't know. Lord, my head is pounding."

"Go home. I'll take care of Trevor."

"Make sure I pay for those favors you call in."

"Of course. That's my business."

"I'm fortunate to have a friend who's so competent. How many scrapes have you saved me from?"

"Starting at Eton?"

"I saved your ass there a number of times, too, if I recall." Bigger and stronger, Jack had come to Austin's aid on more than one occasion; the slender child had not been up to the bullying.

"I know, and I'm grateful. But then I made us both a deal of money in our gambling scheme."

Jack chuckled. "We were good."

"Always. Now, go. You look tired. Everything will be taken care of."

𝔅ELLA ROSE VERY LATE.

Finally, Sarah thought, her impatience having mounted during the hour she'd waited for her aunt to wake. Pushing past the maid who had come from the bedroom to fetch Bella's morning chocolate, Sarah charged into her aunt's boudoir. "I thought you'd never wake," she heatedly exclaimed.

"Do pull that drape back over the window, will you, darling? Alice thinks one actually wants to see the sun in the morning, poor girl."

"I've been waiting ever so long to see you," Sarah crossly noted, jerking the drape over the bright window. "It's almost noon."

"Lord Courtenay was particularly attentive, and didn't let me leave until very late."

"His wife will appreciate your interest. She's busy with Lord Simon, gossip has it. But I don't care about any of those people. I have problems of my own."

Bella struggled up into a sitting position, so she could see her niece more clearly. "Tell Aunt Bella, darling." She pushed a platinum-colored curl away from her eyes. "What can be so important you're frowning this early in the day?"

"I'm more pregnant than I admitted, and now, it seems, Lord Redvers is going to delay us in court until it's going to be *too* late."

Bella sank back against her pillows again and sighed. "Why didn't you tell me sooner?"

"Because I didn't want anyone to know, of course," Sarah retorted, standing at the end of the bed with a scowl for her aunt. "I thought Papa could make him marry me right away."

"Now don't be tantrumish, darling," Bella hastily murmured, her mind racing. "These things can be dealt with. Sit down"—she pointed at a chair near her—"and we'll see what we can do."

"Vincenzo is being difficult, too," Sarah muttered, dropping into the chair with an unladylike plummet.

"Menials are never a problem. I'll speak to him and see that he understands his position."

"He says his family is as well-born as ours. His papa is a court physician."

Bella snorted. "Hardly a position of wealth. Your father is considerably more important than an apothecary. Leave Vincenzo to me. Now as for your, er, other situation. Tell me, how far along are you?"

"Almost four months."

Bella pursed her lips, understanding the time constraints. "Perhaps I should talk to your father."

"Don't. He'll scream at me and tell me how I ruined the family name and prospects, and Mama will weep like she does for anything at all, and what good will that do any of us? Can't we *make* Lord Redvers come up to scratch?"

"Maybe I should go and talk to him."

"Oh, would you? I just know you can make him listen."

"Where's my chocolate?" Bella irritably inquired, faced with disaster impossibly early. "Alice knows I need my chocolate the second I wake." Her head was still painful from the champagne she'd drunk the evening before, and now Sarah had handed her a problem that required clear thinking.

"If you take care of this for me, Bella," her niece soulfully declared, "I'll be in your debt forever."

"Ah, there you are—at last!" Bella waved her maid forward with fluttering fingers and once she'd taken her first sip of chocolate, she proceeded to chastise the servant girl until she was in tears. Shooing her out of the room, she sank back against her pillows. "It never pays to let servants become complacent. Now where were we?" She glanced at her niece over the rim of her chocolate cup. "Lord Redvers will need some very strong incentive to capitulate to your father's demands. I wonder what we can devise to coerce his cooperation . . ."

*W*HILE JACK WAS SLEEPING AWAY HIS HEAD wound and fatigue, and Bella and Sarah were concocting a plan to bring him to the altar, Venus was about to begin her first day back at the hospital in Montmartre.

She'd hardly slept the previous night, her thoughts consumed with images of Jack, her sense of longing so intense, she finally left her bed before dawn, having given up any prospect of further sleep.

While she kept her own apartment in Paris, she was having breakfast at her parents' home that morning. Pleading exhaustion last night, she'd agreed to see them at breakfast and relate all that had transpired in England. The additional days of her holiday would require a tactful explanation. She had no intention of discussing Jack with them.

Fortunately, she had to face only her parents that morning; her siblings were busy with other activities. Only her younger sister, Caroline, still lived with her parents, and she was at the track. Her stepbrother, Chris, was in China at the moment, while Merimee, married and expecting her second child, had gone to the country.

She was greeted warmly by the servants when she arrived.

"Finally, Miss Duras, we have you back," the major-domo, Dumont, said, beaming.

"The weather was particularly beautiful in England," she replied. "It tempted me to stay. How is Yvette doing?"

"She's going to be running again soon. The doctor took the cast off last week." Dumont's daughter had fallen from a tree and broken her leg, and Venus's clinic had treated the young girl.

"It's good to have you back, miss." The footman who took her hat and gloves smiled.

"Thank you, Jean-Claude. Has your fiancée set a wedding date yet?"

"Yes, ma'am." He blushed. "On Midsummer Day."

"Congratulations. I knew she couldn't wait," she pleasantly said.

"Your papa said she can join the staff."

"How fortunate, then, for my parents. Marie is the best seamstress I know."

Venus had always taken an interest in the staff's families, and they reciprocated by viewing her as their personal responsibility. Her parents teased her that the servants knew more about her schedule and activities than they did. But in a way, they were her family, during the times her parents and siblings were traveling abroad. She knew the belowstairs regions intimately.

"Chef made chocolate madeleines for you this morning," Dumont noted as he led her down the hall to the breakfast room. "In honor of your return."

"Gabriel's madeleines are worth a trip back to Paris. I can feel my day improving already."

When she greeted her parents in the sunny breakfast room facing the gardens, she felt her melancholy lighten.

"Darling," Trixi cried, rising in a rustle of yellow striped silk to give her daughter a hug. "How good to see you again. Pasha, look," she joyfully exclaimed.

Pasha was coming around the table to greet his daughter, his smile broad. "The sights in England must have been fascinating, to keep you away so long." As his wife relinquished her hold, he took his turn, hugging his daughter in welcome.

"Your papa knows, of course," Trixi lightly said, sitting down again. "He just wants to tease you a bit."

With a telegraph not only at the shipping office, but in the house, Venus had anticipated that rumors of her affair had reached Paris long before she arrived. "I did have a wonderful holiday." Taking her seat at the breakfast table, she looked at both her parents and smiled. "However, my days of leisure are over, and I'm back home to work again."

"There, I told you, Pasha. She's more sensible than to be taken in by a charming rogue."

"I thought you liked charming rogues," Pasha said to his wife, smiling. Their initial meeting years ago had been unconventional.

"Not for my daughter. Don't look at me like that. It's altogether different."

"What your mother's trying to say is, whatever you want, we want for you."

"I know, Papa. Thank you. I'm really pleased to be back home. Did they tell you what I acquired in England?" The ship had been unloaded yesterday, directly after docking.

"I had all the freight delivered to Montmartre this morning. You'll be greeted with mountains of crates.

"It's so exciting." She leaned forward, her enthusiasm evident. "I brought back so many new pieces of equipment, some absolutely wonderful. It's going to make a big difference in our treatment facilities. Some of the new surgical tools will allow us to better our survival rates. And you'll have to see the operating room lights I brought back. Some run on zinc batteries, although they're too expensive for everyday use. But on those occasions when precise lighting is required, well . . ."

She sat back in satisfaction. "Our hospital will be able to offer the best."

"I'll drive up with you after breakfast," her father offered. "It sounds as though you've brought back a treasure trove."

"Caro and I will come to see everything once she returns from the track. And then you must see the races with us tomorrow," her mother declared. "Your papa's horses have a very good chance to take the first two races."

The talk turned to family matters, and as Venus was brought up to date on the activities of her siblings, she forgot for a time her longing for the man she'd left in England.

Chapter 18

⸺✦⸺

*J*ACK WOKE LATE IN THE AFTERNOON AND immediately heard Peggy's voice.

"I was beginning to think you might have a concussion."

Startled, he took a moment to reconcile time, place, and Peggy in his bedroom. Rolling over slowly in deference to his throbbing head, he saw her seated near his bed, a glass of liquor in her hand.

"It's after five. You slept twenty hours. Are you hungry?"

"Is that brandy? I could use some."

"I suppose I should check with your doctor."

"He wouldn't dare oppose me, anyway. Four fingers will do for a start." A doctor had been called once Jack arrived home, and his wound had been properly dressed.

"Hmpf," Peggy muttered, coming to her feet. But she knew Dr. Litton, and Jack was right. "You should have something to eat as well," she said, moving toward the liquor tray.

"Later. I prefer some numbness first."

"Trevor tried to kill you, I hear."

"Luckily he was never a good shot."

She filled a glass—more than four fingers—and

walked back to the bed. "You're a big man. By the way, Austin sent a note. I read it although your footman didn't want to relinquish it without your approval."

"There's an uneven contest," Jack said with a grin, taking the glass she held out to him.

"That's what I said. I've been having my way for seventy years and wasn't to about to stop for him. Now drink that slowly or you'll get dizzy," she warned, sitting down again and taking up her brandy. "For your information, Trevor is on his way to Van Diemen's Land, Austin said, with a sizable sum of money. Enough, he explained, to live on there in style—whatever that means. I can't imagine there's a scrap of society in such a place."

"Did you also hear Trevor commissioned men to murder Venus?"

"He deserved to be killed for such a low, despicable crime. You're much too generous, and you'll probably be sorry you didn't dispatch him permanently. I don't trust him not to come back even from that distant shore."

"At least he'll be gone for a while," Jack said with a sigh, his own feelings concerning Trevor's life equivocal.

"Let us hope forever. Now, tell me, what's this I hear about you marrying the Palmer gel?"

Jack choked on his brandy. "Jesus, Peggy, give me some warning when you're going to poleax me."

"Is it true?"

"Of course not."

"That's what I told Addie Buchan, who swore she'd seen the marriage license at the Palmers."

"It's a misunderstanding."

"Like the one you had with the Pagets and the Waddingtons?"

"Similar."

"But the Palmers won't be paid off."

"It doesn't look that way. Austin isn't hopeful."

"That ass Palmer has pretensions, that's why. He wants to wash off the stench of the brewery and thinks your title will take away the smell."

"He's wrong. But it looks as though I'll be going to court to prove that to him."

"That'll cost you a pretty penny."

"A price I much prefer to that of marrying his daughter."

She looked at him from under her lashes. "Have any plans to marry someone else?"

"You're wasting your time, Peggy. Venus doesn't want to marry any more than I do. I told you not to play matchmaker."

His godmother gave a dramatic sigh. "You can't blame an old lady for trying."

He chuckled. "Look at it this way, Peggy. I'm just giving you an opportunity to try again with someone else."

"But I like Venus."

"A shame you can't marry her, then."

She didn't reply, her expression causing him a strange unease.

"Don't interfere in my life, Peggy. I'm warning you."

"Have I ever interfered in your life?" she innocently inquired.

"At least ten thousand times, but I'm telling you, not this time, Peggy. I mean it."

"Whatever you want, dear," she sweetly replied.

"When I hear that tone of voice, all the barricades go

up. You're not going to be able to touch me on this one."

"I'm sure you're right."

"I *am* right."

"Yes, dear."

When she said *yes, dear* like that, he was clearly warned. He'd have to talk to his staff and Austin to make sure she didn't ask them to carry out any commissions in his name. But it still left his godmother as a loose cannon in his life.

He'd have to be particularly wary.

IN THE FOLLOWING WEEK, JACK'S ACTIVITIES followed a pattern typical of most wealthy young bachelors who were suffering doubts. He denied rumors both of his involvement with Venus and of his imminent nuptials with Sarah Palmer, refused invitations to society functions, and spent most of his time in the brothels. He preferred Mme. Robuchon's, where he could usually be found once he left the card games at Brookes, although on those days when he found he couldn't sleep, he often held court on one of Lucy's pink satin sofas, greeting those who liked their pleasure early.

After the first night at Lucy's, when he'd sent his favorite courtesan away after no more than a few kisses, everyone understood he wasn't there for the women. Lucy's served as a safe haven from those who were inclined to ask too many questions he either didn't care to answer or couldn't.

His drinking by the end of the week had sufficiently blurred the potent images of Venus to more manageable levels, and when a blond woman approached him, he no longer started.

Ned kept him company at times, and Austin tracked him down twice when he needed signatures or procedural questions answered, but Jack wasn't truly looking for company so much as oblivion. Lucy, middle-aged and motherly, saw that he was fed, coaxing him to eat when he didn't wish it, inviting him into her private quarters occasionally to sleep when he hadn't gone home.

Later in the week, after one of those nights when he'd not found his way back to Redvers House, he woke on the chaise in her sitting room, unshaven, moody, and looking for a drink. Seated at her desk across the small room, she gazed at him with concern. Should she call his servants to come for him?

"Don't you think you've brooded long enough?" she asked.

"Not brooding," Jack muttered, lifting a bottle to her in salute. "Just happen to be damned bored."

"Maybe you need a change of scene. Somewhere other than my place."

The marquis offered her a rare smile. "Are you kicking me out, Lucy? After we've been friends for so long?"

"Go to the country. Breathe some fresh air, clear your head of what's bothering you."

"But then she was in the country with me." He shook his head. "Not a good idea."

"If you're missing a woman, you won't find her in that bottle."

"Don't want to find her."

"Are you sure?"

"Now there's the question of the hour." Raising the bottle to his mouth, he drank deeply.

Jack's reaction to any thought of commitment wasn't uncommon among the young bucks she knew. But if he needed distraction, there were alternatives to drinking himself to death. "Why don't you go fishing?" she suggested. Everyone knew of Jack's love of the sport.

"Can't. She was with me there, too."

"From the sounds of it, you'll have to build some new homes."

"Won't I just," he muttered.

"Why don't I have your carriage sent to take you home?"

"We've known each other a long time, haven't we?" Jack said with a contemplative look, ignoring her question.

She nodded with a lift of her brows.

"And I've spent a good deal of money here."

"You've always been one of my best clients."

"So tell me, Lucy, what's happened to me now that I don't want to touch another woman?"

"Do you want the truth, or something politic?"

His eyes went shut and for a moment she thought he'd fallen back to sleep. "I don't know if I want the truth," he quietly said, his long lashes lifting, the directness of his gaze startling.

"I think I'll tell you, anyway, because you're killing yourself and it's a waste."

He held his hand up, palm out. "Don't."

"Go and find her, tell her you love her, marry her, and start a family so you'll have someone to go fishing with, and I won't have to see you in here again."

"That's not very sociable."

"We've had enough sociable moments in the last ten years. Find something better to do."

"Good advice, I'm sure," he drawled.

She reached for the bell pull. "You'll thank me someday."

"Are you throwing me out?"

The rap on the door was almost instantaneous. The burly man who entered the room a moment later looked capable of taking on an armed regiment.

"I'm sending you to your wedding."

The marquis grinned. "Which one?"

"Not the Palmer chit, you can be sure. I don't allow Lord Palmer in here anymore. The man's vulgar to the bone."

"So it seems. And greedy."

"I'll expect a wedding invitation, although you needn't worry I'll come. But the girls will love to see it."

"Slow down, Lucy. I'm not even sure what day it is."

"Sully will tell you on the way home. See that Lord Redvers is escorted inside his house," she directed.

"Don't trust me not to bolt to the next brothel?"

"Tell Lord Redvers's butler that the marquis is thinking about getting married," she said to her bodyguard. She and Jack's butler, Maurice, were well acquainted, after seeing to Jack's safety and comfort for years.

"What makes you think I'll take your advice? I can stand by myself, Sully, thank you very much," he said, brushing away the man's assistance. "And she doesn't want to get married anyway," he added, bowing gracefully to Lucy. "So you may not get your wedding invitation."

"If I was a betting woman, which I'm not, I'd bet a thousand or two on the lady saying yes."

"I have to ask her first."

"So hurry out of here and see that you do."

"Are you my mother?"

"I could have been, if your father wasn't such a brute and a bastard. Luckily his blood doesn't run true in you."

"Thanks for the reassurance. And you would have been a much nicer mother than the one I had."

"Thank you, dear. Now, I'm waiting for that invitation. Send us one of those big ones, bordered in gold."

Jack laughed out loud for the first time in days. "I'll get Maurice on it right away. And I don't need Sully for a duenna. I can find my own way home."

But Lucy nodded at her bodyguard, and as Jack left the room, Sully followed him.

𝒴OU HAVE A VISITOR IN YOUR STUDY, MY LORD," Maurice said after Jack had been duly escorted inside, after Sully had delivered his message and left. "I told him you weren't home, nor did I expect you soon, but he wouldn't leave. When I ascertained his mission, sir, I had a note dispatched to you at Madame Robuchon's. Would you like to bathe and change first? Are congratulations in order?"

"No," the marquis retorted with a dismissive wave of his hand. "Congratulations are not in order. And I must have missed your message in transit. Who is the man and why is he here?" There was no trace of dissipation or drunkenness in Jack's demeanor; he held his liquor well.

"A most fortuitous visitor, sir, having to do with the young Sarah Palmer. He's her dancing master." Maurice's brows rose in expressive insinuation. "You'll find his information extremely enlightening."

"Bring coffee into my study. I'll see him now."

"Excellent, sir. I've also undertaken to summon Mr. Watts, should you need him."

Jack's eyes widened in speculation at the mention of his barrister. "It's that good?"

"I think you'll find his revelations most welcome, my lord."

"What's his name?" Jack asked, already moving down the corridor, Maurice keeping pace at his side.

"A Mr. Vincenzo Dossi."

"And he knows Sarah?"

"Intimately."

A slow smile lifted the corners of Jack's mouth. "You don't say."

"He's most eager to tell you that."

"Why? Money?"

"I believe he's in love, sir."

Jack's laugh echoed down the hall. "Poor sod."

*W*HEN JACK ENTERED HIS STUDY, VINCENZO sprang to his feet, his pose belligerent, his eyes fierce with temper.

"First, thank you for coming," Jack pleasantly said, his humor greatly improved since speaking to Maurice.

"I didn't do it for you."

"I understand. Please, sit down. Maurice is bringing coffee. Tell me what you want." Jack motioned him to a chair near the windows.

"I don't want anything from you." Indignant that

Jack should think him mercenary, Vincenzo glared at him.

"Let me rephrase that. What can I do for you? And you might as well sit. I won't be able to think straight until I have some coffee."

"You can't have her. She's mine," Vincenzo proclaimed, dropping into a chair, a frown drawing his brows together.

"Just for clarity, let's use names. I don't want to misunderstand anything." Anything this important, Jack thought, exhilarated by the promise of deliverance from the Palmers.

"I'm speaking of Sarah Palmer. You can't marry her. She's having my baby."

"You're sure?"

"Positive, although she's intent on having your title for my child."

"I'm extremely grateful for this information. Would you be willing to testify to this in court?"

"Would it stop the marriage?"

"Absolutely."

"Then I'll do it."

Jack's sigh of relief was audible.

"Only because I want to marry her myself."

"How does Sarah feel about that?" Jack diplomatically inquired, relatively certain of the answer.

"She says she loves me." The young man's voice was adamant. "But her family won't hear of—"

Maurice entered at that point with the coffee tray. Once he'd poured coffee for the men and departed, they resumed their conversation.

"You're a dancing master, Maurice tells me," Jack tactfully noted.

"It's a reputable occupation," Vincenzo defiantly asserted. "My family is respectable, and as well born as the Palmers."

"Lord Palmer disagrees, I presume."

"I haven't spoken to him, but according to Sarah her parents require she marry well, and she only has eyes for a marchioness's coronet. She said I could still be her lover after she's married to you."

"Really?" the marquis said with a dangerous calm.

"I told her I would refuse."

"Did your determination alter her intentions?"

Vincenzo's face fell. "I don't know. She very much wants to be rich."

Rapidly calculating the cost of a court case, along with a possible settlement for the Palmers should they prove recalcitrant, Jack decided Vincenzo might offer better value for the money. "Would Sarah be amenable to a marriage offer from you, should you have an income of, say, ten thousand a year?"

Vincenzo almost dropped his coffee cup. Quickly recovering, he breathlessly said, "Pounds, my lord?" Lire were considerably less valuable.

"Yes, pounds. If you were to take her off my hands, I would be grateful, more than grateful—ecstatic."

"I'll ask her, but she's strongly influenced by her father and her aunt, Lady Tallien."

Jack knew exactly how little ten thousand pounds a year would mean to either of them when weighed against his fortune. Other inducements were definitely in order. "If you could convince Sarah of your new wealth, and if she loved you enough, perhaps you could persuade her to elope. As a wedding gift, I'd be happy to give you a villa I own in Florence."

Tears welled into Vincenzo's eyes and Jack understood his emotion, because he felt like crying, too—for joy.

"Your generosity is overwhelming, my lord."

"I'm selfishly motivated. Don't think me magnanimous without good reason."

"I'll ask Sarah right away, when I see her this afternoon."

"I wish you luck."

"Should she refuse me, I'll still testify for you. Just so she doesn't marry you." Vincenzo smiled. "I'm selfish, too."

"Send or bring me word of the outcome. I can have the money for you anytime, should she agree to marry you, and my solicitor will sign over the deed to the villa immediately after you're married."

"I feel like celebrating," Vincenzo said, coming to his feet with a bound and bowing to Jack. "You've given me hope."

"I understand," Jack replied, rising and offering his own polite bow. "I'm feeling as though my burdens might be lighter soon."

"I don't suppose you've ever been in love," Vincenzo noted. "But it makes life worth living." Jubilant at his new prospects, he fairly glowed.

"Or makes you miserable beyond belief."

"You do know. But I won't be miserable anymore. I'm going to take my Sarah away, and my child. God willing."

The Palmers willing, Jack thought as he watched the exuberant young man leave the room. And they were a much more formidable challenge.

⁂

𝒱INCENZO HAD NO SOONER FLOATED OUT OF the room on his buoyant cloud when Maurice appeared in the doorway with news of another visitor.

"Are you home, my lord?" Disapprobation was apparent in his tone and expression.

"I take it I'm not?"

"It's Lady Tallien, my lord. Demanding as usual. Shall I tell her to leave?"

"No, it will give me great pleasure to see her. Vincenzo tells me he's interested in testifying in court."

Maurice allowed himself a small smile. "Very good, sir."

"Show Lady Tallien in, Maurice, but I'd suggest you clear the corridors for her wrathful departure. I doubt she'll be staying long."

𝐼 SEE YOU STILL HAVE THE SAME IMPERTINENT butler," Bella snapped, her indignation high as she sailed into the room. "I would have dismissed him long ago." She spoke as though Maurice was invisible, although he stood only a few feet away.

"That will be all, Maurice," Jack murmured, watching for a moment until his butler shut the door.

"You're out early this morning." Jack had come to his feet when she entered the room, and he deliberately didn't invite her to sit.

"Since you haven't been home for a week, I thought I'd better take advantage of the opportunity." She surveyed his evening clothes with a jaundiced eye. "Do you keep a wardrobe at Madame Robuchon's?"

"Have you been spying on me? And yes, I do. Doesn't your husband?"

"I'm not in the mood to trade insults, Jack. I've been trying to reach you all week with some important information. My notes have gone unanswered."

"Lucy doesn't forward notes for obvious reasons."

"Can she read?" Derision echoed in her words.

"She's well read, actually. The Greek poets are her favorites."

"How fascinating," Bella sarcastically said. "A blue-stocking whore."

"Unlike society belles who tend to be uneducated courtesans with little conversation."

"And you should know."

"Agreed. Now, if you'd get to the point. I haven't slept well the past week, and I'm irritable."

"Are you missing your latest paramour?"

"I wouldn't tell you if I were. Your news, if you please, and then I'll bid you good day."

"You never used to be so ungallant, dear Jack," she softly murmured.

"But then, I find my previous entertainments no longer amusing."

"Perhaps you're ready to marry, then."

"I didn't know you had a sense of humor."

"Of course I do, which reminds me why I've come. We must discuss your marriage with Sarah."

"Why you, Bella, on this mission? Can't the lawyers earn their keep?"

"I've come to exert some, shall we say, gentle pressure on behalf of my niece."

"I see," he calmly replied. "And what if I don't succumb to your pressure?"

"Then I'll have to make it known that you've sired a love child on Lily Darlington. That *on dit* should dash any hopes she might have of an advantageous marriage. And after the spectacle she made with you at her coming-out ball, who wouldn't believe it?"

"That's nasty, Bella. Would you ruin her life so cavalierly?"

She tilted her head with a theatrical flair. "More pertinently, would you? Come, Jack," she coaxed, shifting to a persuasive mien, "you have to marry someday. Sarah will make you as good a wife as any of the other young chits. She's quite enamored of you."

"And not only me, I hear."

He gave her credit for sangfroid; her expression didn't alter. "I can't imagine what you mean."

"I mean she has a lover," he levelly said.

"Impossible!"

"Someone made her pregnant, and it wasn't me."

"She swears it was."

"You never were gullible, Bella, which means you're party to her lie." He softly exhaled. "You didn't actually think you could succeed, did you?"

Her nostrils flared; all her designs and plans were in jeopardy. "I warn you, Lord Palmer will drag you through the courts."

"I don't think so."

"Then you're wrong," she hotly maintained, "because he has every intention of doing so."

"Have you ever heard of a young man named Vincenzo Dossi?"

He saw her eyes go blank and when she spoke her voice was cool. "No, never."

"Then Sarah's been keeping secrets from you. And I

doubt that, with you here in the role of her emissary. Young Vincenzo tells me he's the father of Sarah's child."

"You'll have to prove that."

He almost felt guilty for the degree of pleasure he was feeling. "Vincenzo was just here."

Her eyes opened wide. "I don't believe you!"

"Believe me. And more to the point, he's interested in testifying in court that he's the father of Sarah's child."

"You paid him off," she accused.

"On the contrary, he offered me his services without charge. Apparently he doesn't want his darling to marry me."

"The damned, impudent cur!"

He'd never seen her face turn red; it didn't become her. "I would have fought the charges in court 'til doomsday anyway. Tell Lord Palmer he might consider looking at young Vincenzo for a son-in-law."

"You bastard! You bloody, cold bastard! You knew this all along!"

"Allow me some small enjoyment." He repressed a smile. "I wish you a pleasant day. I know mine will be." Sketching her a bow, he walked from the room, feeling as though the world had suddenly turned roseate. Austin would be pleased to hear that a lengthy court case had been curtailed.

He was pleased to have his life back, and for the first time in a week, he didn't feel like a drink.

He'd bathed and dined before Austin arrived, and he greeted him in the breakfast room where he was looking over a week's worth of mail. He waved out the servants. "Maurice sent you the good news? Coffee?"

"Yes to both." Austin smiled as he sat down. "But fill me in on the details."

After Jack had elaborated on his conversation with Vincenzo, Austin leaned back in his chair. "You've just been saved a great deal of money, even if your offer to Vincenzo requires payment. Symington would have never settled for so little."

"Do we have to be concerned for Vincenzo's safety? Just a thought, after Trevor's machinations the past few days."

"Why don't I have him moved somewhere, in the event he's needed to testify—although Symington knows better than to pursue this further. And there's always the possibility the young man may elope with the Palmer girl."

"I wouldn't bet on that one either way. But let me know what happens. I'm going home to Castlereagh."

"Finished drinking yourself to death?"

Jack grinned. "I wouldn't do that, with Trevor next in line."

"You need a son . . . against that eventuality."

"It's a thought."

"Why not go to Paris and ask her?"

"Because I don't know if I want to. Nor does she, I assure you."

Chapter 19

———————

*T*HE DAY WAS GLORIOUS. THE DURAS HORSES had all won at Longchamps that afternoon, and now friends and family were celebrating the victories in the garden of the Duras mansion. Venus sat alone inside the house, watching through the terrace doors, not in the mood for festivities. She knew all the guests and normally would have been in the midst of the party, as ready as anyone to discuss and dissect the day's races.

But somehow the animated scene failed to entice her, nor had she taken her normal pleasure in the races that day. Even her activities at the hospital the week past—having all the new equipment unpacked and readied for use—hadn't been as gratifying as she'd anticipated. In fact, one of the doctors had questioned whether she might be overly fatigued, because her melancholy was so apparent.

But fatigue didn't account for her lack of interest in the hospital or races; she'd been sleeping more than usual. In fact, she went to bed early and still found herself oversleeping in the mornings—after invariably dreaming of Jack.

Pragmatic by nature, she wouldn't admit to being lovesick. Nor would it have done her any good to be in love with him, had she allowed herself that fantasy. A man like Jack discarded women with unvarying consistency, the notion of love and romance entirely foreign to him. She'd be foolish to imagine the days of their brief acquaintance had altered the habits of a lifetime.

The sight of her mother walking toward the house brought her out of her musing. Her mother had come looking for her, she knew—her withdrawal hadn't gone long unnoticed. Coming to her feet, she glanced into a gilded mirror above the sofa and forced a smile to her lips. The grimace was so constrained, it made her laugh, so when her mother came into the room through the terrace door a second later, she was pleasantly surprised.

"You must be feeling better," Trixi observed.

"I am," Venus lied, wondering if she would be able to continue her dissembling performance until the last guest departed. "I was just coming out to join you."

*L*ATER THAT NIGHT, AFTER THE PARTY WAS over, Pasha and Trixi sat over a last drink on the balcony of their bedroom.

"We have to do something about Venus," Trixi said, unclasping her lapis earrings and setting them on the small metalwork table.

Pasha looked back from the view of Notre Dame in the moonlight, his brandy glass arrested midway to his mouth. "She won't want us to interfere."

Trixi wrinkled her nose, her fingers on the latch of her bracelet. "She's not been the same since she returned from England. I can't stand to see her so sad."

Setting his drink aside, Pasha said, "What do you want me to do?"

"Should you talk to him? Redvers, I mean."

"And say what, darling? He's not a man who makes a habit of falling in love."

"But Venus is so miserable," Trixi murmured with a small sigh. "I just feel as though we should do something."

"Have you talked to her?"

"I've tried, but she always changes the subject. Did you notice how little interest she had in the races? And afterward, I had to search her out to have her come and join us." She ran her bracelet back and forth between her fingers. "It just breaks my heart to see her like this."

"Why don't we ask her if she'd like to travel with us when we go to Morocco. Vincent will be coming along."

"She's always liked him, hasn't she? You're so clever, darling." Her expression cheered. "Morocco might be just what she needs."

"The trip will be a distraction, at least."

"And perhaps by the time we return, she'll have forgotten Redvers."

𝒱ENUS, HOWEVER, WASN'T SO EASILY CONVINCED the next day, when her parents suggested she accompany them on their trip.

"I'm too busy at the hospital," she said.

"We won't be gone for more than two weeks. You've always liked Tangier."

"Merimee needs my company now."

"She and Gaspard are going to be in the country until July."

"I've promised Felicie that I'd go to Trouville next week for a few days."

"We just don't want you to be unhappy, dear," her

mother replied. "Would you like Papa to talk to Lord Redvers?"

"Dear God, no! Mama, don't you dare even think it! I'd be embarrassed beyond words. Papa, promise me you won't," Venus firmly declared.

"Your mother's concerned with your low spirits. We both are."

"Promise, Papa," she insisted, her gaze unflinching. "Right this minute!"

"Of course I won't, if you don't wish it."

"I most assuredly don't wish it!" she exclaimed and then, recovering her composure, added, "I appreciate your concern, but really, I'm perfectly fine. And I *will* go to Trouville for a few days and sit in the sun and sea breezes so you needn't worry that I've become a social misfit. Felicie always has a houseful of guests, and I promise I'll mingle."

Trixi anxiously regarded her husband. "Why don't we wait and go to Morocco later? Your business will wait, won't it, dear?"

"Mama, don't delay your trip because of me. Papa, go, I'm telling you. Check with Felicie if you don't believe me. I'm leaving with her on Thursday."

"This Thursday?"

"In four days, Mama."

Trixi smiled her approval. If Venus was actually going to attend Felicie's house party, perhaps her broken heart was on the mend. And Felicie always had the most interesting array of guests. Venus was sure to have a good time. "Forgive us, dear," her mother murmured. "Your papa and I just worry."

"I appreciate your concern," she reiterated. "But everything's going well. Did you hear—the new wing at the hospital will break ground next month?"

"Congratulations," her father offered. "Did some new donations come in?"

"A sizable one, from the president of the Bourse. He's a friend of Countess Fleury, one of our benefactors."

And a personal friend of Pasha's as well, but her father said only, "That's good news. Ribot has chosen a useful charity."

THE FOLLOWING DAY PASHA AND TRIXI LEFT for Morocco with a small entourage, and three days later, Venus and Felicie made the journey to Trouville. The city, a fashionable seaside destination on the Atlantic, had recently become the summer mecca for the wealthy. Palatial homes lined the shore, their terraces overlooking magnificent ocean views, the balustraded garden parterres open-air settings for the beau monde to see and be seen, to socialize and exchange gossip.

The seashore, too, was filled with fashionable society promenading along the sand, the natural splendors of nature augmented by colorfully garbed ladies in wide skirts and frilled parasols, the men in their straw hats and pale linen suits neutral foil to the feminine birds of paradise. Unlike the English, who actually swam in the cold Atlantic, the French generally viewed it from a safe distance.

Society had moved en masse to a new locale, escaping the heat of the city, intent on amusing itself with summer pastimes. And Venus was determined to enjoy herself.

———

$\mathcal{J}$ACK'S RETREAT AT CASTLEREAGH HAD GIVEN him the seclusion he wanted, but not the peace of mind nor the relief from his powerful memories. Venus pervasively filled his thoughts and dreams. No matter how he tried to distract himself with an unending array of activities, he couldn't dislodge the potent images from his mind. He had resorted to going on long walks deep into his forests, as though he might ease the plaguing memories if he walked far enough or was tired enough. But distance or weariness didn't prove an antidote, and his restless agitation persisted. Even drinking no longer offered him solace; Maurice had given up bringing him his nightly bottle of cognac.

Too long inured to love, Jack never suspected the tumult he was experiencing might be that tender passion. So long had he been without love in his life, his capacity to recognize it had atrophied. And he continued in his fitful disquietude, not knowing how to comfort himself or how to blot Venus from his thoughts.

As he entered the house one evening, weary in body and spirit, he saw a pile of red leather luggage with a ducal seal in the entrance hall, and inwardly groaned. Even someone he cared about as much as Peggy wasn't welcome now. He found it difficult to be polite; he found it impossible to chat about inconsequential events. All conversation seemed meaningless at the moment.

But he knew his godmother's determination, and he also knew she disliked travel. She was here on some mission important enough to warrant a trip from London.

Glancing up at a sound on the stairs, Jack saw Maurice descending to the entrance hall. "Tell me she isn't staying long," Jack commanded.

Maurice came to rest at the base of the staircase. "The duchess didn't say, sir."

"She brought enough luggage for a month."

"The duchess always travels in state. The amount of luggage doesn't necessarily indicate the length of her stay." Maurice motioned for the footmen and gestured toward the pile of luggage. "I just showed her to the Queen's chamber," he explained. "She always enjoys sleeping in Queen Elizabeth's bed. I mentioned you were out and would see her at dinner."

"I've still time then to muster my defenses."

"The duchess often does have an agenda."

"*Always*, Maurice," Jack muttered. "I suppose the railroads were dismal as usual."

"She'll no doubt entertain you at dinner with her complaints. The list was lengthy even during our brief progress upstairs. I took the liberty to set dinner back a half hour, since I wasn't sure when you'd return."

"Thank you, Maurice. You take excellent care of me."

"We try, sir."

AT DINNER, PEGGY WAS IN GOOD SPIRITS, AND more polite than usual as demonstrated by her unusual reserve in discussing the rail service. Her complaints were moderate and tactfully expressed. The weather had been adequate; her maid, Molly, hadn't forgotten anything; and they'd arrived on schedule. "What a lovely new station you have at Castlereagh," Peggy pleasantly finished, increasing Jack's sense of alarm.

"Thank you," he warily replied.

"You're very welcome." Her tone was bland and affable as though their polite exchange was perfectly normal. "I brought you good news. Sarah Palmer eloped, it seems, with her dancing master." She paused at the lack of response. "You know."

"I know. I'm paying for it." His gaze narrowed. "You didn't travel all this distance to tell me some bit of gossip." Jack waved away the footmen about to serve them. His appetite would be ruined if he was forced to wait throughout dinner for the guillotine blade to fall. "Tell me why you're here, Peggy," he said, "and then we can eat in peace."

"Maurice tells me you've been taking long walks."

"Is that a problem?"

"It's so unlike you, dear."

"I can't see that it matters if I walk."

"And you're no longer drinking." Her tone was apprehensive.

"That worries you?"

"It's hardly like you. Apparently, you're monkish, too. I'll admit, that worries me more than anything."

"I'm sorry my deviation from vice has alarmed you," he sardonically murmured.

"Some say you're ill."

"Then *some* are wrong. I'm perfectly healthy."

"You miss her, don't you?"

"Am I not allowed those feelings?"

"Not with such brooding despondency and such a lack of insight. I swear, Jack," she tartly said, no longer able to contain her exasperation, "do I have to do everything?"

"I think you've done more than enough already," he

coolly replied. "My life is miserable because of your interference."

Ignoring his chastisement, the duchess declared, "Venus is in Trouville."

"How do you know?" His brows turned down in a scowl. "Don't tell me you're writing to her?"

"No, I have friends in Paris. She left for the seashore a week ago."

He pursed his lips, annoyed at her intrusiveness. "I hope she's enjoying herself," he grimly said.

"She's not, according to acquaintances in Trouville."

"If you have detectives following her, Peggy, I'll disown you for good."

"Don't be silly, darling. Why do I need detectives when I have so many friends and the telegraph works perfectly well? By the way, I sent word to have your yacht readied."

"Damnit, you've gone too far this time! I don't *want* you meddling in my life!" He pushed his chair back and came to his feet in a furious surge. A curt nod to the servants sent them scurrying from the room, and when he swung back to face her, his eyes were dark with rage. "You've really overstepped your bounds this time, damnit! Don't you think if I wanted her, I'd go there myself? Don't—"

"Then go," Peggy impatiently snapped. "It's as plain as the tail on a dog why you're moping like a damned schoolboy. And if no one else will tell you the reason why, I will."

"And you know why," he said, his voice utterly cold.

"You love her, you dolt! Why do you think you're more despondent after a month? Why do you shun society and your acquaintances and never even look at a woman anymore? Good God, Jack, only melancholy poets take long walks every day."

"You know that, too." Each word was icy.

"At my age, dear, I've seen it all," she patiently said. "Venus is unhappy at Trouville. You're unhappy here. Why not go to France and at least talk to her? What are you protecting?"

"My freedom."

"Are you enjoying it?"

He walked away, his footsteps echoing in the large room, his moody withdrawal taking him to the windows overlooking the river valley. The moon was full tonight, the nocturnal scene washed in silver, the river a gleaming ribbon meandering through the landscape. As far as the eye could see was his, he thought, and farther still— ten thousand acres on this estate alone.

What good will it do you, a small voice asked, if you're alone? And his loneliness struck him like a blow. The silence of the room surrounded him, his isolation chilling, as his childhood had been—in houses like this, that were never home.

When he turned around, Peggy appeared diminutive at the end of the long mahogany table halfway down the room. She'd always been the only support in his life, the only person he could count on, and for all her meddling, he knew her love for him was unconditional.

An irrepressible hope began rising in his consciousness as he walked back, a tentative smile lifted the corners of his mouth. "I suppose you'll be insufferable if I take your advice and sail to Trouville?"

"Gratified, at least," she calmly replied. "I want you to be happy, and you were with her."

"I'm not guaranteeing anything," he said. "She might

turn me down. Unlike society misses motivated solely by the search for a husband, Venus has a full and active life."

The duchess's eyes sparkled. "I'll lay you a small wager on her answer."

"You'd bet on anything, wouldn't you?"

"Only on sure things. Let me give you a wedding reception once you're back in London."

"She hasn't accepted yet."

"Darling boy, after all your years of charming women, surely when it really matters, you can put all that practice to good use."

His smile reflected a genuine pleasure. "When you put it that way, I'll have to see what I can do."

"There now. It's finally settled. Your captain expects you tomorrow afternoon. May we eat now? I'm famished. The food Molly brought along for our train ride was inadequate, and the smoke and noise are always dreadful for one's digestion, not to mention the terrible delays between London and Oxford that always annoy me. Did I tell you about the time Molly and I were put on the wrong train at—"

Calling his staff back, Jack ordered dinner be served, and between bites and courses he was regaled with the failures and delinquencies of the British rail system.

The Duchess of Groveland, her mission accomplished, was back in form.

Chapter 20

⟨⟨⟨⟨⟨⟩⟩⟩⟩⟩

THE MARQUIS DOCKED IN TROUVILLE AT eight. The choppy seas had caused some delay, but he found lodgings quickly and after a rapid bath and change of clothing, he walked down the promenade to the Comtesse de Casse's home. He remembered her from a Mardi Gras party last year; she was a young woman of affability and charm, like so many French hostesses.

An engagement ring rested in his coat pocket, purchased in London on his way through to Dover, and he'd silently rehearsed a number of different proposals during his journey. But his heart was beating wildly— whether from fear of rejection or from fear of acceptance, he wasn't quite sure. Despite the seeming logic of Peggy's arguments at Castlereagh yesterday, this was suddenly very real. He was taking that final irrevocable step.

And if Venus said yes, he would be shackled for life. The hackneyed phrase brought him to a standstill on the promenade, the flow of strollers passing around him while he gazed out to sea as if looking for an answer in the rolling waves. But no mythic creature rose from the water with words of wisdom, and his ingrained fear slowly gave way to reason. The weeks without Venus had been cheerless. He was here because his happiness had disappeared the day she left, and he wanted her back.

When he arrived at the comtesse's fanciful baroque mansion, he was momentarily astonished at the sizable dinner party in progress. Society was generally more informal at the shore, entertainments featuring casualness over protocol. But apparently, some Russian ambassador was the guest of honor, he was informed by the comtesse's butler, and formal ceremony was required, along with two hundred guests.

He had a message sent in with a servant, but instead of Venus appearing, the comtesse glided from the dining room with swaying skirts and her arms opened wide. After wrapping him in a fragrant embrace, she invited him to join them. "Venus is still dressing, but she'll be down shortly," the comtesse added. "What a pleasant surprise for her."

"I'd prefer talking to Venus first, if you don't mind."

"Heavens, no. The ambassador is still offering toasts—you know the Russians and their drinking. Dinner won't be served for some time yet. But do join us."

His answer was polite but evasive, the charming phrases he uttered so familiar after years of avoiding dinner parties that they rolled off his tongue with ease.

"I don't intend to let you slip away so easily, Lord Redvers," the comtesse observed, recognizing evasion when she heard it. "I'm thinking we might see Venus smile again now that you're here. I understand you're to blame for her blue mood." She playfully tapped his cheek with her fan. "Shame on you."

"Then I must apologize to her, if you'll tell me where she is."

"Now, now, Lord Redvers. She's still dressing."

"I don't care."

"You'll barge in?" Her voice was teasing.

"I promise to knock first. Now, if you'll be kind enough to indicate her room, it will save me the trouble of opening every door upstairs."

"My goodness, darling, you *are* determined." She smiled a knowing smile. Before her stood a man whose heart was captured. "She's in the north rooms, facing the sea. Good luck, my lord."

He'd begun to walk away the moment she'd given him the directions, and he glanced back at her last words.

"Remember to tell her how much you love her before you ask. Women adore a devoted lover."

He smiled. "Is it so obvious?"

"Quite, Lord Redvers. Do come down later and we'll help you celebrate."

A SENSE OF SITUATION WAS ALL-POWERFUL AS he climbed the stairs and turned down the corridor. Did every man feel this agitation before proposing—caught in limbo between hope and fear? Sure and yet unsure when actually contemplating a future beyond tomorrow? He inhaled deeply, forcibly suppressed his indecision, reminded himself that genuine, true feeling was at the heart of his journey, and flexing his fingers as though readying himself for combat, strode forward.

*H*OW COULD SHE POSSIBLY ENDURE ANOTHER dinner party? Venus thought. How could she smile for an entire evening and pretend to be listening to conversations when she didn't care what anyone had to say? How many endless luncheons and dinners and dances had she attended in the days of her sojourn in Trouville without feeling any pleasure whatsoever? Why couldn't she feel the same exhilaration as others did in the endless round of summer activities—tennis, croquet, sailing, teas, and musicales?

This evening, she'd shamelessly lied, pleading a lame horse to explain her tardy arrival at Felicie's dinner party—in truth, she'd been desperately wishing she could stay away forever. She'd lingered on the dunes until late, her mount grazing on the sea grasses while she'd looked across the Channel and wondered what Jack was doing. Struggling with jealousy and longing, she tried not to think of his return to his former way of life, or of the women who were assuaging his desires. She attempted instead to focus on the positive events in her life, the charity work that had always given meaning and purpose to her life. But her mind would treacherously return to thoughts of Jack, to memories of their days together, and she could no more stop the poignant recall than she could hold back the tides.

When the sun had almost disappeared, she first noticed the chill of evening overcoming her. And she'd hurried back, knowing she was going to be late for Felicie's party.

Now, bathed and adorned for the evening, she'd dismissed her maid, finding it impossible to actually go downstairs and smile all evening. Sitting at the window, her gaze unfocused on the crashing surf, she contemplated possible ways to avoid the festivities.

Could she plead a headache, or would Felicie disregard such feeble resistance? What type of illness could suddenly and believably appear? Would a sprained ankle suffice?

A knock on the door interrupted her hopes for deliverance, and she grimaced before she called out, "I'll be right down."

At the sound of the door opening, she swiveled around, ready to apologize for not appearing sooner. But the words died in her throat.

Coming into the room, Jack shut the door. Dressed for the evening, he looked as he had so many times before: tall, powerful, darkly handsome, his allure so potent she could feel the familiar ache in her heart.

"How did you find me?"

His smile was the one she remembered so well. "Peggy—who else."

"She made you come?" She shouldn't be so abrasive. A sensible woman would be more gracious.

"She can't make me do anything."

Her pulse rate shifted, began to beat in a wild tattoo. "So you decided to visit Trouville on your own?" Her governesses would have chided her for her lack of charm.

"Only when I heard you were here. You look wonderful. Unfashionably tanned and glowing. I've really missed you," he softly added.

"I've thought about you rather a lot, too."

"Good because I'm—" He paused, took a deep breath, a rueful smile quirking his mouth. "I planned a dozen different ways to say this on my way across the

Channel, but at the moment, all the fine phrases escape me. So I'll just ask." He blew out his breath. "Will you marry me?"

"You sound uncertain."

"I'm not even sure of my name right now. My brain seems to have ceased functioning. But you look even better than I remembered, and that's saying a lot. I'm also feeling happy for the first time in weeks"—his grin had a small-boy innocence to it—"so say yes."

"It's very tempting . . ."

His expression changed: his eyes took on a shuttered look. "I told Peggy you'd say no."

"I'm not saying no."

He hadn't moved from the door. "You're not saying yes."

"I'm concerned about—" She hesitated.

His brows rose.

"Your past . . . your reputation, your entire way of life."

"I'm different now. You made me different. Ask Peggy. She was the one who insisted I come, because she was worried about my hermit's life."

"I knew she made you come."

"No." The shake of his head was minute. "She could never make me do something I didn't want to do. Her concern was mainly with my monkish ways."

"Monkish?" The word held a world of promise, and the urge to smile bubbled up inside her.

"Absolutely monkish. And you?" He quickly held up his hand. "Forgive me. It's not an issue."

She quirked one brow. "You don't mind if I've slept with someone?"

"Of course I do, but *your* past isn't in controversy."

He suppressed a smile. "Although I'd like to call out any man who's touched you."

"At the risk of augmenting your ego, you've spoiled me for other men."

He abruptly pushed away from the door, moving toward her as though her words had given him the assurance he needed. Reaching her, he took her hands in his and drew her to her feet. "Then marry me, because I need you to make my life complete. I long for you every minute of the day and dream of you at night. I'm thinking that must be love," he said, his gypsy eyes audacious.

"What if it isn't?" He sounded too cavalier and charming. "I'm not sure either of us knows what we're doing."

"I do."

"Easy to say. Neither of us has ever been in love before. Think of the loss of independence."

"It's terrifying. I know. I drank several cases of brandy contemplating that loss of freedom. But, look, we're happy together and miserable apart. It seems pretty simple to me."

"I'm not so sure it will be simple. I remember you saying once, 'I'm going to need some ground rules.' And I do now."

"Such as?"

"Exclusivity. You can't look at another woman. I won't have a marriage like—" she pulled her hand from his and gestured vaguely "—so many others."

"Nor will I." He recaptured her hand, possessive and wanting the comforting touch of her. "You can't flirt with other men. I can't guarantee my sanity should you."

"Are we immature and juvenile? Others seem to be

blasé about fidelity." She understood the rules of a society where nothing mattered but appearances.

"I'm not a tolerant man," he softly declared.

"Nor would I be blasé about the Bellas of your world," she firmly countered.

"Then we're agreed," he said. "Set a date—soon."

Her smile was teasing, her gaze joyful. "What if I want a large wedding?"

"Then we'll have a large wedding—soon."

"That's not such an easy task."

"I'm sure Maurice can help. And Peggy, of course. She can move mountains if necessary. How does next week sound?"

"Impossible!" She leaned back a little so she could better gauge his seriousness. "My parents are in Morocco."

"We'll bring them home."

He *was* serious. "There are other complications, too, darling, including our schedules. Where will we live?"

"Don't keep bringing up trivialities," he calmly said. "Adjusting our schedules isn't an issue. Nothing's an issue as long as you marry me. I'm going to have much more time now that I've given up vice. So I'm completely at your disposal."

She didn't even know if she should quibble anymore after his gracious recanting of his previous amusements, but she really did have a certain inflexibility in her schedule. "I'm going to have to spend at least two weeks each month in Paris," she stated.

He shrugged. "It shouldn't be a problem. How do you feel about children? Austin tells me I should think about an heir, with Trevor next in line."

Startled, she looked at him in mild bewilderment. "That sounds slightly pragmatic."

"Sorry. I haven't gotten used to the idea of babies yet."

"I, on the other hand, often see babies born at the hospital."

"Really," he said, clearly uneasy with the subject.

"Although I've never considered a child of my own."

"If you'd rather not," he quickly interjected.

She gently squeezed his fingers. "I'd like to very much."

"Really?" he said again in an altogether different tone. "Are you sure?"

"As sure as I am that I love you."

"I like the sound of that," he murmured, his voice husky and low.

She turned her ear to him in teasing response.

"I love you more."

"Then everything's perfect."

"Greedy minx. You always want more."

"Surely not a surprise to you."

"On the contrary, it's one of my greatest pleasures."

"Happy?" she whispered.

He nodded, suddenly struck with the full glory of unalloyed joy. "I never knew."

"Nor did I, not about this kind of bliss. Thank you for coming."

"Thank Peggy."

"I will. She loves you, too."

"I'm a very lucky man."

And he was. Even those most cynical at first over the marriage of the notorious Lord Redvers had to agree.

He was indeed lucky in love.

NOTES

1. See page 1. Exhibitions in themselves were nothing new. Trade fairs had been held in Europe for centuries; Paris had been presenting an Industrial Exhibition every five years since the early nineteenth century; Ireland had been displaying Irish agriculture, arts, and manufactures every third year since 1829; and England had held its first exhibition of Art Manufactures in 1847, with successive ones in 1848 and 1849. But the Great Exhibition of 1851 was the first international rather than national exhibition.

As Henry Cole notes with typical Victorian superlative and grandiosity, "The history of the world, I venture to say, records no event comparable in its promotion of human industry, with that of the Great Exhibition of the Works of Industry of all Nations in 1851. A great people invited all civilized nations to a festival, to bring into comparison the works of human skill." (Gibbs-Smith, Charles. *The Great Exhibition of 1851.*)

The organization of this giant enterprise, the inclusion of every important type of manufacture, its appeal to all classes, the stimulation of trade, the creation of a new excursion style of travel, the educational benefit, and not least the profit of 186,000 pounds when the exhibition was over made it a historic achievement.

The building, entirely of glass over an iron framework,

enclosed a space of eighteen acres. It was 1,848 feet long and 456 feet wide; the height of the nave was 63 feet, the transept 108 feet—tall enough to cover the three full-grown elm trees that had been left to grow inside. On opening day, May 1, 1851, half a million people waited in Hyde Park to see the Queen officially open the exhibition. To preserve order on the occasion, only season ticket holders were admitted to the building. Twenty-five thousand men and women packed the aisles and galleries of the Crystal Palace. In the words of *The Times* the next day: "There was yesterday witnessed a sight the like of which has never happened before and which in the nature of things can never be repeated. They who were so fortunate as to see it hardly knew what most to admire, or in what form to clothe the sense of wonder and even of mystery which struggled within them. The edifice, the treasures of art collected therein, the assemblage and the solemnity of the occasion, all conspired to suggest something even more than sense could scan, or imagination attain." The article goes on with the sublime self-glorification that placed an Englishman in the center of the universe: ". . . Some were most reminded of that day when all ages and climes shall be gathered round the Throne of their Maker; there was so much that seemed accidental, and yet had a meaning, that no one could be content with simply what he saw."

In this magnificent Crystal Palace that awed on countless levels, the exhibitors numbered 13,937 (British Isles and Empire 7,381; foreign 6,556). There were over 100,000 exhibits. In the period the exhibition was open to the public, May 1 to October 11, 1851, the total number of visitors was 6,039,195 with the average daily attendance 42,831. The building was taken down during the summer of 1852

and rebuilt in a modified form at Sydenham, where it remained until it burnt to the ground on November 30,
1936.

2. See page 20. In 1851, dueling was illegal in both
France and England, although duels often took place.
Should a participant not be of lofty enough social status,
he would more likely find himself on trial for murder if his
opponent died. In 1808, for instance, a Major Campbell
was hanged for killing a Captain Boyd over an argument
concerning the correct way of giving a command. At the
time a writer observed that the catastrophe would leave a
salutary lesson to mankind.

However, the following year, Lord Castlereagh, the Secretary of War, sent a challenge to Canning, the Secretary
of State for Foreign Affairs, and a duel was fought at Put-
ney Heath. Canning was wounded and the encounter ter-
minated. The Duke of Wellington and the Earl of
Winchelsea fought a duel in 1829. Another notable duel
was between the Earl of Cardigan and Captain Tuckett in
1840, and the impunity with which Cardigan and the two
seconds flouted the law resulted in highly critical public
opinion concerning the institution of dueling. Two more
well-known fatal duels in 1841 and 1843 led to the forma-
tion of the Anti-Dueling Association, and the Queen and
her government became involved. The chief result was
publication by the War Office of articles forbidding dueling, and judges and juries became more determined to con-
vict duelists of murder.

Nevertheless, the practice continued. Even the Prince
of Wales was involved in the illegal activity, offering a
challenge to Lord Randolph Churchill in 1876 over the
Aylesford Scandal, asking him to name his seconds and

meet him with pistols at some convenient spot in France. Duelists often found it prudent to go abroad after 1844 to fight their duels, or at least flee to the continent for a time until the scandal subsided. Not until the close of the nineteenth century did dueling virtually disappear from the cultural scene.

3. See page 23. Considerable ambiguity exists over the wearing of drawers in the nineteenth century. Although drawers were for sale as indicated by ads in ladies' publications early in the century, their use was not universal until much later. One of my favorite observations is that of King Victor Emmanuel visiting the court of Napoleon III in 1855—at the height of the wide-skirted caged crinoline fashions. Following a number of the Empress's ladies-in-waiting up a flight of stairs, he had a clear view of their bottoms under the tipped cages of their skirts. And he remarked that he was delighted to see the gates of paradise were always open. First-person accounts are always enlightening in terms of dating fashion. In *The History of Underclothes* by C. Willett and Phillis Cunnington, in the chapter covering 1857–66, the authors mention, "If drawers are worn they should be trimmed with frills or insertion"; the "if" is indicative of their irregular use. In general, too, the French were less prudish and constrained about their bodies than the English, so I'm assuming Venus Duras would be sans drawers at this time.

4. See page 27. The condom as a birth control device emerged in wide usage only after the vulcanization of rubber in 1844.

5. See page 187. The Derby run on Wednesday, May 21, 1851, is wonderfully described in the May 24, 1851,

issue of the *Illustrated London News*. It's fascinating to see and feel and read the same edition of the magazine that contemporaries of the event held in their hands. The pages are yellowed, the engraved illustrations fabulously detailed and numerous, the atmosphere and sense of place striking. The events in my story mirror those that actually took place on that day so long ago, in terms of weather, horses, spectators, and the actual race.

6. See page 192. There really was a man who won seventy thousand pounds on the Derby race that year, the equivalent today of 4,200,000 U.S. dollars. According to the *Illustrated London News*, he was Sir Joseph Hawley, owner of Teddington, the actual winner of the Derby. Teddington was a chestnut horse, bred in 1848 by Mr. Tomlinson. His sire was Orlando, winner of the Derby in 1844. The engraving in the *Illustrated London News* portrays a lean, beautiful, gleaming thoroughbred with his jockey up.

ABOUT THE AUTHOR

SUSAN JOHNSON, award-winning author of nationally bestselling novels, lives in the country near North Branch, Minnesota. A former art historian, she considers the life of a writer the best of all possible worlds.

Researching her novels takes her to past and distant places, and bringing characters to life allows her imagination full rein, while the creative process offers occasional fascinating glimpses into the complicated machinery of the mind.

But perhaps most important . . . writing stories is fun.

Look for Susan Johnson's
new historical romance
TEMPORARY MISTRESS
Available in fall 2000

Fleeing from relatives who would force marriage on her,
heiress Isabella Leslie seeks refuge in an infamous London brothel. There she decides on a shocking course of
action—to preserve her independence, she would shred
her reputation to tatters so no suitor would ever dare
offer for her hand. And only one man can help her with
the deed: Dermott Ramsay, earl of Bathurst, London's
most accomplished libertine.

Turn the page for a sneak peek.

He was never nervous. It was impossible that he could be nervous. Good God, where was his valet when he needed him? This cravat was impossibly wrong. "Charles!" he shouted. "Dammit, what were you thinking when you tied this thing!"

"Sorry, my lord," Charles apologized, coming back into the dressing room at a run, six fresh cravats draped over his arm. "I'm sure the next one will be tied to your satisfaction."

But it wasn't, of course, because nothing at the moment was completely satisfying, and once Dermott was dressed to an acceptable degree of correctness, Charles disappeared downstairs to regale the servants with a detailed account of the earl's toilette, down to his three changes of evening coat and the crushing of the offending cravats under his heel.

"She must be somethin' real special," a footman said. "He ain't never had no—"

"Hasn't ever," the housekeeper corrected.

"Ain't never," the footman repeated, wrinkling his nose at the housekeeper who considered herself the superior person belowstairs, "had no light o' love to Bathurst House. And what with the cook cooking for hours now and the wine steward ordered to serve only the very best—"

"And the flowers," the upstairs maid declared with feeling. "I've never seen so many flowers."

"I'd say she's a Venus for sure," another footman maintained. "Or like that Helen of Troy whose face launched a thousand ships, they say."

"Well, we'll soon see, will we not," the butler, Pomeroy, intoned in his haughty basso. Rising to his feet, he surveyed his staff with a piercing gaze. "Places everyone," he ordered. "She's due to arrive in fifteen minutes." After a meticulous straightening of his shirt cuffs, he turned from the table and moved to the stairs that would bring him into position in the entrance hall.

Dermott stood at the window of the north drawing room, his third glass of brandy in his hand, his gaze on the street below, feeling as though he were going into battle. His pulse was racing, his nerves were on alert; the tension in his shoulders strained the superfine fabric to a degree that would dismay his tailor. Draining the glass of liquor, he felt the heat flow down his throat with relief; at least one familiar sensation struck his brain when all else was chaos. The clock chimed the hour and he glanced at the bronzed winged victory with a timepiece between her feet. Where the hell was Miss Leslie? It was seven.

Had she changed her mind? Had Molly changed it for her? Had he thrown his entire establishment into turmoil for nothing? The scent of lilies suddenly overcame him and glancing about the room, he saw a great number of very large arrangements. Like a funeral, he thought. "Shelby!" he bellowed.

His secretary came round the corner so instantly he must have been standing outside the door. "Have the maids take some of these damnable flowers away," Dermott barked. "They smell."

"Yes, sir. Would you like to greet your guest in some other room? The scent may linger even if the vases are removed."

At Shelby's propitiating tone, Dermott realized how

rude he'd been. "Forgive me, Shelby. You can see how out of practice I've become at paying court to a lady. And no, this room is fine. Here, you take one of these," he said, handing his secretary a large vase of flowers. "And I'll take another and that will be sufficient to make this room look less like—"

"A funeral?"

"Exactly."

The two men were at the top of the staircase, about to descend to the entrance hall and dispose of their vases when the front door opened and Isabella stepped into the grand marble entrance hall.

Dermott swore at the bad timing.

She looked up.

The butler looked up as well and, wide-eyed, surveyed his employer, who stood with a large vase of lilies in his hand.

"Are those for me?" Isabella sweetly inquired.

Dermott grinned. "If you want 'em. Although I warn you, they smell," he said, moving down the stairs.

"I'd be surprised if they didn't. Don't you like lilies?"

"Not this many." Reaching the bottom of the stairs, he offered them to her with a bow. "For your pleasure, my lady."

"One of many tonight, I presume." Her warm gaze met his over the flowers.

"Your wish is my command," he murmured.

"What a charming concept. I do look forward to the evening."

"As do I, Miss Leslie." He handed the vase to Pomeroy and reached for the ties on her cloak, a possessive gesture, symbolic perhaps of the fact that he was the taker and she the takee. Standing very close as he untied the velvet ribbon, he said so low the words were for her alone, "I've waited a long time."

"I pray you won't be disappointed." But her tone was playful rather than conciliatory and his gaze rose from the tangled knot.

"No chance of that," he whispered. Slipping the bow open, he slowly undraped the cloak from her shoulders as though he were unwrapping a personal gift.

The young footmen audibly gasped, but none received a reproach from their superiors, for all eyes were trained on the young lady. Isabella's white lace gown was so sheer, her body was only partially concealed. The risqué décolletage appeared more in the nature of a tenuous support for the plump mounds of her breasts, and the entire garment was held in place with two small silver shoulder bows. The imminent threat of gravity added a delicious element of suspense to the ensemble.

"My compliments, Miss Leslie," Dermott murmured. "You have taken all our breath away."

"As do you, my lord. You quite turn my head." He looked large and powerful dressed in perfectly tailored black superfines, his rangy form shown to advantage, his linen crisp and white, gleaming in the candlelight, the diamond at his throat so large it could only have come from India.

"Might I offer you a glass of champagne?" he asked as heat fairly crackled in the air.

"That would be very nice," she purred. "For now . . ."

He acknowledged the delectable words with an appreciative smile and offered his arm. "Miss Leslie."

"My lord Bathurst." Dipping a small curtsy, she placed her hand on his wrist and they both felt the jolt.

Inhaling deeply, Dermott wondered how in the world

he was going to repress his carnal urges when the little minx was deliberately leaning into him so her breasts were almost spilling out of her gown. Dinner, he thought. "Dinner," he said to Pomeroy. "We'll have dinner now."

"Now, my lord?" The schedule had been specific. Champagne and brandy first, then dinner at nine.

"Now."

"Yes, my lord." Pomeroy escorted them to the dining room, knowing the chef was going to tear his hair out with dinner pushed up two hours. On the other hand, he reflected, the earl and his lady seemed oblivious to all but each other. There was a good possibility they wouldn't notice what they were eating.

The dining room positively gleamed, Isabella thought as they entered the large chamber—the cherry wood walls, the massive silver plate on the sideboard and table, the crystal goblets marching in a row beside the two services on the mahogany table, the gilt frames on the paintings adorning the walls, the twin chandeliers of Russian crystal that dripped from the high-coffered ceiling. She felt as though she'd entered a shining Aladdin's cave.

"Do you always eat in such splendor?" she asked, slightly in awe of such magnificence.

It took him a moment to answer because he rarely ate at home and when he did, he generally shared a tray with Shelby in his study. "Actually, no." In fact, he couldn't remember when last he'd eaten in this room. "Would you rather have dinner somewhere else?"

In bed with you, she thought, still trembling from his touch, but it wouldn't do to be so forward. She'd been told men never liked women to give orders. "This is very nice. Really."

"Would you like a glass of champagne?" he asked because he badly needed a drink.

"Oh, I would very much. Thank you."

With a nod, he indicated Pomeroy to serve them. "The room seems warm or I'd suggest we sit by the fire. Although you're probably not warm," he added with a smile, surveying her scantily dressed form.

"Actually, I am. Dreadfully warm—I mean, the *room* is indeed warm."

Her stammering was charming. "So we'll sit away from the fire."

"Yes, please, I'd like that."

Suddenly she seemed very young, very different from the seductive minx in the entrance hall, and he felt an odd disquiet. "How old are you?"

"Twenty-two."

His sigh of relief brought a smile to her face.

"I didn't realize age mattered."

"It's bad enough— Just set the tray down, Pomeroy. We'll serve ourselves." As the butler walked away, Dermott continued. "It's bad enough you're a virgin. I'm not, however, about to bed some adolescent." A grin broke across his face. "Although you definitely don't have the look of a child, Miss Leslie. And I mean it in the most complimentary way." He handed Isabella a stemmed goblet of champagne.

"Molly thought you'd like the gown," Isabella said, a half-smile lifting the corners of her mouth. "Do I look sufficiently seductive?"

"In that dress? Completely, wholly, exuberantly. And white-interesting," he murmured over the rim of his glass.

"A metaphor, I believe." Her blue eyes sparkled. "Molly's idea again."

"She sets the stage well."

"I am also well trained, sir," she sportively noted. "Although not to your standards perhaps. Your reputation is formidable."

He slid lower in his chair, feeling faintly disgruntled at the reminder of their disparate lives. "I wish you weren't a virgin."

"I could relinquish my virginity to someone else first if you like."

"No," he snapped.

"You could watch," she suggested, innuendo in her tone.

"Not likely," he growled.

"Or we could get this over with as quickly as possible."

"You have a sense of humor, Miss Leslie."

"Molly says I'm allowed to be as selfish as I wish because you can take care of yourself."

"Meaning?" he asked, grinning.

"Meaning you are an accomplished libertine."

"I can't argue with you there."

"Why?"

"Why?" he repeated.

"Why do you do it?"

What a startling question. "Why not?"

"You engage in debauch without thinking?"

He shrugged. "Mostly."

"I've thought quite a deal about tonight."

"In your case, I have too. Don't look so surprised. I don't as a rule"—he smiled—"engage in debauch with virgins. So you see, tonight is different."

"How different?"

One dark brow rose as amusement flared in his eyes. "Is this a catechism?"

"Do you know?" She wanted her question answered.

"As a matter of fact, I don't. I don't have the vaguest notion why you fascinate me."

"I fascinate you?"

He shrugged again. "It seems so."

"Because of this?" She swept a hand over her gown.

"Definitely a factor," he said with a boyish grin. "I confess your good looks are a most potent lure for me."

"Then we can both be accused of being shallow," he sportively affirmed. Although he knew better. He'd slept with scores of great beauties and never felt what he felt right now.

"Do you actually want to eat?" she asked all of a sudden.

His heart missed a beat. "You decide," he carefully replied.

"I'd rather not eat right now. I'm too excited."

He set his glass down, slid upright in his chair and gazed at her with a look that was faintly quizzical and wholly carnal. "What would you like to do instead?"

She bit her lip, debating how to ask and then in a rush, said, "May I see your bedroom?"

His pulse rate leaped, but he schooled his expression to a well-bred courtesy. "Certainly," he said, coming to his feet.

"If you don't think me too forward."

"It's not a problem." Offering her his hand, he drew her up from the chair.

"I wish I could be calm. I'm so nervous."

Her hand was small and warm in his and it took effort to maintain his composure. "Should I bring a bottle of champagne with us?" He smiled. "For your nerves."

"Maybe you should, although I already had some wine at Molly's before I left—to calm myself—and I'm not sure when I'll get tipsy."

"You may get tipsy if you like," he genially offered, picking up the bottle from the iced container. "I've always found the world looks considerably better after a bottle or so."

As they stepped into the hall, Pomeroy materialized from the shadows.

"Postpone dinner," Dermott instructed. "I'll ring when we're ready."

"Very good, sir." The chef was going to burst into tears.

"I wonder if I might be a *little* hungry," Isabella apologetically said. The aromas of dinner were wafting up the dumbwaiter in the hall, enticing her.

"Something light?" Dermott suggested.

"That would be wonderful. I think I smell chicken."

"A little of everything," Dermott ordered.

"Now, sir?"

Dermott looked at Isabella, then back at Pomeroy. "Now," he said.

"I do apologize," Isabella remarked as they began ascending the stairs.

"No need. Pomeroy will take care of it. That's what he does."

"Our household was rather small compared to yours. And not so formal. I confess, I'm quite intimidated."

"By Pomeroy? Don't give it another thought. If you're hungry, you can eat. It's as simple as that. What else do they have to do? Hell, I'm hardly ever home."

"Don't you like your home?"

He glanced around the cavernous staircase and entrance hall, at the multitude of ancestors staring down on them from the walls, and the cupola fifty feet above them. "I suppose I do. Never thought about it."

"And yet you're never home."

"Too quiet."

"You require stimulation?"

He laughed. "You might say that, darling. Come, this way." Tugging on her hand, he led her down the corridor toward a huge painting of a man in Elizabethan dress with a hunting dog.

He'd called her darling. The word strummed through her brain, warming her senses even while she told herself to discount charming words from charming men.

He stopped before two massive carved doors just short of the huge painting and tucking the champagne bottle under his arm, opened the door. "Welcome to my wing, Miss Leslie," he said, ushering her into an enormous drawing room.

"This can't be your bedroom."

He nodded toward another set of double doors. "It's in there. The earls of Bathurst apparently used this room for—" He grinned. "I haven't the foggiest idea. Come, I'll show you my bedroom. It's built on a slightly more intimate scale."

Only slightly, she realized as he opened the doors. The idea of intimacy must have been in terms of royal levees. The bed was mounted on a dais, crowned with a gilt coronet draped in crimson brocade. Enormous gilt chairs covered in a similar brocade were placed along the walls, as though courtiers had watched their master sleep. Windows ten feet high were draped in swags and tassels and more of the crimson brocade. A large desk sat in the middle of a Persian carpet off to one side. Obviously a working desk; papers were strewn over its surface. The ceiling must have been twenty feet high, the mural adorning it that of a bacchanal.

"Do you actually sleep here?"

"Cozy, isn't it?"

"For two hundred people maybe."

"Let me show you my dressing room." Taking her hand again, he led her across the carpet, custom woven for the dimensions of the room, and opened a normal-size door into a normal-size room.

His stamp was revealed on every detail of the room, from the riding boots on a stand at the end of the bed to watch fobs tossed on a tray atop his bureau and the portrait of him as a child tucked away in a corner. The bed was small, made for a single person and covered in blue Indian cotton. There was a desk here as well, more cluttered than the one in the imposing bedroom outside. And books. Everywhere. On shelves, on chairs, stacked in piles on the floor.

"Forgive the mess," he apologized. "I don't let the staff move my things. If they clean up too much, I never can find anything."

"You read."

He smiled. "Is that all right?"

"Forgive me. I was surprised, that's all. May I look?"

"Certainly." He offered her entree with a small bow and then took himself to a small liquor table. He set down the bottle of champagne, poured himself a brandy, spilled an inch or two of champagne into a glass for her and sat down to observe her tour of his room.

"Fielding," she said with a smile, holding out a small volume to him. "I love him."

"He observes the realities with a charming sense of the absurd."

"Yes, does he not. And Richardson. You like him too?"

"When I wish to pass the time. He has less humor and his heroines always meet disastrous ends." He shrugged.

She picked up another book. "I love Voltaire too."

"You are enamored of reading then," he said, taking pleasure in watching her excitement.

"Oh, yes, very much. It was my access to a world I'd never know otherwise."

"You lived with your grandfather, Molly said."

"Yes, we had a cozy life, but not an exciting one. Business and books, books and business. I'm sure you'd find it very boring."

"I contend with my share of business as well, although my secretary, Shelby— I forgot to introduce you downstairs. You turned my head completely and my manners went calling."

"I love when I turn your head."

"Like you love books."

She turned around to face him, her eyes wide. "Not in the least, my lord Bathurst. In a completely tumultuous, tremulous way that defies description."

"I know."

"You do?"

"It's most odd."

"But lovely," she softly intoned, "like a cozy fire on a cold night . . ."

"Not exactly." There was nothing cozy about the lust drumming through his brain. "Molly's told you what to expect tonight, hasn't she?"

"For an entire week, my lord. Oh, dear, have I kept you waiting with all my talk of books?"

"You needn't call me my lord. And you haven't kept

me waiting," he politely lied, discounting his week-long impatience.

"I suppose you'd rather do something else than listen to me prattle on about books. But I confess, I'm not exactly sure how to . . . begin. It's all well and good," she nervously noted, "to be schooled in seduction, but when one actually is onstage, as it were . . ."

"Come, sit and have your champagne. We'll decide how to begin later."

"Yes, sir."

"Please, my name is Dermott."

"Yes, sir"—she fluttered her hands—"I mean, Dermott."

He'd not had a lover say yes, sir to him before and while Miss Leslie might be experiencing a degree of trepidation, he wasn't exactly on familiar ground either. "Drink some champagne," he noted, handing her the glass. "And tell me about your map library."

His deliberate effort to put her at her ease was successful, and within moments she was conversing in a completely natural way. He asked questions, she answered. And before long, he was refilling her glass and she was leaning back comfortably in her chair and smiling at him in a deliciously sweet way. It unnerved him transiently, sweetness having never been a trait that attracted him, but she was exceedingly sensual as well.

"So you see, if Magellan had had better maps, he might have survived."

"Would you like to see those in my library?"

"Now?"

"We've plenty of time." He had no intention of making love to a trembling virgin. In fact, on more than one occasion since meeting Miss Leslie, he'd tried to talk himself out of making love to her entirely.

They took their drinks with them, and Dermott guided Isabella to a secret door concealed in the masonry of the fireplace surround and holding her hand, preceded her down a narrow curving staircase that opened into the library below. His maps were arranged in large shallow drawers and after Isabella had exclaimed over the rarest of his collection, he showed her the maps of India he was updating.

"I could help you," she excitedly said, lightly touching some mountain elevations he'd added to a section of northern India. "I've some very good inks that will last forever. Well," she added with a small grimace, "when I return home I'll be able to give them to you. Grandpapa had them specially mixed in Paris."

She had no way of knowing that taking out the maps of India had been a watershed he'd not been able to cross since returning to England. Gazing down at her head bent low over the table, her golden hair shining in the lamplight, he felt an affection he'd not experienced since he'd lost his family. How could this slight young woman so touch his feelings when none of the scores of women he'd made love to since his return had so much as engaged his interest?

He moved away, not wishing to feel what he felt. Replenishing his glass, he walked to the windows overlooking the terrace and stared out into the starry night.

"I've bored you again," Isabella remarked, putting the maps away.

The small sound of the drawer sliding shut forced him to speak. "I'm tired, I think."

"I've said something wrong," she murmured, coming up to him. "I apologize."

"It's nothing you said. Molly tells me I'm moody."

"Then I shall entertain you," she brightly declared.

"Surely you're not thinking of singing." A smile creased his face.

"I don't see a piano in sight."

"Luckily."

"You don't like female entertainments?"

"Not of the cultural kind."

"Ah . . . then perhaps I should show you how these bows open." She reached up to her shoulders.

"Not yet." Quickly placing his hands over hers, he arrested her action, not sure he was ready, not sure an artless virgin could fill the void in his black mood.

"Yes, sir—er, Dermott," she corrected. The warmth of his hands on her shoulders, the weight of them, his closeness made her tremble. Her wanting him no longer seemed casual if it ever had been, no longer a practical decision, but deep, specific, and defenseless. "When?"

Never, he should say. Her virginity was a vast deterrent, and his own troubled memories were disquieting.

"I want you . . . ever so much," she whispered, gazing up at him with wistful blue eyes, taking a half step forward so her body brushed his.

"This could be a mistake." Irresolute, skittish, he hesitated.

"You promised," she pleaded.

The innocent longing in her eyes, the lush feel of her body against his weakened his already equivocal resolve. His body automatically responded to her nearness, his erection rising between them.

"You *do* want me," she breathed, moving her hips against his rigid length. "I can tell. . . ."

She was temptation incarnate—the look, the feel of her—and gripping her shoulders, he reluctantly pulled her closer. Her sweet scent filled his senses; her soft breasts pressing into his chest whet his appetite for more; her hips brushing against his throbbing erection fed his lustful cravings.

She slid her hands from beneath his and reaching up, placed them on his shoulders. "I'm going to kiss you now, my lord," she murmured, as though she had a schedule to keep.

And when she rose on tiptoe to reach his mouth, it was impossible to resist. His hands drifted down her back, cupping her bottom, and pulling her hard against his body, he softly growled, "You'd better be sure." His voice took on a faint drollery. "Then at least one of us will be."

"I'm sure." Her eyes were untouched by doubt, her mouth only inches away.

Wanting to be kissed.

He lowered his head slowly, as though she were dangerous.

"Kiss me," she whispered, tightening her grip on his shoulders, drawing closer.

And he impetuously obliged, covering her mouth in a restless, hotspur kiss that didn't charm or take heed of her innocence, but instead fed his own rash urgency. A greedy, incautious kiss that ravished and roused and tantalized.

She sighed into his mouth, unafraid, audacious in her wanting, reveling in his need. Melting against him, she ate at his mouth, tasted him deeply as though he was hers to savor and relish and he was the reason she'd waited so long for her first kiss.

It was half a lifetime away from Dermott's first kiss and heated or not, flame hot or blazing, it wasn't enough.

He wanted more.